VALIANT HEART

THE FRONTIER HEARTS SAGA

COLLEEN HALL

Copyright © 2024 Colleen Hall. All rights reserved.
No part of this book may be reproduced in any form or by any electronic or mechanical means, including information storage and retrieval systems, without written permission from the author, except for the use of brief quotations in a book review.

ANAIAH FROM THE HEART An imprint of Anaiah Press, LLC
Edited by Eden Plantz
Cover design by Eden Plantz
Book design by Anaiah Press, LLC

Valiant Heart is dedicated to my brother, Tim. Without his knowledge of antique aircraft, this book wouldn't have been possible. He patiently answered my questions about so many details I couldn't learn from research alone—minute trivia that helped me add realism to the airplanes Rafe and Will flew. His enthusiasm for antique aircraft was contagious and inspired me to honor the aerial pioneers who climbed into those fragile machines and paved the way for modern flight.

ACKNOWLEDGMENTS

So many people have helped me during the writing of this book that I have a whole community of supporters. Their input and prayers are invaluable. My beta readers provided honest feedback in the early stages of the manuscript and tactfully pointed out blind spots in the plot. They offered suggestions when I ran into a plotting snag or have a problem with the conflict. I can always turn to Cindy Jantz, one of my earliest supporters from childhood, when I have a plotting problem that needs to be hashed out. Her observations boost me over any mental blocks that hinder my narrative. Andrea Eliasson and Wendy Johannes also offer sound feedback.

Many friends prayed me through this manuscript and the editing process—my Shepherd Group at church, my fellow writers in my American Christian Fiction Writers group, Jim Russell, Donna Andersen, Marie Himka and many more. I couldn't have done it without their prayer support.

Thanks also to my family, especially my sons whom I can rely on whenever I have a technical problem or getting out my newsletter.

And special thanks to editors Eden and Kara, who always take my writing efforts to the next level with their professional input.

CHAPTER 1

Colorado Rockies
Early June, 1922

Would Rafe talk to her? Would he even acknowledge her? Had the intervening years lessened the damage done to her husband by his aerial battles against the Hun?

The words Rafe had spoken before he'd walked out of her life just days after they'd been reunited at the Great War's end still rang in her ears. "Live your life, Daisy. I'm no good for you. I'm damaged."

Those words had haunted her for four long years.

Daisy Wild Wind gazed at the Rocky Mountain scenery outside the steam train's grimy window. She didn't notice the view.

Each turn of the train's wheels took her closer to the inevitable confrontation with Rafe. Her stomach clenched at the prospect of meeting her husband. She hadn't notified Rafe of her plan to return to Summit. When she'd considered informing him of her homecoming, her courage had failed. To arrive unannounced had seemed the better option and would give him no opportunity to obstruct her intentions.

The train's shrill whistle announced their arrival in Summit. When the engine had ground to a halt at the town's small station, the few other passengers who'd made the trip gathered their possessions and filed down the steps. Frozen in her seat, Daisy remained in the rail car, alone. While she battled the urge to abandon her dreams, she gulped in a deep breath.

At last, she rose. Her legs shook, and she gripped her handbag with icy fingers, but she straightened her shoulders and lifted her chin. When they'd been together and she'd stood beside Rafe, the top of her head hadn't even reached his shoulder. Now, she'd need every bit of height she could manage when she faced him, just to give her courage.

Daisy navigated the coach's stairs and stepped onto the station's wooden platform. Her three suitcases and her black medical satchel had been stacked alongside the tracks at the platform's edge. In Summit's sleepy sanctuary, she could leave the luggage there until she knew where she'd be staying. Turning her back on her baggage, she descended to the boardwalk and strolled along the single street.

The boardwalk ended just past the hotel. Daisy halted at the edge of the walkway and glanced up the slope to the mine. Where would she find Rafe? A peek at her wristwatch confirmed the time as midafternoon. Unless Rafe had changed his work habits since the war, he'd most likely be at the mine now. She'd start her search there.

Would she find Rafe in his office, or would he be in the shaft's dark belly? Her stomach flipflopped again. Would he be angry? Cold? Distant?

Her palms grew clammy, and she almost turned back.

Perhaps she should take a room at the hotel first. She could always find Rafe later.

She gave herself a stern reprimand and castigated herself for being a coward. Taking a hotel room now would only postpone the inevitable confrontation. Besides, once she listed her name in the hotel registry, speculation would fly. She didn't want Rafe to learn of her presence through the gossip mill.

Daisy left the boardwalk and took the first step toward the mine, then another, and another in the long trudge up the slope. Each step increased her trepidation until her pulse raced, and her heartbeat pounded in her ears. Her breath came sharp and fast.

On either side of the road just before the final incline to the mine stood two spacious clapboard houses. Wide verandas with spool-picketed railings fronted each home.

She turned her attention to the house on the right. She and Rafe had lived there for three short years before the Great War disrupted their lives. The sight of the house brought all the memories of the joy and grief she'd experienced within its walls crashing back. She couldn't bear the pain. With one hand pressed against her chest, where her heart wept in silent agony, she tore her gaze from her former home and forced herself to continue her trek.

She reached the mine. As she halted at the bottom of the steps, Daisy tried to quiet her hammering pulse. Her whole body trembled as though buffeted by a strong wind. She gripped the railing to steady herself.

What Rafe would look like after four years? Had he changed?

Daisy forced herself up the steps and across the porch. She reached the door, then let herself into the bare reception area. No one sat on the bench beside the door. She and Rafe would be undisturbed.

The door to Rafe's office on the left wall stood open. Frozen where she stood, Daisy stared at her husband's office door. She swallowed, hard, and closed her eyes. Her ears buzzed, and darkness swam at the edges of her vision. She leaned against the side of the bench to steady herself. Unable to face the coming scene without the Lord's help, she sent a silent prayer heavenward.

Her pulse steadied, and she opened her eyes. With her gaze fixed on the office door, she crossed the reception area and halted just over the threshold.

Rafe sat at a battered oak desk, his head bent over the paperwork stacked in a neat pile on a green felt blotter. She'd forgotten what a big man he was, long-limbed and wide shouldered, and how he owned the space around him just by his very presence. Sunlight from the window just beyond his desk burnished his face with a tawny glow. A few silver strands now mingled with the black curly hair at his temple. Lines that hadn't been there when she'd last seen him bracketed his mouth. His sculpted features and bold nose appeared harder than she remembered.

Daisy froze. The sight of her husband, after so long a time apart, hit her with the force of a sledgehammer. Her heart battered her ribs, and her knees threatened to buckle. Light-headedness made her lean against the doorframe. Her love for him, love that she'd hoarded close to her heart ever since he'd left for France, burst forth, like a dam overflowing. A desperate need to touch him—to thread her fingers through his springy hair, to trace his face with her fingertips, and to curl her fingers around his shoulders—consumed her. She yearned to say his name, but the word jammed in her throat.

As if he sensed her presence, he lifted his head and

pinned her with a stare. For just a heartbeat, his dark eyes glowed before his expression shuttered, and his face became an impassive mask. In that instant, he had never resembled his half-Cheyenne father more.

Daisy gripped her handbag as if it were the only thing that held her upright. After an awkward beat, while a deafening silence filled the office, she found her voice. "Hello, Rafe."

Seconds ticked past before he replied, his voice as expressionless as his face. "What are you doing here?"

"I came to see you."

"Why?"

"I'm your wife."

Rafe sighed and tossed his pen onto the blotter. "Only in a legal sense."

"We're married in the sight of God. We took sacred vows together."

His firm jaw set, Rafe stared at her without replying.

Daisy lifted her chin and stared right back, something she never would have done when they'd first met. She'd been too timid in those long-ago days to be so bold as to challenge the indomitable Rafe Wild Wind. When he didn't speak, she plowed on. "We both believe the marriage vows we took are binding for a lifetime. I don't think you've changed so much that you don't believe that anymore."

After a pause, in which he regarded her with an unblinking gaze, Rafe replied in a cool tone. "Apparently, I still do. I haven't offered to divorce you."

"But you won't live with me as my husband."

He shook his head. "I explained once why I can't live with you."

"That was four years ago. Haven't the years made any difference?"

Rafe rose. His presence filled the room. "I'm not having

hallucinations anymore, if that's what you mean. And I don't hear men screaming in my head. But nothing changes what I did during the war."

"You told me you were like your father. Well, your father may have killed many people during his warrior days, but once he found the Lord, he put all that behind him. Can't you do the same?"

Rafe declined to reply. Instead, he rounded the desk and crossed the room with unhurried strides.

As he approached, Daisy couldn't help but admire the way his faded blue flannel shirt molded his muscled shoulders and deep chest. Worn denim jeans encased his long legs. His heeled leather boots thudded on the bare floor in a definite masculine manner. She had never ceased to wonder how she'd captured this virile man's heart. In that moment, she wanted nothing more than for Rafe to fold her in his arms and hold her close, to whisper that he still loved her.

He halted before her and gave her a slow perusal through narrowed eyes. With Rafe standing so close, Daisy had to tilt her head to look into his face. She tried not to fidget at his inspection or let his chilly deportment intimidate her.

His slow gaze traveled from her new patent leather Mary Jane shoes to the drop-waisted green dress with pink polka-dots she'd purchased for this occasion. His glance flicked over the single strand of faux pearls that dangled to her waist. When his attention reached her hair, nearly concealed by her felt *cloche* hat, his perusal halted. "What have you done to your hair?"

"I bobbed it." On a daring impulse, she'd had her blonde hair cut and styled in a bob that curled under her chin and framed her elfin features. Bangs feathered across her forehead.

"I can see that. Why?"

"I hoped you'd like it."

"Does it matter whether or not I like it?"

His indifference nearly drove Daisy to despair. "It matters to me. I wish it would matter to you."

"I liked your hair long, but bobbed hair is all the rage these days. I suppose you have to keep up with fashion."

"I hope you'll grow to like it."

"Why?" Rafe propped his weight on one leg and hung a thumb from his belt. "Are you staying in Summit?"

She nodded and met his impassive gaze, ignoring the urge to fidget with her necklace. "I've been working in the Denver hospital and have just graduated from medical school. I have a doctor's degree. I thought I'd set up a practice here."

"Doc Irby won't like it. And I can't imagine too many people taking to the notion of a woman doctor."

"They'll have to get used to it."

Rafe shrugged. "You'll have a tough time of it. And while you're here, don't get any ideas about getting back together with me. I'm still no good for you."

"Why don't you let me be the judge of that?"

"You don't know what's good for you."

"I know you're good for me, Rafe. You always were the best thing in my life. And I'm not going to give up on us. Ever."

"Suit yourself, but don't blame me when your hopes go down in flames."

Daisy touched his face with a tender gaze and refused to let his words wound her. "When did you become such a cynic? I know the man you were before the war is still there, underneath all that bitterness. Together, we can find him."

"I'm a lost cause, Daisy. Don't waste your efforts on me."

"I've prayed for you every day these past four years. I believe the Lord will honor those prayers."

Rafe didn't reply.

Not daring to push him further, Daisy changed the subject. "I've just come from the Slash L. I spent some time with your parents before I came here. Your mother sends her love."

"She writes to me every week."

"Of course, she does. She loves you. I'm to tell you that she and your father will visit sometime this summer, whenever your father can find time to leave the ranch. He's been occupied with heading up all three branches of the ranching operations since your great-uncle Clint died."

"In that case, I doubt they'll make it out here this summer."

Daisy tried for a gentle tone. "Your mother would appreciate it very much if you'd visit them."

"She knows I won't."

"Why, Rafe? Why can't you go back to the ranch? At least spend Christmas there. Cole and Garnet would love to see you."

"I can't inflict my presence on the family."

"And when did you start to think more of yourself than of your family? They don't care that you're damaged. They love you anyway. Your mother grieves because you won't see them. You're being selfish to stay away."

A dull flush crept up from his shirt collar to the roots of his hair. She'd pushed him too far, but she refused to stand down.

"You've changed since the war. The Daisy I knew would never have said anything like that." he shot back through clenched teeth.

"The Rafe I knew wouldn't have made my saying it necessary."

They eyed each other in stiff silence, while tension roiled the air between them.

After a moment, Rafe shook off the emotion that held them in thrall.

He took her elbow and turned her toward the door. "Now that we've thoroughly insulted each other, let's get you settled. Where are you staying? Did you take your things to the house? If so, I'll move into the hotel."

Daisy clamped her lips at the bruise his comment left on her heart. She wouldn't let his aloofness deter her resolve. He'd heal, and they'd be reunited. She'd make sure of it. "My luggage is still at the train station." She dug in her heels.

When she refused to take another step, he glanced at her and quirked an eyebrow.

She met his gaze. "Rafe, I won't move into the house until we can live there together as husband and wife."

He snagged his black felt cowboy hat from its peg by the door and settled it over his curly hair. "Then you'll have a long wait."

CHAPTER 2

Once outside and on the road, Rafe lapsed into silence. He held her elbow in a firm grip and towed her along beside him. His long strides ate up the ground. Trying to keep up, Daisy trotted at his side. When they passed their former home, she refused to look at the house again. To do so would only bring more pain.

She glanced at the house on the opposite side of the road. Her brother-in-law, Cole Wild Wind, had commissioned that house for his wife, Garnet, though they'd moved to the Slash L Ranch after the Great War. With the death of his cousin in the war, Cole had assumed the responsibility of running the cattle business side of the ranch.

Curtains fluttered at the open windows, so the house wasn't empty.

"Rafe, who's living in Cole and Garnet's house? There are curtains at the windows."

"Mr. Montgomery is renting the house. He's the proprietor of the new mercantile store. He's widowed and lives there with his daughter."

With that comment, Rafe fell silent again, and Daisy didn't have breath for more conversation. After a few more strides, she jerked at his arm. "Rafe, please slow down. I can't keep up."

The Rafe she'd known before the war would have been more solicitous for her welfare. She missed the old Rafe. His mother would be appalled at his behavior.

Without apologizing, he slowed his gait.

Daisy gasped a few breaths. "I'm sorry. I'm not used to the mountain air."

Rafe halted and looked down at her. For a heartbeat, the emotionless mask cracked. A glimmer of regret crossed his face before he once again assumed an impassive expression, though he recollected his manners. "No, I should be the one to apologize. I should have remembered that you've just arrived and haven't had time to adjust to the altitude." He paused.

Hopeful for something more personal, Daisy held her breath.

"I forgot you're such a little mite. You couldn't keep up with me if you tried."

"I always felt I was slowing you down. Especially when you taught me to skate. Or to ride a horse."

Rafe snared Daisy with a look that brought back their shared past and the memories that simmered just below their verbal conversation. "You never slowed me down."

The air between them crackled.

Daisy couldn't tear her gaze from his face. Drenched by the hot June sun, they stood in a high mountain valley staring at each other. Seconds hung suspended while they neither moved nor spoke. She gloried in the tortured appearance of Rafe's countenance. At least, in this moment, he couldn't hide the truth of what he felt. He might do his best to cultivate a disinterested air, but the truth of his feelings for her ripped away his shield.

Rafe shook his head as if to free it from the unwelcome emotions and took her elbow again. He turned her toward the town. "Come along." His gruff tone belied his unfeeling air. "Let's get you settled."

They reached the hotel and stepped onto the boardwalk. Rafe turned her toward the hotel door and reached around her to open the portal. She entered ahead of him, and he shut the door behind them, then crossed the reception area to a high wooden check-in counter with an ornate oak-paneled front. Placing both palms flat on the desk's top, he addressed the clerk. "I'd like to rent a room."

The clerk reached for a fountain pen lying beside a lined registration book. "Certainly, Mr. Wild Wind. And for whom would you like to rent the room?"

"Mrs. Daisy Wild Wind." Rafe's firm voice didn't falter over her name.

Daisy had come to a halt beside Rafe. At his words, the clerk cut her a sharp glance. Avid speculation gleamed behind the man's spectacles. The gossip mill would hum tonight. Word that Rafe Wild Wind's absent wife had arrived in Summit after a four-year separation would be too delicious a tidbit not to spread.

Rafe ignored the clerk's curiosity. He gestured toward the open register. "I'll sign that for my wife."

The balding man collected himself. "Yes, certainly, sir." He pushed the register toward Rafe and handed over a black fountain pen. "Just sign on the last line."

While Rafe signed her name in his bold scrawl, the clerk took a key attached to a large brass ring from a row of hooks on the wall behind the desk and offered the key to Rafe. Her husband laid down the pen and shoved the registry back across the counter.

"Your wife will have room number four on the second floor. The door is at the head of the stairs."

"Thank you." Rafe turned away from the reception desk and took Daisy's arm again. He drew her to the center of the room. With his voice pitched low, he bent his head and spoke into her ear. "Stay here. I'll get your things from the train station."

"I left three suitcases and my medical bag on the platform."

Rafe nodded and released her arm, then crossed to the door and stepped onto the boardwalk. Daisy watched him stride past the window in the direction of the train station.

With the hope that the clerk wouldn't engage her in conversation, she stood in the center of the reception area and ignored his avid scrutiny. The trip from Denver, coupled with her emotional reunion with Rafe, had exhausted her. She had no desire to satisfy the man's curiosity or to field his questions. Turning her back to the counter, she gazed about the reception area.

An attempt had been made to bring Eastern civilization to the hotel. A patterned rug in woven jewel tones covered the bare wooden floor, and a potted fern in a large Chinese-style ceramic vase filled one corner. Wicker furniture with emerald-green seat cushions lined the walls. Lace curtains fluttered at the open windows.

Daisy had just decided to sit when the door opened, and Rafe filled the aperture. He carried two of her suitcases and had her black medical satchel tucked under one arm. Behind him followed one of the railway stewards with her trunk. She hurried to Rafe's side and pried her doctor's bag from beneath his arm. "Here, let me take that."

The three of them wrestled her luggage up the curving staircase. In the second-floor hallway outside her door, Rafe tipped the steward and thanked him for his help. The man saluted, clicked his heels, and vanished down the stairs.

Daisy brought her attention back to Rafe, who loomed in the hall amid her baggage. "I'll have to get used to that all over again."

"Get used to what?"

"How people so eagerly follow your every request."

"Money talks."

She shook her head. "It's more than that. You and Cole both have a gift of leadership. Men jump to follow your every command."

Rafe shrugged. Reaching into his back jeans pocket, he pulled out her room key and inserted it into the lock. Her door swung inward, and he motioned for her to precede him.

She stepped into the room. In the wall directly ahead, two tall windows with sheer curtains overlooked the dusty street. Behind her, Rafe deposited her suitcases beside an oak wardrobe near the door, then pulled her doctor's bag from her grasp and tossed the black satchel onto the bed.

Daisy turned her back to the windows. With the bed behind her, they faced each other from the distance of a couple paces, though the invisible chasm that separated them loomed as an impassable abyss. An awkward silence hung in the air.

She took a step closer to her husband. "Thank you, Rafe."

"For what?"

"For not putting me back on the train."

"I don't think putting you on the train would have done any good. You're a determined little thing." Despite his hard tone, one corner of his mouth twitched.

"And I'm determined to win you back."

He sighed and swiped his hat from his head, then rumpled his curly hair. "Don't, Daisy. You'll only get hurt."

"I've already been hurt. Don't you think you hurt me when you left me alone in Denver four years ago? And what I've lived with since then?"

"I'd hoped you'd moved on."

"In one way, I have. I went to medical school and became a doctor, but my heart still belongs to you. My heart will always be yours."

"Then we're at an impasse. I'm just a husk of a man with nothing to offer you. Don't waste your love on me."

Recalling the tortured expression on his face during their walk to town, Daisy refused to accept his words. "I don't believe that. I know the love we had is still there. It may be buried, but it's there."

Rafe shifted his weight to his other leg and propped his fists on his hips. "Stop, Daisy. What we had is in the past. Our years together were the best years of my life, but our relationship is finished. Over." His impassive expression decried any emotion she might have seen earlier. "I'm sorry I can't be a true husband to you, but there it is. The sooner you accept the truth, the better it will be for you."

He turned his back to her and crossed to the door. With one hand on the brass knob and the other holding his hat alongside his thigh, he glanced at her over his shoulder. "Set up an account for yourself at Katie's place. No matter that we're not living together, you're still my wife, and I'll assume responsibility for your care. I'll pay your hotel bill and your tab at the café."

Daisy shook her head. "Once I get my medical practice going, I'll support myself. At least until we reconcile."

A cold mask settled over his features. He shoved his hat onto his head. "We won't reconcile. Get used to the idea." He opened the door and stepped out, snapping the portal closed behind him.

Without his presence, the room felt cold and empty. Daisy clutched her arms about her middle and nearly doubled over from the pain his repudiation caused. She staggered to one window. Despite his rejection, she hoped to catch a glimpse of him as he left the hotel. She brushed aside the filmy curtain and scanned the street. Horses pulling wagons, cowboys, and men dressed like miners passed along the road. Muffled sounds drifted up from below.

Moments later, Rafe stepped onto the boardwalk beneath her window. He paused to roll his shoulders as if to loosen them before he swung to the right. He'd taken three strides toward the mine when, through the window's glass, Daisy heard a muted feminine voice call his name.

Rafe halted and pivoted. A tall, willowy woman with hair that gleamed like polished brass hurried toward him from the direction of the new mercantile store. She walked with an unconscious grace that Daisy couldn't hope to emulate. The woman halted a mere breath from Rafe and curled her fingers about his arm in a too-familiar gesture. She smiled up at him, leaning into him in a manner that suggested intimacy. In response, Rafe grinned down at her in a warm fashion that he hadn't accorded to his wife. He thumbed back his hat and stood planted on the walkway, his head cocked, and made no move to disengage the woman's hand.

With her heart thudding against her ribs, Daisy stared at her husband and the woman wrapped together in a private tableau. The woman's posture bespoke an ardent familiarity with the tall man at her side. As she spoke, she ran a palm over his shoulder. Rafe nodded at whatever she said.

Daisy fisted her hands and squeezed until her nails bit into her flesh. She couldn't watch a moment longer. With her eyes closed, she wheeled from the window and leaned against the wall. The scene of her husband and the unknown woman seared the inside of her lids. A blaze of jealousy such as she'd never thought possible to feel crashed over her in a scorching tide. Who was that woman? How dare she touch Rafe in such a familiar manner! And how could Rafe allow her to touch him that way? He was a married man.

She and Rafe might not have lived together as husband and wife since the Great War, but he was still married. Didn't he consider himself bound by their vows?

Daisy breathed through her nose until her heartbeat slowed and the scalding resentment receded. Only then did she peer around the window frame to look into the street again. The boardwalk baked in the afternoon sun. Both Rafe and the woman had gone.

CHAPTER 3

Darkness shrouded her hotel room. Daisy sat cross legged on the bed, the covers tucked around her waist. In an unending loop, the display she'd witnessed earlier between Rafe and the *chic* mystery woman played over and over in her mind. Sleep eluded her as the vision of her husband with the other woman tortured her.

She hadn't considered the possibility that Rafe had found someone else in the four years since they'd parted. His attitude toward the woman hadn't seemed especially lover-like, but nonetheless, a warm relationship must exist between them. The woman had made their rapport obvious for anyone to see. The likelihood that her husband might no longer love her had never occurred to her. Now, the prospect daunted and left her feeling hollow.

The memory of the last time she'd seen Rafe four years ago seared her soul. She recalled the episode in their hotel room after a parade in which her husband, being one of the Army Air Services' top aces, had been hailed as a celebrity.

The scene flashed through her mind, as fresh as though she'd experienced the incident yesterday.

"I'm no fit husband for you, Daisy. You'd be better off without me." Rafe had stood tall and stiff across the Denver hotel room. He still wore his flyboy's belted, olive-drab tunic jacket and buff-colored wool jodhpur pants tucked into high boots. The long white aviator's scarf worn by all the flyboys wrapped about his neck. One end dangled over the front of his uniform tunic.

She'd stared into her husband's lean face. Who was this cold-eyed stranger who'd come home from the Great War in place of the teasing, tender man she'd married? Where was the Rafe Wild Wind who'd loved and courted her despite her lack of pedigree? She, the maid of a New York socialite, had somehow captured the heart of the handsome Rafe Wild Wind, half owner of a Colorado uranium mine and one of the heirs of the Slash L Ranch. Where had that man gone?

She'd managed to croak a reply. "What . . . what do you mean?"

Rafe had gestured toward the hotel room's window, which overlooked the street down which the triumphal parade had just marched. Decked out in full military uniform, Rafe had been one of the flying aces honored in the parade. "That farce out there . . . people cheering and waving, making heroes out of us. We're not heroes. If they only knew the truth . . . we're killers. Aerial warfare is nothing more than mechanized slaughter. How many young men died in the skies over France? Or in the trenches? And for what? What did we accomplish with all our killing?"

Speechless, Daisy had stared into her husband's taut face. She circled the bed and crept toward him. "Rafe, the war is over. The killing has stopped." Reaching out, she laid her palm on his chest. Beneath the tunic's wool fabric, his muscled chest felt firm and warm beneath her splayed fingers.

He flinched at her touch. His dark eyes burned down at her. "It's still in my head. It's all in my head. I live it over and over again. The machine gunfire, the screams. . ."

"You just got home. The war is still fresh. I'm sure that in time, it will fade."

Rafe spun away from her, and her hand dropped to her side. She stared at his wide shoulders and the back he now presented to her. He tossed his next words at her like a hand grenade.

"I'm flawed, Daisy. I'm no fit husband for you. You're so sweet, so gentle. I don't deserve you."

She darted around him and gripped his upper arms. Shaking him a bit, she forced him to meet her gaze. "Rafe, I've changed, too. I'm not the same girl you married. Don't forget I've been there, as well. I was a nurse on the front lines. I've experienced war and seen what trench warfare does to men. You're not the only one who's changed."

For a heart-breaking moment, she thought he wouldn't reply, but then he spoke in a flat monotone. "You didn't kill anyone. You saved lives."

"You only did your duty. You fought for America, for freedom, and to defeat the Hun."

A heavy silence settled between them before he replied, "I found out one thing. I am my father's son."

"What do you mean?"

"My father was a feared Dog Soldier. He was very good at killing people. And so was I."

"Rafe, our country was at war. Killing the enemy isn't murder. You only did what you had to do."

His mouth clamped in a tight line. "I'm damaged, Daisy. I don't think I'll ever be whole." With gentle fingers, he pried her hands from his arms and put her away from him. "I don't know what I'll do next, but I'll do it alone."

Was he telling her that he was leaving her? Chills rippled across her skin. "Rafe, what are you saying?"

"Live your life, Daisy. You'll be happier without me. I don't even know who I am anymore."

Desperation overcame panic. She didn't want to lose her husband now, not after he'd survived the Great War. "No, I won't be happier without you! We belong together. We'll work together to help you heal."

"I'm an empty shell of a man who would snuff out your joy. I'm dead inside with nothing to offer. You have so much to give. You're kind, and giving, and you love nursing. You can help many people with your skills." His face tightened, and he stared at her with empty eyes. "I'm tainted. Living with me would contaminate you. I'd drag you down to my level."

Daisy stepped right up to him. He held himself still, erect, and threw up an emotional barrier she couldn't breach. "Rafe Wild Wind, you weren't reared to quit. I know you're not a quitter. Don't quit on me, on us. We can work this out."

He shook his head. "It's too late for us. The war destroyed the man I was."

She stared into his face as numbness crept through her limbs. He meant to leave her. She made a last, desperate attempt to change his mind. She'd grovel, she'd beg. She couldn't hold onto foolish pride at this moment. "Rafe, don't you love me anymore?"

At her words, his expression softened. His gaze roved over her features, touching each one with tenderness. He replied in a tone so gentle, her heart broke. "I don't know. I loved you once, Daisy, and your love for me made it possible to keep going, to get into my plane and take off on each mission." He palmed her cheek with one large hand. "But the war and the killing snuffed out any feelings I once had. I'm just a hollow husk, and I don't want to drag you down to where I am. I'm sullied. I'm no good for you."

She clung to his shoulders, trembling, and turned her face into his palm.

"When you decide what you want to do, set up a bank account and send the information to me at the mine office. Each month, I'll deposit enough money for your expenses. Or go to the Slash L and stay with my family. They'll be happy to have you there."

He smoothed her blonde hair away from her face and sifted his fingers through her tresses. As though committing her features to memory, he seared her with a hot perusal before he leaned down to place a gentle kiss on her forehead. "Goodbye, Daisy."

"Rafe, no, please no. Don't go." Her voice broke.

He released her and stepped around her. The door closed behind him. The *snick* of the latch sounded absolute in its finality. She stood alone in the empty hotel room.

Scalding tears sprang to her eyes and spilled down her cheeks. She tottered to the bed they'd shared the night before and collapsed on the coverlet. She'd known Rafe had been struggling with inner torment when he hadn't touched her. In the few days they'd been together since they'd both returned to the States from war-torn France, he hadn't touched her as a husband should. He'd been distant, aloof. Though she had a war's worth of loving stored inside waiting to be shared, he'd shut her out. She'd yearned to be loved as he'd loved her during the few short years they'd had together before the war had separated them, but he hadn't touched her.

Without Rafe, her world fell in ashes at her feet.

Men's voices and hoofbeats drifting up through the open window from the street below jarred Daisy from her memories and back into the present. The memory of the scene with

Rafe dissolved as the hotel bedroom assumed reality's solid features. The blankets snuggled warm and soft about her. Through the gloom, a mirror atop a dresser just beyond the foot of the bed threw back a dim reflection of herself. Across the room, a tall wardrobe stood beside the door. She wasn't in the Denver hotel room of four years ago. She was in Summit. The year was 1922, not 1918.

After seeing Rafe with the woman on the street and experiencing his coldness toward herself, Daisy's resolve faltered. Could her marriage be restored? Perhaps moving to Summit and hoping for a reconciliation with her husband had been a fool's errand.

She scrubbed her eyes with the heels of her hands and flopped back onto the pillows. Only after sending a heartfelt prayer heavenward did she find peace enough to sleep.

CHAPTER 4

Daisy stepped from the hotel and paused on the boardwalk, debating whether or not she should go to Katie's Café for breakfast. Katie would be ecstatic that Daisy had returned to Summit, but she wasn't ready to confess her situation to her friend, so she ignored her growling stomach and decided breakfast could wait.

She glanced to her left. While she'd been gone, Summit had grown since its pre-war days. Now two mercantile establishments gave the town's citizens a choice of stores to patronize.

Two eateries now competed for customers' business, and a bank had sprung up across the street. Summit now boasted an official post office, right beside the bank, as well as a boot shop and saddlery shop.

Daisy turned her attention to the right. The dirt track that bisected the town and led to the mine had been widened to street width. Beside the hotel, a clapboard church lifted its spire toward the sky. To the left of the road clustered the homes where married miners lived with their families.

She turned her gaze to a spot hidden by the mining

community, but in her mind, she could see the image as clearly as if her eyes beheld the reality. Without conscious direction from her, her feet moved of their own accord off the boardwalk onto the dusty street. She pressed on to an overgrown lane just beyond the miners' homes and turned onto the grassy path. At the end of the track, a small graveyard drowsed in the sunlight.

At the sight, grief tightened her chest. Her throat clogged. She fought down her anguish and focused instead on her surroundings. Perhaps if she thought about the mountains' beauty instead of what waited for her in the cemetery, she could maintain a measure of composure.

The bright sun shimmered in the clear air. She breathed deeply, delighting in the dry pristine quality. No motor car fumes nor garbage scent tainted the atmosphere. Beyond the meadow, fir and spruce trees grew up the mountains' shoulders as far as the timber line. A ring of jagged mountain peaks that stabbed their rocky spines into the sky encircled the valley.

Daisy came to a stop and brought her gaze back to the cemetery. A whitewashed picket fence enclosed the burying ground. Rough wooden crosses or flat wooden slabs marked the graves of those who had died while living in Summit. Since she'd left, the community had lost several people.

She pushed open the gate and forced her reluctant feet to carry her inside. Making her way to a spot near the back fence, she halted at the foot of a tiny grave. Her chest constricted, and a sudden hot gush of tears obscured her vision. She dropped to her knees beside the grave and swiped the moisture from her eyes.

A slab marker with the words "Molly. Beloved Daughter of Rafe and Daisy Wild Wind. Gone to Heaven, Aged Two Years" had been burned into the wood. The short mountain grass over the grave had been mowed, and someone had put wildflowers in a tin can at the tombstone's base. *Rafe*. No one else would have cared enough to make the gesture.

Amidst her grief, the knowledge that Rafe cared enough to maintain their daughter's grave and put flowers at her marker told Daisy that emotion still existed beneath her husband's cold façade. The observation cheered her. Rafe wasn't a hopeless case, as he'd insisted.

Daisy settled on the grass and drew her knees up beneath her jade green and white striped cotton dress. With her arms linked around her drawn-up knees, she contemplated her daughter's grave and the paths her life had taken since Molly had died.

Molly had contracted whooping cough the spring she'd died. None of the doctor's remedies had saved her. Her daughter's death had ripped Daisy's heart asunder and left a hole that couldn't be filled.

Her life would have been very different if Molly hadn't died. If her daughter had lived, she would have stayed in Summit and waited out the war. She wouldn't have gone to France and lent her nursing skills to the wounded and dying on the front lines. She never would have attended medical school and become a doctor, yet she wouldn't have traded her daughter's life for a medical degree. Even now, she'd gladly give up her degree if doing so would bring Molly back to her.

And Rafe? After the war, would he have stayed with her for their daughter's sake? Her knowledge of his character told her that however difficult it might have been for him, her husband never would have left them. They'd have been a family.

Another wave of grief at the might-have-beens left Daisy shaken. She rested her forehead on her knees and closed her eyes, while the June sun warmed the back of her neck. She clung to the knowledge that in a believer's life, all things are ordained by God. None of the hardships she'd suffered had been an accident. The Lord had seen her through the grief of the past years, and He'd sustain her now.

The squeak of the gate's hinges alerted her to the fact that she wasn't alone. She froze, hoping she wouldn't be disturbed. Footsteps swished toward her through the grass and halted at the foot of Molly's grave.

Daisy scrambled to her feet and whirled. Rafe stood not three feet away. The brim of his cowboy hat shaded his face, and the sun at his back cast a long shadow toward Molly's tombstone.

He scrutinized her with an intent gaze. "I thought I'd find you here."

Daisy wanted to ask him about the woman who'd detained him on the sidewalk the night before, but she refrained. Antagonizing him wouldn't help win him back. Instead, she nodded. "I had to come."

"I know." His gentle tone soothed her heart's aching sorrow.

She gestured toward the tin can with its cheery blossoms. "Thank you for putting flowers on Molly's grave. And for mowing the grass."

"That's the least I can do." He hung his thumbs off his jeans' back pockets and stood with elbows akimbo, feet planted wide. The breeze fingered his blue flannel shirt and made the fabric ripple around his torso.

They stood in silence, both looking down at their daughter's grave.

Daisy swallowed around another lump, then glanced at her husband. "She would have been eight years old now." Her voice broke, and she gulped. "She had your curly hair."

"And your blonde hair and blue eyes."

"She would have been tall." Daisy's eyes misted at the thought of what Molly might look like now.

"Not if she took after you instead of me."

Their shared memories, and the history that entwined their lives, ensnared them both. They couldn't look away from each other. The past collided with the present and gripped them in a whirlpool of emotion. Neither could deny the yearning that pulled at them.

Rafe returned his attention to the grave. His silence wrapped them both in their mutual past.

Quietude pressed with a heavy hand between them, while a droning bee bumbled its way to the blooms in the tin can.

A question that had nagged at Daisy since her husband had gone to France burned on her tongue. She hesitated, then took the plunge. "I have to know—if Molly hadn't died, would you have joined the war? You were old enough so you didn't have to fight. And you never said why you went."

Rafe's head jerked up, and his glance swung to her face. An arctic chill filled his eyes. After a moment, he turned his gaze away to the high-country meadow as if he couldn't bear to look at her a moment longer.

Daisy waited while tension seethed between them.

At last, he spoke in a tight tone. "I don't know. I thought I was doing the right thing when I went to France and joined the Lafayette Escadrille. After all, the Huns were sinking our ships, and America hadn't yet entered the war. I felt honor-bound to fight. I saw it as my patriotic duty." He paused, while silence hung in the air, before he continued in a husky voice. "And I couldn't stay here after Molly died. I had to get away."

"That's how it was for me, too. After you left, and with Molly gone, I just couldn't stay in Summit."

The year had been 1916. Rafe had gone to France, and weeks later, he'd been fighting Germans in the sky.

Silence enveloped them again.

Daisy had to look at something besides her daughter's final resting place. She turned her attention to the meadow beyond the picket fence. A three-sided aeroplane hangar with a peaked roof housed a red two-seater biplane not far beyond the cemetery. A swath of grass had been mowed down the meadow's length to make a makeshift runway. She cut a glance at her husband and gestured at the craft. "You're still flying?"

He followed her glance and nodded. "The plane is faster than taking the train. I use it mostly for business." He looked back at her, and warmth lit his eyes. "Besides, I like flying."

Rafe tipped his head to one side and perused her from her shoes to her hair.

The breeze played about her head. Air currents lifted a few blonde filaments and wafted them across her face. Daisy brushed aside the wayward strands and tried not to fidget. She hoped Rafe approved of the other new dress she wore today. She felt fashionable in its dropped waist and sash knotted about her hips, its straight style and Peter Pan collar.

At Rafe's continued scrutiny, Daisy tried not to squirm. Something about the way he looked at her, about the intent expression on his face, captivated her. When their gazes snagged, heat arced between them. The air hummed while they yearned toward each other. A flame lit Rafe's eyes, and as if in a trance, he curled one palm about her shoulder. Daisy quivered in response. She waited for him to speak, to tell her that he still loved her, but the moment passed. With a shake of his head, her husband dropped his hand to his side.

A hush dropped between them. Daisy took a trembling breath and tried to collect her composure.

"I want to take you to Montgomery's Emporium and get you outfitted with some new things." Rafe's change of subject caught her unawares.

Daisy cast him a startled look. "New things? Why?"

He sighed. "Have you forgotten that I oversee your bank account? I know where you spend every penny, and except for the two outfits you wore yesterday and today, you haven't bought any new clothes in four years. All of the money has gone to pay for your tuition, medical books, and clinical supplies. You've spent only enough on yourself to house and feed you."

"You spied on my expenses?" Her voice rose.

"Not because I didn't trust you. I know you well enough to realize you won't throw money away." The hint of a smile cracked his face. "My accountant is a bit fussy about keeping track of where the money goes."

"Oh. I see."

"Will you come with me?"

Was Rafe offering her an olive branch? Or did he want her to dress in a manner that would befit the mine owner's wife? Whatever the reason, she wouldn't turn down an opportunity to spend time with her husband. "Of course."

Stooping, she placed a kiss on the grave marker's rounded top and cast a final look at her daughter's resting place.

Rafe waited until she'd collected herself, then took her elbow in a gentle clasp and turned her toward the gate. They passed through and ambled down the track toward the street. His fingers on her elbow brought back memories of their courtship. Daisy tried not to let him know how much she enjoyed his touch.

They reached the town and stepped onto the boardwalk. Halfway down the block, Rafe turned her toward the new mercantile store. As they passed its plate glass window,

Daisy stared into the aperture. In the display area behind the glass stood the latest in marketing techniques—a life-size female mannequin—dressed in a fashionable outfit. The owner of this shop must have money to spare if he could afford to transport a mannequin all the way to Summit.

The words *Montgomery's Emporium* had been painted on a sign above the door in black letters outlined with gold. Rafe opened the door, and with his hand riding the small of her back, he escorted her inside. A bell above the door jingled their presence.

Daisy cast a glance about the crowded interior. This store sold merchandise a cut above the typical rural general store. Its inventory included the usual supplies that mining and ranching housewives or their husbands needed, but luxury items mingled with utilitarian objects. Fancy lamps, bric-a-brac, paintings, rugs, children's toys, even store-bought underwear stocked the shelves.

A woman emerged from a room behind the counter and greeted them with a smile. "'Mawnin', Rafe honey. It's a little early for you to be shoppin', isn't it?" Her drawl flowed through the air like warm honey and hinted at the deep South. She rounded the counter and strolled toward them.

Daisy halted. A hot tide surged from her belly upward to her hairline. She knew her fair skin couldn't conceal her flush, but she was helpless to stop the heat that consumed her. Her palms grew damp.

Rafe's hand at her back urged her forward. Daisy took one more grudging step and stopped again. His hand dropped to his side.

"Morning, Edith," Rafe replied with the easy familiarity that one accorded a close friend.

"I'm not shopping for myself. I'd like you to outfit my

wife. She needs some new things, something appropriate for Summit."

Daisy stared at the woman who had halted beside Rafe. This was the same woman who had waylaid her husband outside the hotel yesterday afternoon. Her willowy height made Daisy feel diminished. Finger waves styled her gleaming bobbed hair. Her blonde eyebrows had been plucked to make them thinner, then darkened. A line of ebony kohl rimmed her eyelids, and she'd applied soot to her lashes. Her cheeks glowed with rouge that had been applied with an artful hand. Scarlet lips formed a perfect Cupid's Bow. Daisy disliked her on the spot.

And her dress—her dropped-waist dress of dusty rose voile must have cost more than the two new ones Daisy had purchased put together.

"Rafe, you have a wife?" The woman turned her attention to Daisy, taking her measure in one sweeping glance. Conscious of her face—bare of cosmetics—and her lack of pedigree, Daisy felt judged and dismissed, although the woman took care not to betray her feelings to Rafe.

Rafe's features reddened, and he tucked his hands into his back pockets. "I do have a wife. Edith, I'd like you to meet Daisy." Rafe nodded toward Daisy. "Daisy, meet Edith Montgomery. Her father owns the mercantile."

As Daisy acknowledged the introduction, she recalled that Rafe had told her the Montgomerys were renting Cole's house. *Cole's house*, which was located just across the road from Rafe's own dwelling. Daisy's jealousy kicked up a notch.

Edith extended her hand. Crimson nails decorated her fingertips. "Gracious, Miz Wild Wind. You certainly are a surprise. Some of us here in Summit wondered if you really existed. I heard the gossip that you'd come back, but since

Rafe didn't mention it, I didn't believe it." She cut an arch glance at Rafe. "Rafe nevah talked about you."

After a brief handshake, Daisy dropped Edith's hand. "I've been attending medical school. Now that I've graduated, I intend to set up a practice here in Summit."

"A doctah! Well, Doc Irby takes real good care of us." Edith's drawl drew out her words. "But you're so brave to have a career."

Daisy thought it time to deflect the focus from herself. "What brought you to Summit, Miss Montgomery? Life must seem very dull for you here."

"Mah daddy has the consumption. His doctah's in Charleston advised him to go West if he wanted to live. So, we sold everythin' and came here. Summit suits us." She cast another look at Rafe. "I don't find it dull."

Though Daisy distrusted the smile Edith Montgomery gave her, a smile that revealed perfect white teeth, she attempted a civil reply. "A dry climate is our usual remedy for tuberculosis. I hope your father has been doing well since you moved here."

"Why, bless your heart for askin'." Edith's Cupid's Bow lips curled up. "Mah daddy's doin' just fine. He's so much better, we've decided to stay here. We'll nevah go back to Charleston."

Rafe stirred. "If you could help Daisy, Edith, I'd appreciate it. Get her whatever she needs and put it on my account."

"Really, Rafe, I can choose my own clothes." Daisy frowned at her husband.

"I'm sure you can, but Edith can cut your shopping time in half. She knows what she has in stock. I'll wait here for you." Rafe settled himself in a rocking chair beside the central wood stove and crossed one booted ankle over his other knee. The look they exchanged was poignant with memories of the early days of their marriage when Rafe had accompanied her to the shops in Denver, outfitting her for life in the West. Their forays into Denver's stores had been a grand adventure. They'd walked arm in arm, and Rafe had given his approval to every outfit she chose. Laughter and kisses had set the tone for those light-hearted days.

Daisy turned away and followed Edith to the section near the store's front where women's clothing hung.

Rafe had settled into the chair with a determined air, and Daisy knew him well enough to realize he'd wait there until she'd completed her shopping. No protest from her would dislodge him.

Edith surveyed Daisy's diminutive form. "You're not very big."

Daisy ignored the urge to bristle. Edith's tone hinted at disapproval, as if her size were a black mark against her character and some deficiency in her make-up accounted for her lack of height. She couldn't stop the retort that sprang to her lips. "Rafe doesn't care. He likes me this way."

Edith cast her a pitying look but said nothing. She pulled a garment from the rack and held it up against Daisy's front. "This one might do."

Daisy took the dress and eyed the apparel with critical appraisal. Her days as a socialite's maid had given her an eye for fashion and fabric. She knew quality, and she'd developed her own sense of style. She shook her head. "Not this one." She hung the frock back on the rack.

The bell over the door tinkled again. The women glanced over as a man wearing a chambray work shirt and denim pants entered. With a quick look around, the man spotted Rafe and hurried in his direction.

Rafe rose and stepped toward the newcomer. They met in

the center of the store at the end of a counter that held children's toys. They conferred, while Rafe listened with bent head. At the end of their conversation, Rafe gave an order, and the man loped from the mercantile. The door banged shut behind him.

Rafe strode toward the women, skirting several shelves and racks of merchandise. He came to a stop beside the plate glass window in which stood the mannequin. "There's been a minor emergency at the processing plant. I have to go. Daisy, don't worry about spending too much money. Get whatever you want. Edith will take good care of you." With a mock salute to the women, he bade them farewell. "Ladies . . ."

He wheeled and headed out of the mercantile.

Daisy watched while the door shut behind him, leaving her alone with the woman who had put her hands on him the night before.

CHAPTER 5

Rafe's departure left behind an awkward silence. Daisy and Edith faced each other as two contestants sparring for the same prize.

Daisy took the offensive. "You really don't need to help me. I can choose my own wardrobe. If I have any questions, I'll ask."

"But Rafe specifically put you in mah care."

Being in the charge of the beauteous Edith was a condition so unappealing that Daisy recoiled. Drawing on her years of watching her former employer deal with undesirables, she drew herself up to her full height and looked down her pert nose at the other woman. "Thank you, but I'd prefer to dress myself. You may go."

Edith propped her hands on her hips. Amusement lit her face, and her lips twitched, but she didn't leave. "Rafe has moved on, you know. He's nevah mentioned you in all the years I've known him."

"I won't discuss my husband with you."

Edith shrugged. "Suit yourself. It won't change a thing."

A tall, rangy man with thinning auburn hair emerged from

the back of the mercantile. "Edith? Do you need help out here?"

Edith gripped Daisy's arm and dragged her to the back of the emporium. They halted before the high wooden counter. "Daddy, guess who's come to live in Summit?"

Daisy appraised Mr. Montgomery's health with a professional eye. Edith had been right when she'd said that her father had recovered from the consumption. His ruddy color bespoke health. Though he was thin, he showed none of the muscle-wasting emaciation typical of tuberculosis patients. Living in the dry mountain air had benefited his constitution.

She brought her attention back to the conversation.

"This is Miz Wild Wind, Rafe's wife."

Mr. Montgomery's forehead wrinkled as he turned his attention to Daisy. "Rafe's wife? I figured the gossip to be nothin' more than a rumor." He looked her up and down. "We thought you must be dead."

Edith nodded. "In this case, the gossip is true. His wife has come back to Summit."

Mr. Montgomery seemed to collect his manners. He came around the counter and took Daisy's hand. "Forgive me, Miz Wild Wind. Hearin' that you've come home took me by surprise. We weren't expectin' you."

And why should he be expecting her? That both these people assumed they figured largely enough in Rafe's esteem that they should be privy to his personal affairs rankled. She allowed Mr. Montgomery to hold her hand and forced a smile. "I kept my return a surprise."

"She's a doctah, Daddy."

Mr. Montgomery looked down his thin nose at Daisy. "Well, now. A woman doctah! And do you intend to practice medicine here?"

"I do."

Mr. Montgomery pulled at an earlobe. "I wish you well, but folks around here have nevah seen a woman doctah before. It may take them a while to get used to the idea."

"I know I'm a novelty, but I assure you I'm a competent physician." Daisy aimed another smile at them both. "If you'll excuse me, I must get on with my shopping." She made a dismissive motion when Edith stepped toward her. "No, I'm sure you have work to do, so don't feel you must help me. If I can't find something, I'll ask."

Daisy browsed among the shelves and racks. Rafe had told her to spare no expense, so she decided to take him at his word. With Edith Montgomery having all but declared that she considered Rafe to be hers, a new wardrobe would be a necessity. She could never compete with Edith in glamor and sophistication, but she wouldn't concede the field without a fight. Her future, and Rafe's, were at stake.

Most of the clothing at Montgomery's Emporium didn't measure up to Denver standards, but Daisy found a few items that met her approval. She chose two gingham dresses with dropped waists and one skirt and blouse set. She piled new underwear and hose onto the mound of apparel on the counter.

Edith rang up her purchases and bagged them. Daisy left the shop with her booty and returned to the hotel.

In her room, she dumped the parcels on the bed and sank onto the coverlet. Her thoughts circled around again to last night's question. Had returning to Summit been a mistake? Would she lose Rafe after all? Upon reflection, she concluded that he most likely interpreted Edith's interest as a close friendship. In his dealings with the Southern belle that morning, he'd betrayed no hint of a romantic interest in her. Besides, he wouldn't have taken his wife to the shop if he'd had feelings for Edith, would he? The Rafe Daisy had known would never have been disloyal to his wife, and in her heart, she felt he'd remained true to his wedding vows despite their separation.

Still, the fact that he hadn't mentioned he had a wife distressed her. How could he have gone four years and not mentioned her? Had he truly put her behind him? A vision of the years stretching before her while she and Rafe remained married in name only presented a bleak future.

Daisy stiffened her spine. If, after all she could do to win Rafe back, he refused to live with her as her husband, she still had her medicine. The Lord had gifted her with a talent for healing, and she'd practice medicine with or without Rafe. Somehow, she'd manage to get through each day, just as she'd done for the past four years.

She hung her new dresses in the wardrobe and packed her underthings in the dresser. Then she gathered up the flyers she'd had printed in Denver and left the hotel. The flyers would advertise her as a reputable doctor. The first step in establishing a practice in the town would be to let people know of her availability.

At the livery stable near the train depot at the far end of town, she began her mission. She stepped through the open double doors into the barn's dim interior, redolent with the scent of hay and horses. Several horses stood slack-hipped in their stalls. They swished their tails at the ever-present flies, and they cocked their ears at her when she entered.

Did Jeb Harte still run the livery? He'd be sure to remember her, though she didn't see him in the building. The sharp *pang pang* of metal on metal sounded from the yard behind the stable, indicating that someone was outside. Picking her way through the shadowy interior, she headed toward the double doors at the stable's rear. Outside in the adjoining corral, she spied Jeb in his open-sided farrier's shed that backed up to the barn's outside wall.

He stood at a blacksmith's anvil, shaping a glowing horseshoe with a mallet. A tall bay gelding stood cross-tied between two posts near the anvil.

As Daisy ambled toward the farrier's shed, she took care to avoid the horse droppings that littered the dirt. She halted when she reached the shed and waited for Jeb to acknowledge her.

Jeb gave the horseshoe a final whack. With a pair of tongs, he thrust the red-hot metal into a tin bucket filled with water. The shoe sizzled. Only when the metal had cooled and he'd laid the shoe on a wooden shelf nailed between two support posts did Jeb peel off his gloves and look in her direction. He dropped the gloves onto the shelf and strolled from beneath the shed's shelter. His thick leather farrier's apron flapped with each step.

"I heard you'd come back." He thrust out a large paw. "Welcome home, Mrs. Daisy."

His greeting warmed her as his hand engulfed her own. "Thank you, Jeb. It's good to be back." After a hearty shake, she pulled her hand free.

He eyed her with friendly interest. "Are you here to stay?"

"I plan to."

He looked away from her and glanced at the mountain peaks that ringed the valley, then ripped his cowboy hat from his head and swiped an arm across his sweaty forehead. As he settled his hat on his head once more, he returned his attention to her face. He cleared his throat. "Well, Mrs. Daisy, I wish you all the best. Maybe you can do something with that husband of yours. He's been mighty unhappy since he came back from the war."

"I know he has. I hope I can help him."

"If anyone can, it will be you, and not that minx from Charleston." Jeb narrowed his eyes at her. "That gal has plans to rope your husband. Have you met her?"

"Yes, this morning." If Jed Harte was confiding his concerns to her, Edith's interest in Rafe must be obvious to everyone in Summit. The thought added another layer of anxiety about her husband's involvement with the sultry Southerner.

"Now that you're back, take that husband of yours in hand and remind him that he's a married man. Not that I fault him. He's done nothing, but that Montgomery gal is tryin' her best to hogtie him." Jed cleared his throat again and shuffled his feet. "I've said my piece. Now, what can I do for you? Do you need to rent a horse?"

Daisy shook her head and held out a flyer. "I've been to medical school, and now I'm a doctor, I wondered if I could put one of these on your cork board?"

Jeb took the flyer from her and scanned the paper. "You're a doctor now? And you a woman! And such a little mite!"

Daisy gritted her teeth. The way people carried on about her being a woman doctor, one would think she had two heads and was a member of a freak show. "Yes, I'm a doctor, and I intend to set up a practice here. These flyers are to let people know I'm in business. I thought since a lot of people come to your livery, it would help if I could leave a flyer on your board."

Jeb ran a palm around the back of his neck and shrugged. He pushed the ad back into her hand. "Sure, help yourself."

When Daisy had tacked her ad to the cork board beside

the door, she stepped back and eyed her handiwork. Her handbill rubbed shoulders with ads for horses and cattle, farming equipment, seed, and saddlery. She sighed. Most of Jeb's customers were men. A man would never consider soliciting the services of a female doctor.

CHAPTER 6

Undaunted, Daisy squared her shoulders and left the livery. Next on her list was Katie's Café, the café she remembered from her earlier days in Summit. Katie ran the café, and her husband supervised a crew of miners. Katie had become one of her particular friends during her years in Summit before the Great War and would support her efforts to establish a medical practice. A member of Katie's family might even be one of her first customers.

At the café, Daisy hurried through the dining area and found her friend bending over the stove in the kitchen. She rapped on the open kitchen door.

At the knock, Katie straightened away from the oven and turned. Her face lit when she saw Daisy, and she opened her arms in welcome. "Daisy, come here and let me give you a hug!"

Daisy rushed into her friend's embrace, and the women hugged, hard. Just that simple human contact reminded Daisy of how lonely she'd been during the past years. She'd so longed for affection and warm human contact. Both had been denied her. Now Katie's kindness proved to be her undoing.

Katie disentangled herself from Daisy's clutching arms and put her hands on her friend's shoulders. She gave Daisy a sympathetic look. "I think you need a cup of tea and a good coze."

"Shouldn't you be working on tonight's meal?" Daisy sniffled.

Katie shook her head and steered Daisy toward a long wooden worktable. She pulled out a stool. "The meal can wait." She pushed Daisy onto the stool and busied herself heating water, then pulled two tin mugs from a row of shelves beside the stove.

Daisy watched while Katie prepared the tea. The homey sight calmed her.

When the water was hot and the tea was steeping, Katie brought the teapot to the table and settled on a stool beside her friend. "Now, tell me why Rafe has been here in Summit all alone for the past four years, and you've been somewhere else. Where have you been, anyway?"

"I've been going to medical school."

Katie lifted her eyebrows toward her hairline. "Medical school!"

Daisy nodded.

"And what did Rafe have to say about that?"

"Nothing. I didn't tell him. We haven't been in contact. He didn't even know I was coming back to Summit."

Katie pushed back a strand of brown hair that had come loose from her braid and reached for the teapot. She poured tea into both mugs and shoved the sugar bowl toward Daisy.

Daisy ladled a spoonful of the sweetening into her mug and stirred. When both women had their tea fixed to their liking and had sipped, Katie prodded her friend.

"You might as well tell me all of it. Why haven't you been living here with Rafe?"

The story tumbled out. Except for Rafe's family, she'd discussed her personal life with no one in all the years since the war. Sharing her heartache with Katie somehow made the pain more bearable.

"I can't say I'm surprised that Rafe left you. He's changed since the war." Katie took another sip and cast a concerned look at her friend. "When he first came back, he was jumpy. Loud noises set him off. He's over that now, but he's hard. There's no "give" to him. He's working himself to death. And he hasn't been to church."

"Rafe has stopped attending church?"

Katie nodded.

The news grieved Daisy. Their shared faith had been one of the things she and Rafe had valued. "Has he ever mentioned me?" The question nagged as she speculated about whether or not Edith had told her the truth on that score.

"Not so I've heard, although I don't see much of him. He takes his meals here sometimes, but I don't rub shoulders with him. Any of the new people who have come to Summit since the war probably don't even know he's married, although amongst those of us who know you, there's been plenty of speculation about where you might be. No one has dared to ask Rafe, though."

Daisy's shoulders slumped, and she stared down into her mug. Edith had told the truth, then. Rafe hadn't mentioned her.

Katie cast her a shrewd look. "So you've met Edith Montgomery."

Daisy lifted her gaze to her friend's perceptive face. "Yes, Rafe took me to Montgomery's Emporium this morning to do some shopping."

"Don't blame Rafe for Edith's flirting. He hasn't encouraged her, although he could do more to discourage her. I don't think he realizes what she's about."

"How could he not realize?"

Katie shrugged and rolled her eyes. "He's a man. Men can be blind where women are concerned. He's friends with the Montgomerys and plays chess with Edith's father every Sunday afternoon. He often takes Sunday dinner with them, and he spends the holidays with them, so it may be that he looks on Edith as a sister."

Daisy cast a doubtful look at her friend. Edith's dealings with Rafe had nothing sisterly about them. "She made it plain that Rafe is a close friend of her and her father."

"They're his kind of people. They come from money."

"I can't compete with her." Daisy sighed.

Katie squeezed her hand. "Of course, you can. You already have an advantage over Edith—you're his wife. He loved you once, and I'd wager he still does. Your Rafe is a man who stands by his commitments. He won't let Edith steal him away from you." She sat back and picked up one of the flyers Daisy had laid on the table. "Now, what do you plan to do with that medical degree you earned?"

When Daisy had shared her plans, Katie chuckled.

"Good for you. Doc Irby needs some competition. He's an old fossil, but he's a favorite of the children. He keeps peppermint candies in his pocket and hands them out to the youngsters. And the men like him because of his tonic, which is mostly whiskey."

"Whiskey!"

"Yes, whiskey. It doesn't cure his patients, but it sure makes them feel good. At least for a while."

Daisy stared at the stack of flyers, then glanced at Katie. "Doc Irby must have come to Summit after Dr. Keller left to help with the war effort." Dr. Keller had been Summit's doctor and had taken her under his wing when she first came to town, full of ambition to be a nurse.

"Yes, Doc Irby arrived soon after you'd gone to aid the wounded."

"Did you know Dr. Keller died of the Spanish flu right after the war?"

Katie shook her head, and her mouth turned down. "The news never reached Summit."

"I worked under Dr. Keller in France, right on the front lines. Once Rafe left me after we returned to the States, Dr. Keller's memory inspired me to get my medical degree and become a doctor." Regret for the doctor's death tugged at Daisy. "If he'd lived and returned to Summit, I could have partnered with him after I got my license to practice medicine. Instead, I'm here alone."

Katie grimaced. "And Summit is stuck with that quack Irby."

Silence fell while the women sipped their tea. After a few moments, Katie stirred and glanced at Daisy.

"Since a road has been put in all the way to Summit and city folk have motor cars, tourists come up here during the summer. It's a bit early yet, but before long, they'll come driving up that road." Katie propped her chin on one hand and looked at Daisy with her head cocked. "And six days a week the train runs up here for the day trippers."

"So Summit has been discovered?"

"You might say that. The hotel is full during the summer months. You may get a few customers from the tourists."

"I suppose so."

"Every few weeks an over-confident young man who's driving too fast misjudges a curve and goes over the edge. You might be able to put the pieces back together. Doc Irby certainly can't."

"Katie! I don't want that kind of business!"

Katie shrugged. "Families come with their children. We have the usual assortment of sniffles and tummy aches when families are here."

"I hope Doc Irby doesn't give those children some of his patent medicine." The thought of children being administered anything containing whiskey horrified her.

"He doesn't know how to do anything else."

Daisy shook her head. "In any city, he'd be out of a job."

"That's why he stays here."

"What do the tourists do while they're here? Summit doesn't have much to offer."

Katie laughed. "I can tell you've been away a long time. Things have changed around here. For a generous fee, Rafe allows people to tour certain sections of the mine. Some of the miners serve as tour guides whenever a group is scheduled."

Stupefied, Daisy stared at her friend. "People actually spend money to go down into that dark hole?"

"Yes. Only it's not as dark as it used to be. Rafe's had electric lights installed in the tunnels, especially those sections that are open to the public."

Daisy's thoughts jumped to how the whole town had benefited when the ore refinery had been built when Rafe and his brother had been active partners, and hydroelectric power had been installed to run the refinery. Now, all the businesses had electric lights, and she'd enjoyed electricity in the home Rafe had built for her.

"Picnic tables have been built beside the lake so families can eat boxed lunches there," Katie continued. "And the T Bar Ranch takes in boarders. Some people like a taste of the ranching life, and with beef prices so low, the extra money helps. Rafe gives aeroplane rides, too. You'd be surprised at how many pretty young things love to go up with the handsome ace."

The news hit Daisy in the stomach. Hearing about Rafe's life during the years she'd been gone brought many surprises, not all of them good. She propped an elbow on the table and covered her eyes. "I've been gone too long. Maybe it's too late for our marriage to be mended."

Katie patted her shoulder. "Never think that. I'm only telling you so you know how things are with him."

Daisy dropped her hand to her lap. "What else?"

"As far as I know, he's declined all social invitations from those pretty young things. He hasn't been seen with any of them outside of his cockpit, though not for lack of trying on their part. Your husband is quite popular with the girls."

Daisy could well imagine the truth of that statement. Rafe's handsome features and engaging ways, his smiles and thoughtfulness, had won her own impressionable heart. Since the war, an aloof attitude and an air of command combined with his good looks must make an irresistible challenge for modern young ladies who felt society's rules were meant to be broken.

Katie continued her narrative. "In addition to our July Fourth celebration, the tourist season's highlight comes during the last week of August. The town puts on a fete to commemorate summer's end. Your husband and the Montgomerys are the planning committee."

One more thing to throw Rafe into Edith's orbit. Dismal discouragement gnawed at Daisy.

"The town sponsors a barbeque, a parade, and a dance. Your husband gives plane rides all afternoon. The highlight of the night is a fireworks show."

"And how does Rafe manage not to burn down the mountains with his fireworks?"

Katie giggled. "Your husband is a very enterprising man. All of the fireworks explode over the lake. Still, we've had a brush fire or two."

"I can see that Summit isn't the quiet town I remember."

"Not in the summer. Winter is a different matter."

Daisy shivered as she recalled the brutal winters the town endured when massive snowfall closed the roads and railroad for the winter months. Only the hardy could survive a Summit winter.

She drained her tea and set down the mug. Scooping up her handbills, she hugged her friend. "This conversation has been very informative. Thank you for the tea and for listening to my woes. Now, I'd better see how many more of these ads I can pass out this afternoon."

CHAPTER 7

After the service on her first Sunday in Summit, Daisy paused at the foot of the steps outside the church. To the newcomers, she'd become an object of speculation. Those who had known her from her earlier days welcomed her. Although curiosity about her relationship with Rafe overshadowed their encounters, no one brought up the topic. The whole town knew she'd returned and that she and Rafe weren't living together. The affair provided endless juicy conjecture. She tried not to mind being the subject of gossip, but the scrutiny still rankled.

Edith and her father stopped beside her. Daisy tried not to let the *chic* Edith, who wore a dropped-waisted silk dress of deep violet, overshadow her. A velvet bow nestled in the V between Edith's Peter Pan collar, and embroidery decorated the garment's pockets. A straw cloche hat with a violet silk flower over one ear hugged her bright hair.

"Good mawnin', Miz Wild Wind." Edith curved her lips in a patronizing smile. "The weather is fine today, don't you agree?"

"Very fine." Daisy cast a glance at the cloudless sky. She

wanted to fan herself, but she wouldn't do so in Edith's presence. In her silk dress, Edith looked cool and polished and made Daisy feel hot and rumpled in comparison.

"I see the good people of Summit are makin' you welcome."

"Everyone has been very kind. Of course, I still have friends here, so I'm not a complete stranger." Edith needed a reminder that Daisy had allies.

"I'm sure you'll be right at home in no time." Mr. Montgomery patted her shoulder.

"Actually, I feel at home here already."

Edith took her father's arm. "It's been nice chattin' with you, Miz Wild Wind, but Rafe is comin' to dinner, so we'd best get on home. Have a good afternoon."

Mr. Montgomery tipped his Homberg hat to her and allowed his daughter to tow him away.

Deflated at Edith's news, Daisy watched them walk to the road and then turn in the direction of their rented house—the house just across the street from Rafe's home.

That Edith had dropped the news Rafe would be their dinner guest hadn't been an accident. The flirt had inserted that morsel into their conversation with deliberate intent to let her know Rafe would be spending his afternoon with them, while she remained alone in the boarding house.

Daisy turned away and trudged to her hotel room. The hollow feeling that had burgeoned in her chest expanded. In the hope that Rafe would attend the church service that morning, she'd dressed with care. She'd donned her new green dress with the pink polka dots and had worn her long faux pearl necklace. She'd taken special care with her bobbed hair, wanting to look her best for him. He hadn't come.

In her room, Daisy tossed her purse and her Bible onto the bed and sank down on the crocheted white coverlet. Her shoulders slumped. Her thoughts turned to Rafe, who'd be spending the afternoon with Edith and her father. Scenes of Edith flirting with Rafe tortured her. Would Rafe share with Edith the fond smile he'd given her on the boardwalk? No doubt they'd engage in cozy conversation, and Edith would push the boundaries of acceptable behavior. Daisy fisted her hands in her lap, and her stomach churned.

She jumped to her feet and paced to the door, then spun and crossed the room again. At the double windows, she halted and brushed aside a swath of lacy curtain to stare down at the street. With the town's businesses closed for the day, the sunny road drowsed in the heat.

She pivoted from the window and returned to the bed. Lifting her Bible, she clutched it to her bosom as she crossed to the rocking chair in the corner. She sank into the chair and opened the Scriptures. As it had many times during the past four years, a time of meditation in the Word and prayer helped to restore her peace.

She laid the Bible on the lamp table beside the bed and left the room. She'd lost her appetite the moment Edith had mentioned that Rafe was spending the afternoon with her and her father, but perhaps she could choke down a few bites at Katie's Café. More than the food, Katie's breezy cheerfulness was just what she needed.

* * *

The next morning, Daisy donned the serviceable dark skirt and plain white blouse she wore when she worked. Even though she had no patients yet, she wanted to look professional. Outside, she strolled up and down the boardwalk, letting people know she was available. She'd tacked her flyers on the cork boards of all the businesses in town and handed them out to curious people along the boardwalk, but no one had requested her services.

People stopped to chat, eager to have a word with the newly returned wife of the town's preeminent citizen. Daisy suffered their attention and kept a smile on her face, though she wished she could avoid the notoriety. She'd just disentangled herself from a conversation with a curious matron with several children clustered about her skirts when she spied a portly, middle-aged gentleman strolling toward her.

The man wore a dark suit and a straw boater hat. A tidy mustache curled up at each corner of his mouth.

One of the little girls standing beside the lady tugged at her mother's arm. "Mamma, there's Doc Irby. Can I ask him for a piece of peppermint?"

"Yes, dear. I see he's already passing out candy." All the children abandoned their mother and scampered toward the doctor.

The lady cast an apologetic glance at Daisy. "Doc Irby is a great favorite with the children."

"I can see why." Daisy watched the doctor approach.

Numerous youngsters bobbed around him like corks on water. The physician gave each child a piece of peppermint and a pat on the head. As he neared, she turned a professional eye on him. From his ruddy cheeks and the veins across his nose, he must imbibe too much of his own tonic.

Doc Irby halted beside her and looked her up and down. His eyes glinted behind his spectacles. "You must be the new doctor in town."

"Yes, I am." Daisy extended her hand. "I'm Dr. Wild Wind."

Doc Irby took her hand in both of his. "Well, well. A woman doctor. Times are changing, eh?"

"This is the twentieth century, not the Dark Ages." Daisy couldn't keep an edge from her voice.

Doc Irby chuckled. "So it is. I think there'll be enough room for both of us in this town."

"I hope so. I'm not going anywhere."

The doctor winked at her. "You've got more to keep you here than doctoring."

Daisy didn't rise to his gambit. She turned the conversation in a pharmaceutical direction. "I've heard people speak of your famous patent medicine. I wondered if I might purchase a bottle?"

Doc Irby beamed at her. "Of course, of course! My tonic is good for what ails you. It will cure any ailment the human body can devise."

The good doctor had a bit of the huckster in him as well as whatever medical knowledge he might possess. Daisy began to see why the simple mining folk had confidence in him.

He patted his suit jacket's pockets. "I just happen to have a bottle of my patent medicine right here. I never leave home without one." He produced a flat green bottle from a pocket and presented it to her with a flourish.

Daisy took the bottle. "Thank you, Dr. Irby. How much do I owe you?"

With an expansive gesture, he waved away her offer of payment. "Not a penny, my dear. This one's on me."

When they'd parted, Daisy hurried to her hotel room. With the door closed behind her, she unscrewed the lid and sniffed. Strong whiskey fumes wafted from the bottle's neck and stung her eyes. She averted her face and blinked. As Katie had warned her, the tonic contained a high whiskey content. She took a cautious sip. Beneath the whiskey flavor, the taste of herbs layered on her tongue.

She recapped the bottle and stuffed it in a dresser drawer. Although whiskey seemed to be the main ingredient, perhaps there were enough herbs to help with some ailments. She could guess what some of the herbs were that the doctor brewed into his tonic, but she couldn't identify them all. To prescribe the tonic to random physical conditions could be dangerous. The wrong herb for a specific illness might have a negative reaction. With a shake of her head at the doctor's phony medicine, she left the room.

Rafe remained elusive for several days, and Daisy didn't catch a glimpse of him. From her experience with being married to him, she knew that responsibilities at the mine occupied most of his time. Though he now lived as a bachelor and might sometimes take his evening meals at Katie's Café, she didn't encounter him there. His absence from the café couldn't be that he intentionally tried to avoid her. The Rafe she knew would never stoop to such a tactic.

Toward the week's end, she decided to track him down. She needed to see him on a professional matter, and she couldn't wait.

That morning as she prepared to leave her hotel room, she swung the wardrobe door wide and contemplated her clothing with a critical eye. With Rafe in mind, she searched through her ensembles for one that would set off her figure. Which outfit should she wear? Which garment would flatter her most? After much agonizing over the choice of attire, she donned a skirt and blouse set, one of the new outfits she'd purchased from Montgomery's Emporium. The long blouse of dusky blue fell to the bottom of her hips and was encircled with a low-slung tie belt. The skirt of checked dusky blue and orange swirled just to her calves. She glanced in the mirror and freshened her golden hair.

She dropped her gaze to her lips. What would she look

like if she painted her lips in the fashionable Cupid's Bow style and colored her cheeks with rouge? Would she be daring enough to darken her eyelids with kohl and her lashes with soot? What would Rafe think of her then?

Whirling away from the mirror, she banished the image her imagination conjured. What Rafe would think of her if she used face paint didn't matter, since she'd never bolster the courage to try. Besides, she didn't think Rafe would approve of her wearing cosmetics.

Nerves twisted Daisy's stomach as she left the hotel and hiked to the mine. She hadn't seen her husband since the morning he'd escorted her to Montgomery's Emporium. That had been over a week ago. Once having seen him again, she missed him with an aching misery. She anticipated the coming encounter with a mixture of hope, yearning, and dread. She hungered for their meeting to be civil, or perhaps even warm. More than likely, however, Rafe would resort to the cold stranger who'd taken the place of the husband she'd married.

She hesitated outside his office door and closed her eyes, then took a deep breath to bolster her courage. With only a moment's dawdling, she opened her eyes and stepped over the threshold. She halted. The office was empty.

The letdown nearly undid her. She almost lost her courage and fled. With a firm grip on her runaway emotions, she banished her misgivings. Rafe must be attending to business in the mine or at the refinery. She'd wait for him. Crossing the office to a wooden chair in front of his desk, she sank down onto its hard surface and tucked her legs beneath her, prepared to wait for her husband's return.

The walnut mantel clock on the shelf ticked away the minutes. The chimes had just jingled the ten o'clock hour when voices sounded in the reception room. Daisy recognized

Rafe speaking. The second voice she didn't know. She clenched her fists in her lap. She'd hoped he'd be alone.

Rafe and the other man stopped just outside the office and conversed for several minutes. Then silence fell and footsteps crossed to the mine's door. The door opened and shut. The other man had left.

Daisy felt Rafe's presence before he spoke. She turned her head and saw him looming in the doorway. Feeling at a disadvantage sitting down, she rose to her feet and faced him. They stared at each other across the room, his face closed, and his eyes shuttered.

At last, he spoke. "What are you doing here?"

"Do I need a reason to see my husband?"

"I can think of no reason why you should seek my company."

Daisy despaired. Would he never accept that she still loved him and wanted to be with him, even without the reason that had brought her to his office? "We're husband and wife. Spouses usually spend time together."

Rafe tossed his black felt cowboy hat onto its peg beside the door and crossed the room with his habitual easy grace. He rounded his desk.

Daisy watched him with hungry eyes. She wanted him to come to her, to touch her with love and tenderness the way he once had done. She ached to touch him in return, to feel his flesh beneath her fingers, but he put the desk between them and looked her up and down without emotion.

"I told you not to expect things to change between us."

"We can't both live here and completely avoid each other."

"I'm not avoiding you. You're simply not a part of my life."

His words crushed her. Her heart must bleed from the

blow he'd just dealt her. Did he feel nothing for her? How could he cut her from his life—she, with whom he'd created a child—yet welcome Edith into his circle? Edith, with whom he seemed to enjoy an easy familiarity but who had no legal ties to him.

Daisy stepped closer to the desk and reached toward him. "Rafe . . ."

For a heartbeat, his veneer cracked once again and revealed his own pain. His tortured expression betrayed that he suffered as she did. Their separation caused him anguish. Only that glimpse into his heart eased Daisy's misery. Perhaps she could hope, after all.

Her hand dropped to her side. "I have something to discuss with you."

Rafe had mastered his emotions. No trace of his real feelings showed when he replied. "I'm listening."

"As a doctor, I need a place to sterilize my dressings and equipment. There's no place for me to do that at the hotel. I wondered if I might use the kitchen at the house."

For long moments, he regarded her with a thoughtful expression. Finally, he spoke. "I'm usually away from the house in the mornings. You can use the kitchen then."

That Rafe wanted her to use the house when he'd be less likely to encounter her stung, but at least he'd agreed. "Thank you. I'll go tomorrow."

"Do you have any patients yet?"

"No, but I've been visiting the miner's wives. I hope they'll come to trust me, and I want to be prepared. If someone has an emergency, I won't have time to sterilize bandages or instruments."

Her husband gave a stiff nod and pulled out his chair. He sat, then reached for a stack of papers and pulled it toward him.

She'd been dismissed. Hoping that Rafe might at least bid her farewell, Daisy stood poised before the desk for several moments, but he didn't look up. When he continued to ignore her, she whirled and stalked across the room. At the door, she glanced back.

Rafe sat unmoving, his head bowed.

CHAPTER 8

Daisy stood at the bottom of the veranda steps with her black doctor's bag in one hand while she scrutinized the house where she and Rafe had lived for three years. He'd had the house built before they married, so they'd moved in after their wedding trip and had lived there together until Rafe had left for France.

Memories, some joyous and some heartbreaking, filled her. She dreaded going inside, but she put one foot on the bottom tread. Another step followed, and another, until she reached the top. She stepped onto the veranda and halted. A white railing with spooled pickets encircled the porch. Two slat-backed wooden rocking chairs occupied the space to her left. On the other side, beside a stack of split firewood, hung a swing attached by chains to the ceiling. Everything was just as she remembered.

Memories made her heart clench. She and Rafe had spent many evening hours in that swing. When her daughter had been a baby, she'd sat in those rockers and held Molly on her lap. Tears pricked at the edges of her eyes at the thought of her lost child.

Shaking off her maudlin thoughts, she approached the sturdy wooden door with hesitant steps and stared at the bronze knob. This home contained the sum total of her married life. Once she turned that knob and entered the house, there would be no going back. Her heart would be vulnerable to whatever recollections assailed her.

With a deep breath to steel herself against the inevitable emotional onslaught, Daisy turned the knob. The door swung inward, and she stepped over the threshold. She closed the door and lowered her doctor's bag to the floor.

The house remained as she remembered it. To her left, an open door led into the kitchen, and beyond the kitchen was the dining room. The spacious great room where she stood took up most of the right side of the house. Across from the dining room door, a curving set of stairs with a mahogany banister led to the second floor, and past the stairs was Rafe's personal office, the one he'd used while they'd lived here together. At the end of the house, another door led to the back yard.

Their upstairs bedroom at the front of the house overlooked the valley. Molly had been conceived and born in that room, in their bed. Her room had been next to theirs. Two other bedrooms comprised the upper floor. She and Rafe had planned to fill every room with children.

Daisy paced into the great room. Comfortable leather furniture invited one to sit. Above a coal stove on the outside wall hung a pair of elk antlers. A brown and white spotted cowhide rug sprawled over the floor in front of the stove. Clear Colorado sunlight streamed through the windows and made the room glow.

Nothing had changed. Rafe had left everything as it had been before the war. His essence filled the house. He'd tossed a dark green flannel shirt over the back of a roomy leather chair and left a pair of sturdy work boots at the foot of the stairs. She could almost imagine that Rafe was upstairs and would come thudding down, calling her name.

As she stood behind the chair whose back faced the kitchen, she ran her palms over the soft leather. She'd touched this seat countless times in her three years of living here. When her foray reached Rafe's shirt, she hesitated. Then, as if in a trance, she stretched out a hand and gripped the soft flannel. She lifted the shirt and clutched the garment to her heart. She breathed in his scent, which still clung to the fabric.

Memories swirled through her head and made her dizzy. She staggered around the chair and collapsed onto the seat. With Rafe's shirt clenched in her arms, she doubled over and gave way to the memories that wrenched her. Tears scalded her eyes. She laid her forehead on her knees and let the tears soak her skirt. Gasping sobs tore at her throat. Her shoulders shook.

When the last sob had been wrung from her, Daisy sat up and swiped at her eyes with the heels of her hands. She breathed deeply and pushed up from the chair. With loving hands, she draped the shirt over the back of the chair where Rafe had left it. For several heartbeats, time ceased to exist as reality blurred with her imaginings. In her fantasy, she and Rafe still lived here, together, as husband and wife. She'd pick up his discarded clothing and put his boots under the bed, as she'd done countless times when she'd lived here.

The sound of men's voices on the road outside jarred her back to reality. The present intruded onto her dreaming. With a final touch of his shirt, she sighed and walked to the stairs.

Gazing up, she thought of the bedrooms above. Should

she take that journey into the past? Did she have the strength to stand in the room she'd shared with Rafe, or to peek into Molly's bedroom? Her bruised heart cried out that she'd suffered enough. Now wasn't the time to inflict further pain. She'd save that pilgrimage for another day.

Daisy turned away and retrieved her doctor's bag. She carried the satchel into the kitchen and set it on the table in the middle of the room. A quick glance showed her that Rafe had left this room untouched as well. The same red and white checked gingham curtains fluttered in the breeze at the open windows. Matching checked oilcloth napery covered the table. Unwashed dishes from several meals littered the cast iron sink beneath the windows.

When she'd carried in an armload of kindling from the porch and lit a fire in the oven, she pumped water at the sink into a large metal pot and set it on the stove. While the water heated, she delved into her black leather bag. She pulled out bed sheets that had been torn into strips and rolled into bandages and laid them on the table. A stethoscope, a metal tongue depressor, and a reflex hammer followed. Cotton wool, scalpels, catheters, a bottle of carbolic, and plaster bandages joined the pile. She laid a jar of chloroform with a dropper bottle and a metal container that held a syringe and needles soaking in methylated spirits beside her other supplies.

When the water was boiling, Daisy dropped anything that could be sterilized into the water except for the sheets. She'd do them in the next load. While her instruments boiled, she leaned against the table and looked around. When she'd lived here, Rafe had employed a cook for her, so she'd never had to slave over a hot wood stove, though she'd fixed a few meals for the two of them on the cook's days off. She knew her way around this kitchen. Working here again soothed her. She closed her eyes and let the tensions flow away.

She'd just finished fishing her instruments out of the water with a pair of tongs and had laid them on a clean towel on the sideboard to dry when a knock sounded at the door. Curious about who could be calling at this late morning hour, she dropped the tongs onto the towel and hurried to the door. She swung the portal wide.

Edith stood on the veranda, a pie plate covered by a dishcloth in her hands. When dismay flitted across her face before she schooled her expression to cordiality, conflicting emotions warred in Daisy's breast. The other girl had expected to see Rafe instead of her. Catching Edith off guard gave Daisy a sense of guilty satisfaction, though Edith's chic appearance made her uncomfortably aware of her own serviceable doctor's outfit.

Not pleased to see the woman who had designs on Rafe at his door, Daisy kept her voice cool. "May I help you?"

"Is Rafe here?" Edith's tone held a bite.

Daisy shook her head. "He's at the mine. If you have business with him, look for him at the office."

"I was sure he said he'd be here . . ."

"He's not."

Without waiting for an invitation, Edith breezed past her into the great room. A waft of expensive perfume followed in her wake. She pivoted to face Daisy. "I brought him a rhuba'b pie." With the tin pie plate balanced in one hand, she lifted a corner of the dish towel so Daisy could inspect the dessert.

Daisy and Rafe had their own rhubarb patch while she'd lived here, and she'd baked rhubarb pies for him. For another woman to make him treats rankled. Daisy reached to take the pastry from Edith. "I'll see that he gets it."

Edith swung the dish out of her reach and strolled into the

kitchen as if she belonged there, hips swaying. "Nevah mind. I'll tell him it's here." She crossed to the pie safe in the corner and deposited her offering there, then closed the door. As she whirled to face Daisy, the hem of her patterned voile dress flared about her calves.

The two women stared at each other across the room. What did a wife say to the woman who had designs on one's husband? Daisy didn't have time to dwell on the issue, for Edith took the initiative and launched into her opening salvo.

"It's no good, your tryin' to win Rafe back. He doesn't love you anymore."

If Daisy hadn't seen the misery on Rafe's face the day before, she might have believed Edith's words. "If he doesn't, that's between him and me. I doubt he'd confess such a thing to you."

Edith curled her painted lips. "How do you know that? You don't know what we are to each other. And you've been gone so long, it's a wonder he hasn't forgotten you."

"As I mentioned once before, I won't discuss my husband with you."

Edith shrugged. "If you love him, leave Summit. Rafe is too good for you. You'll only hold him back."

Daisy almost recoiled at Edith's spite, but she refused to give the other woman the satisfaction of knowing how her words wounded. She watched while Edith prowled the kitchen, opening drawers and poking into the cupboard. When Edith stopped by the medical instruments drying on the sideboard and reached to pick up the tongue depressor, Daisy stepped forward. "Don't touch that! I've just sterilized those instruments!"

Edith froze, then backed away. "Well, I'll just go on now and find Rafe. I can let myself out."

Daisy trailed behind while the other woman sauntered into the great room.

Just before Edith reached the door, she detoured to the chair where Rafe had tossed his shirt and snatched up the garment. "I declare, men are such messy creatures." She shook out his shirt and folded it. "They always leave their things wherever they get done with them." She laid the shirt on a lamp table beside the chair and made her unhurried way to the door. At the door, she halted and cast a glance at Daisy over her shoulder. "Think about what I said."

When the door had shut behind Edith, Daisy expelled a breath. Her insides roiled. Edith's visit had left her more shaken than she cared to admit. Her familiarity with the house told Daisy the other woman had been inside more than once. Had she ever been here alone with Rafe?

Daisy shut down that line of thought. To allow visions of Rafe and Edith alone together in the house where he'd lived with Daisy would only make her angry. She had to trust her husband's integrity.

With her lips clamped, Daisy stalked to the lamp table where Edith had put Rafe's folded shirt. She snatched up the shirt and shook out the folds, then stepped to the chair. With great care, she arranged the shirt over the fat leather chair back the way Rafe had left it. She wouldn't allow Edith to touch her husband's clothing. As long as she and Rafe remained married, she'd be the only woman to handle his garments.

After she returned to the kitchen, she sterilized the bandages and hung them on the clothesline in the back yard. Later, after they'd dried, she'd iron them and roll them into individual packets so they'd be ready when she needed them. Before she left, she poured the hot water she'd used to sterilize her instruments into the sink and washed the dirty dishes

Rafe had used. With loving care, she dried each plate, fork, and glass and put them away in the cupboard.

Rafe might not like the fact that she'd washed his dishes, but she wanted to leave her own mark on their home, something to let him know she still cared.

CHAPTER 9

Summit Town
Late June, 1922

As her heart ached, Daisy pulled the faded blooms from the tin can at Molly's headstone and tucked several stalks of mountain chiming bells into the makeshift vase in place of the dead blossoms. The tiny blue and pink flower clusters brightened the grave. She stared down at her daughter's resting place for several moments before she left the cemetery.

On her way back to town she turned into one of the streets in the neighborhood where the mining families lived. She'd been visiting the community, hoping to get to know the wives and their children. Perhaps bonds of friendship and trust would allow these women to let her help them.

She reached a house where a thin woman was hanging wet laundry on a rope strung between two posts. A spotted dog barked at her from the front porch. Daisy halted beside the picket fence that encircled the yard. This lady was one of the wives with whom she'd tried to strike up a friendship. "Good morning, Mrs. Johnson."

Ada Johnson glanced her way but didn't pause in her task. She bent to reach into her woven clothes basket and extracted one of her husband's blue chambray work shirts. "'Morning, Mrs. Wild Wind." As she spoke, she attached a clothespin to one of the shirt's shoulder seams.

"May I help you, Mrs. Johnson? I could hand you the clothes. That way, you wouldn't have to bend over to pick them out of the basket."

From her earlier visits, Daisy had noticed that Mrs. Johnson often paused in her work to place her hands at the small of her back and rub there. And no wonder that Mrs. Johnson had a backache, Daisy thought. Although Rafe provided better than average housing for his married workers, he couldn't afford to install electricity or running water in each home. The wives had to carry water from the lake and haul it to their homes, then heat the water for washing clothes, dishes, or bathing. And heating water was no easy task. All the wood used for cooking and washing had to be chopped, a thankless task left to the wives.

In comparison to the life these women experienced, her married life had been idyllic. Her home had been heated with coal. Rafe had electric lights installed. He'd paid one of the mine worker's sons to chop wood, so they always had a supply of kindling for the kitchen stove. She'd never had to chop a stick of kindling in all the time she'd lived in Summit. A pump at the kitchen sink guaranteed she never had to haul water. Her husband had hired a cook for her. The cook had also done the laundry, so she'd been spared the task of laboring over a washboard. Hot water had never been in short supply, so she'd been able to bathe more than once a week.

Although she'd had some light household tasks, her life had been privileged compared to these women.

Daisy gazed down the pitted street from one house to another. The less-than-sanitary conditions in which most of these people lived could lead to illness. An epidemic of smallpox, typhus, or scarlet fever could spawn in this community and sweep through Summit. Visions of battling an epidemic made her shudder. She did her best to encourage cleanliness whenever she visited the mining community.

Now, she pushed open the gate and strolled into the yard without waiting for Mrs. Johnson's permission. She reached the basket. "Here, I'll help you with the clothes."

Mrs. Johnson stretched and put one hand at the small of her back. She grimaced. "That would be a pure pleasure, Mrs. Wild Wind. My back is aching something fierce today."

Daisy plucked another work shirt from the pile of damp clothes in the basket and held the garment out to the worn woman beside her. "What have you done this morning?"

Mrs. Johnson took the shirt and shook it out before she attached it with a clothespin to the line. As she talked, her hands were never idle. "Well, I got up before sunup and cooked my man his breakfast. Then I hauled water so I could wash the dishes. That used up most of my wood, so I chopped enough to heat water for the washing. I had to haul more water to do the laundry. Then I stripped the sheets off the beds while the water heated. Before I could start the washing, Benje dropped a bowl and cut his foot on the glass before I could sweep it up."

Daisy halted in the act of plucking an item of clothing from the basket and stared at Ida Johnson. These poor mining wives endured such drudgery, apparently without complaining and without any hope for an easier life. She recalled her task and handed the woman a child's pair of overalls. "I can see why your back aches. My back hurts just listening to you."

Mrs. Johnson swiped back a hank of limp brown hair that had come loose from her bun before she took the overalls from Daisy. Her faded cotton dress hung loose on her too-thin frame. "That's so kind of you, Mrs. Wild Wind, but don't you worry about me. Your husband treats his men real fine, and he pays his workers a fair wage. My Tom is making more money working here than he would at any other mine. I'm glad to do my part to help Tom."

Daisy scowled and bent to pluck another work shirt from the basket so Ida wouldn't see her expression. Tom could do more to lift the load from his wife, but she refrained from commenting. Her doctor's curiosity wondered how badly Benje's foot had been cut and what his mother had done to treat the wound. "Mrs. Johnson, tell me about Benje. How badly was he cut?"

Mrs. Johnson frowned as she considered the question. "It seemed deep to me."

"And what did you do for Benje after he cut his foot?"

"Well, I wiped the blood off with my apron. The cut still was bleeding, so I gave him my apron and told him to press it to the wound. Then after it stopped bleeding, I put a little honey on it and tied a dishcloth around his foot."

Daisy tried not to shudder. "Honey is good, but did you clean the wound?"

"Well, yes, I poured water over his foot first. He'd been walking outside barefoot, so his foot was dirty."

"Would you mind if I take a look at Benje's foot?" She handed a bedsheet to the other woman.

Mrs. Johnson hesitated as she hung the sheet on the line.

"If the cut is too deep, he might need stitches. And the injury should be disinfected." Could Mrs. Johnson be persuaded to overcome her reluctance to consult a doctor about Benje's injury? A doctor meant money, something not usually factored into a mining family's expenses. And Daisy wasn't the genial Doc Irby, who probably would be the family's first choice of physician. "I won't charge you anything. I just want to take a look."

Still, Mrs. Johnson hesitated. She pinned the last piece of clothing to the line and faced Daisy with a frown. "Well, I guess it can't hurt."

"Thank you, Mrs. Johnson. You won't be sorry." Daisy scooped up the clothes basket and followed the other woman inside through the back door. A short hallway with a bedroom on either side led to a living room and then a kitchen at the front of the house.

Benje, a freckle-faced, tow-headed urchin of about ten years sat at the table. His glum expression told Daisy he'd rather be outside playing with the other boys than sitting indoors with his foot propped on a chair.

"This is my Benje." Mrs. Johnson laid a hand on her son's shoulder. "Benje, this is Dr. Wild Wind."

Daisy laid the clothes basket down and extended her hand to the boy. "I'm glad to meet you, Benje. And you may call me Doc Daisy."

His blue eyes rounded. "Are you really a doctor?" He took her hand and gave it a shake.

"Yes, I'm a doctor. I went to school to learn how to be one, and I have a certificate that says I'm a real doctor." She took back her hand and propped it on one hip. "Your mother tells me you cut your foot this morning. Would you mind if I take a peek?"

Benje cast a worried glance at his mother. "Is it all right if the doc looks at my foot, Mama?"

Mrs. Johnson gave her son a tired smile and tucked a hank of hair behind her ear. "It's all right, son."

Daisy knelt beside the chair where the boy's foot rested. She loosened the knot Mrs. Johnson had tied in the dishcloth and unwrapped the makeshift bandage. With gentle fingers, she examined the injury.

Benje had stepped on the glass with the heel of his foot. The laceration was a clean cut, although deep. Daisy glanced up at the boy's mother. "The wound should be disinfected, and it needs a couple of stitches."

Distress twisted Ada Johnson's features. "We can't afford a doctor, not for this. It's just a cut."

"Yes, it's just a cut, but it still needs attention. If that wound isn't treated, Benje will get an infection, and then you'll have a more serious situation to deal with. And the cut does need stitches to heal properly." Daisy pushed to her feet and smiled at the taller woman. "I promise I won't charge you for my services."

Mrs. Johnson nodded a reluctant assent. "All right." She wrung her hands. "I can't imagine what Tom will say."

"If Tom gives you any trouble, send him to me." She patted the woman's shoulder. "I have to get my medical bag from the hotel. I'll be right back."

In her room, Daisy checked her supplies. Her bag contained suturing needles, sutures, alcohol, ethyl chloride spray for local anesthesia, dressings, and soap. She snapped the bag closed and swung out the door.

Mrs. Johnson waited in her kitchen, trying to comfort Benje's fears.

Daisy dropped her bag on the table and smiled down at Benje, whose freckles stood out against his pale face. "I'll make this as painless as I can, Benje. And I know you'll be a brave boy. Think of what a story you'll have to tell your friends."

Benje brightened at the thought of the yarn he could spin for the benefit of his buddies.

Daisy turned her attention to his mother. "Do you have any water left from your washing? I'll need to cleanse my hands."

Mrs. Johnson appeared surprised at the notion that Daisy would wash her hands before treating her son, but she indicated a pot on the stove. "There's some water over there."

After she'd crossed to the cast-iron stove, Daisy ladled warm water into a tin wash basin on the sideboard. Using the soap from her bag, she scrubbed all the way to her elbows, taking care to clean beneath her fingernails. When she'd cleansed her skin to her satisfaction, she knelt beside Benje once more and looked into the boy's face. "I promise not to hurt you more than necessary."

Reaching into her black leather bag, she pulled out the ethyl chloride spray. "This will help to numb your foot before I stitch."

She set down the spray bottle and began to cleanse the wound. While she worked, Mrs. Johnson's younger children gathered around to watch. The youngest, a toddler with a wispy blonde braid and patched skirt, stood beside Benje's chair with her thumb stuck in her mouth. Daisy tried not to dwell on the fact that the little girl reminded her of her own lost daughter.

She turned her attention to the business of tending to Benje's cut. Mrs. Johnson shooed her brood back outside and hovered at Daisy's shoulder. The whole procedure took less than half an hour. Benje flinched when she inserted the needle for the first stich, but after that, he remained bravely stoic. When she'd finished and snipped off the last thread, she squeezed his knee. "You were a very brave boy, Benje. I don't think your friends would have been half so brave."

He beamed at her and grinned at his mother. "Doc Daisy said I was brave, Mama."

Mrs. Johnson hugged her boy. "You were, son. You were very brave." She turned to Daisy. "Thank you for helping us, Doc Daisy."

"I was happy to help, Mrs. Johnson."

The other woman touched Daisy's arm and gave her a shy smile. "Please, call me Ada."

When Daisy had repacked her bag and left instructions with the miner's wife about keeping the wound clean, she left the little house in an exuberant state. She'd finally been able to use her medical skills, and she hoped word would spread to the other mining families. A huge step toward building trust in the community had been taken this day.

* * *

Daisy sat at a rear corner table of Katie's Café, her back to the wall. Her satisfaction over having helped her first patient that morning still lingered. Before she moved to Summit, she'd left the job she'd had in a large hospital while she attended medical school. Now she missed the opportunity to help people each day that working in a hospital afforded. Treating Benje that morning had reminded her of why she'd become a doctor.

She took a bite of venison stew and watched as a group of young people arrived at the café. Their banter filled the dining room, and they treated each other with easy familiarity. Since she didn't recognize them as any of Summit's residents and their clothing marked them as city folk, they must be some of the season's motorists that Katie had predicted would arrive. The freedoms young people enjoyed now never would have been allowed before the war.

A few single miners straggled in and took seats at one of the tables. As the room started to fill, the women whom Katie had hired to help her scurried about serving the customers.

A dark-haired man entered the café. His tall form filled the doorway, and his wide shoulders blocked the evening's light. *Rafe.* Daisy's stomach clenched. She hadn't seen him since their conversation in his office. During the intervening days, she'd missed him with every fiber of her being.

Would he acknowledge her? Would he even see her, tucked away in this corner?

He removed his black cowboy hat and stepped forward. His gaze scanned the dining room. Daisy waited to see if he'd notice her. Her heart pounded.

The moment his gaze connected with hers, Daisy stopped breathing. Nothing else in the room existed except the two of them.

He gave her a terse nod and made his deliberate way toward her across the dining room. When he passed the table where the young people sat, the girls giggled and cast sheep eyes at him. One of them rose from her chair.

"Oh, Mr. Wild Wind!"

Rafe halted and turned toward the young lady, a pert red head with curly hair and kohled eyes.

"My friends and I are wondering if you'll be giving plane rides this summer. We're hoping you'll take us up again in your aeroplane."

Rafe stood with that self-contained stillness he'd learned from his half-Cheyenne father and looked at the girl. Daisy, who knew him well, noticed that he tightened his fingers on the hat he held down along his jeans-clad thigh, the only indication of annoyance he betrayed. His aloofness must be a challenge to these modern young things, to whom a handsome man such as Rafe represented a dare.

The girl stared back, her expression expectant. Just when her smile began to waver at the edges, he replied.

"If you're still here on Saturday afternoon, I'll take you up. I give rides on Saturdays during the summer."

The girl's smile widened, and she addressed one of her male companions. "We'll be here, won't we, Ron?"

Ron, a handsome young man in a tweed jacket, shrugged. "I hadn't planned to stay here that long, but if you have your heart set on going up with the ace, we'll be here on Saturday. I can always do some more fishing in the meantime."

The red head faced Rafe again. "You can count on us. We'll be here."

Rafe nodded and turned to continue his way across the room.

"Oh, Mr. Wild Wind."

Rafe stopped and glanced at the girl over his shoulder.

A bright expression filled her face. "Would you care to join us? We can make room for you."

The other girls giggled once more.

Rafe made them wait before he responded. "Thank you for the offer, but I already have a seat." He turned his back on the group and made his way toward Daisy's table. When he reached her, he halted and stared down at her. "Do you mind if I join you?"

Did he really think she'd refuse him? "Of course not. Sit down."

Without replying, he hooked a booted foot around one of the chair's back legs and jerked. The chair scraped backwards along the floor. Rafe dropped his long length into the seat and laid his hat, brim up, on the table between them. "I'm only trying to spare you the gossip that would result if I ignored you. We've caused enough gossip already."

"Whether you avoid me or sit with me, people gossip. Now the townspeople will be wondering if we're getting together again."

He shrugged. "What did you expect when you came back here?"

"I expected exactly what's happening. I don't like it, but I can live with it."

"Well, I wouldn't be a gentleman if I ignored you, so here I am."

"Thank you." His inference that he merely shielded her from gossip rankled, but she tried to appreciate his motive. She would have preferred that he took his meal with her because he craved her company.

Daisy peered past his shoulder to the table where the young people sat. The women all stared their way and whispered amongst themselves. "I think you've created a storm of gossip with those girls. Right at this moment they're wondering who I am and why you're sitting with me."

Rafe didn't bother to turn around. "They shouldn't be surprised to see me with a woman. They've seen me with Edith."

"I'm not Edith."

He leveled a look at her that silenced her.

One of Katie's workers came to take his order, and the interruption defused some of the tension that had sprung up between them. When he'd ordered the venison stew, Daisy blurted out the first thought that sprang to her head.

"Those young people must have been here several times before if they know your name."

Distaste twisted his mouth. "They've come up at least once every summer since the war. They're city people who travel the mountains during the summer now that motor cars make touring our country easier. They expect us locals to cater to them. If they want a plane ride, they expect a plane ride."

"And I'm sure you charge them well for the privilege," Daisy said. "The Rocky Mountains are beautiful, but I think those young ladies find more than the mountains attractive." She couldn't help but tease him a bit.

The old Rafe would have responded with a humorous quip, and the dimple in his cheek would have flashed, but the Rafe who had taken the place of the husband she'd married only gave her a flat look and shrugged. "They're angling for entertainment. I don't intend to be that entertainment."

"Well, I don't blame them for finding you attractive. I was smitten by your handsome face when I was their age."

His expression turned grim. "Daisy . . ."

She gave him a defiant glare. "It's true, and I still find you handsome. I think that touch of gray at your temples makes you look more distinguished than ever."

The waitress brought his dinner then, and he applied himself to the stew without bothering to reply.

While he took the edge off his hunger, Daisy watched him from half-lowered lids. What could they talk about? If they were still living together as husband and wife, what would she have told them as they sat over the dinner table? She would have shared the fact that she'd treated her first patient that morning. Why couldn't she tell him about that now?

"Rafe, I had my first patient today."

He swallowed the bite of fluffy bread he'd been chewing and laid down his spoon. "Tell me about it."

Daisy launched into her tale. Sharing something with her husband that was close to her heart almost made her forget they no longer lived together, that both war and years separated them. With Rafe sitting across the table from her, she lived only in the moment. What mattered was that she had an opportunity to share her passion for healing with the man she loved, the man who, at this moment, looked at her as though he cared.

A thrill made her heart soar. She couldn't help but think Rafe had softened just a bit.

CHAPTER 10

Summit Town
Early July, 1922

"Doc Daisy! Doc Daisy! Come quick!" A man whom Daisy recognized as the owner of one of the outlying ranches burst through the door of Katie's Café.

He carried a mid-sized mongrel with a bristly coat of brown patches mixed with white. A brown spot covered half of the canine's face. One ear stood up, and the other one drooped. At this moment, blood stained the dog's fur and had besmirched the towel wrapped around him.

Daisy leaped from her seat at the round table where she and Katie had been enjoying a cup of tea more than a week after her dinner with Rafe. She hadn't seen her husband since then. "Mr. Bentley! What's happened to your dog?"

"Cougar, Doc Daisy. It jumped us when we came on it sudden. I was checking my cattle in the high meadow when I came on a cougar that had killed a calf. Mack here rushed the cat and got mauled." With gentleness at odds with his big frame, Jim Bentley lowered the dog to the table. "I got that cat, though."

Daisy shot a quick glance at Katie to see if her friend resented a bloody dog being deposited on one of her dining room tables. Katie shrugged and spread her hands in a helpless gesture.

"Wouldn't you rather have Doc Irby treat Mack?" As much as she needed patients, Daisy wanted to be sure the rancher wouldn't regret using her services. She wanted confirmation that Mr. Bentley wouldn't blame her if she couldn't save his dog.

"Doc Irby's out of town on another call. You're all I have to save Mack." Jim Bentley stroked the mutt's matted fur with loving tenderness.

"Very well, I'll do the best I can, but I don't know if I can save him until I examine his injuries."

The rancher nodded, trusting that Daisy would give his dog the same care she would have afforded a human patient. In cattle territory, everyone knew a working ranch dog was worth its weight in gold.

"Mr. Bentley, we'll have to move Mack. I can't treat him here."

Katie protested. "Do you dare move him? I have room for you to work on him here."

Daisy shook her head. "In a little while, you'll have customers coming in looking for a meal. I don't want to tie up your kitchen and dining room with dog hair and blood."

"Well, if you're sure . . ." Katie didn't insist on donating her facilities after Daisy pointed out her possible loss of business.

Daisy considered her options. The only place she could treat Mack would be the kitchen at Rafe's house. She didn't have time to check with her husband to see if he'd mind her turning his kitchen into an operating room, so she'd deal with Rafe later. Right now, the dog needed medical attention.

She touched Jim Bentley's arm. "I'll run up to my hotel room and get my bag. Take Mack to Mr. Wild Wind's house and wait on the veranda for me."

With those words, she darted from the café and jogged to the hotel, dodging foot traffic along the boardwalk.

Katie had been right about the tourists. With June nearly over, the town's population had swelled to almost double its normal size. Motor cars chugged down the street. Families filled the vacant hotel rooms. On her dash to the hotel, Daisy squeezed between tourists who clogged the boardwalk.

When she burst into the hotel lobby, the clerk stared at her from behind the reception desk. A family with three young children in the middle of the room pulled their offspring from her path as she barreled past them toward the stairs.

"Why is that lady running?" one of the youngsters asked.

"I'm sure I don't know," his mother replied. "She was very rude."

Daisy didn't stop to explain. She dashed up the stairs to her room and snatched up her medical bag. She kept the satchel restocked after each use, with the utensils sterilized and ready to be used. As she wheeled toward the door, she glanced at her reflection in the dresser mirror. She wore a yellow and white gingham dress with a Peter Pan collar and dropped sash tie belt, one of the dresses Rafe had paid for from Montgomery's Emporium. She sighed. She didn't have time to change into her doctor's skirt and blouse. Perhaps her white surgeon's apron would keep most of the blood and fluids from her clothes, but she resigned herself to the fact that she'd probably ruin her dress.

Outside her former home, Jim Bentley's horse stood

ground tied near the bottom veranda step, head hanging. Lather coated its sides, and sweat dripped from its flanks. A crowd of men had gathered at the base of the veranda steps. Word must have gotten out that the lady doc was going to treat the ranch dog, and the town's loafers had gathered to watch the show.

Daisy pushed her way through the throng and hurried up the steps onto the porch. Mr. Bentley waited near the door, his face drawn with worry. Daisy gave him a reassuring smile as she brushed past him and reached for the knob. "Bring Mack inside."

In the kitchen, she dropped her bag on the sideboard and spread a sheet over the oilcloth-covered table, then patted the table. "Put him here."

At the sink, she pumped water into a deep cooking pot. "When this water gets hot, I'm going to scrub my hands. I'll need your help with Mack, so you'll have to scrub, too."

Jim Bentley nodded and didn't question her.

"Now, bring me some kindling from the veranda. I'll need wood to heat this water."

The rancher disappeared onto the porch and returned with his arms full of kindling. Daisy loaded the wood into the stove's firebox and struck a match to the sticks. She lifted the pot of water onto the stove, then pumped water for a second pot.

While the water heated, she shrugged into her white doctor's apron. After tying the strings in the back, she secured a white kerchief about her head, then leaned over the table to examine Mack.

The loafers who had gathered about the veranda steps had followed Jim Bentley into the house, and now they crowded into the kitchen.

"You gonna save that mangy dog's hide, Doc Daisy?" One of the men hooted while his companions guffawed.

Daisy shut out their comments and focused on her patient. She unwrapped the towel from around the dog and dropped it on the floor. The cougar had ripped open the dog's hip to the bone, and claws had torn a gash along Mack's ribs. She'd have to pull together torn muscle and ligaments. To stitch up the animal would require patience and a great deal of suturing. She'd use tough canvas thread for the skin, but catgut for the inner stitches.

She lifted her head and looked at the rancher as she eased away from the table. "Even if Mack pulls through, I can't guarantee he'll be able to drive cattle like he used to. I don't know if he'll even be able to run."

"It don't matter. Just save him."

With the water steaming, Daisy ladled some into the wash basin and instructed the rancher on how to wash. While he scrubbed, she laid out her instruments. When Jim Bentley had cleaned his hands and arms to her satisfaction, she dumped the dirty water down the sink and poured more for herself. She cleaned her hands, beneath her fingernails, and up to her elbows. Though her patient was a canine, she wouldn't do less for him than she would do for any human.

She'd just finished washing and had turned toward the table when the loafers standing about the kitchen grew silent. Curious about the cause, she glanced up. Rafe stood in the doorway.

Their glances locked, and Daisy forgot everyone else. The air seemed to have been sucked from the room, and for a moment she forgot to breathe. Then reason returned, and she gulped in a breath. From his lack of expression, she couldn't tell whether or not Rafe was angry at her invasion of his kitchen.

He stepped into the room. At a quiet word from him, the crowd melted away, leaving her alone with her husband and Jim Bentley.

Rafe approached the table and spared a look for the dog, then turned his attention to her. "What can I do?"

Her heart leaped as though he'd just declared his love. Her feminine instincts, and her knowledge of Rafe, told her that those simple words put the love he felt for her into action. He may not have acknowledged that emotion, but that didn't lessen its reality. "First, you can scrub up."

She poured clean hot water into the wash basin and demonstrated how she wanted him to wash. Turning to the table, she plucked a strip of an old sheet that she'd torn into lengths from her bag. She held out the cloth to Mr. Bentley. "Tie this around Mack's muzzle. I'm going to hurt him, and I don't want any of us to get bitten."

While the rancher tended to his dog, Rafe shook water from his hands and moved to her side. "I suppose you want me to hold him down."

Daisy nodded. "If you'll hold down his hindquarters, Jim can handle his front end. Mack trusts him, so it will be better to have Jim by Mack's head."

With a nod, Rafe circled the table. When she gave the signal, he gripped the dog's hips with a strong but gentle hold.

While the men pinned the canine to the table, Daisy washed Mack with warm water and wiped away the encrusted blood. Pale red liquid ran over the tabletop and dripped onto the floor. She ignored the splashes that stained her apron. Picking up her scissors, she snipped off any hair that could get in the way of her stitching.

She laid down the scissors and picked up the bottle of

carbolic acid. "I'll have to douse the wounds with carbolic to kill the bacteria. It will be painful."

The men nodded and took a firmer grip on the patient. Daisy dripped the antiseptic into the torn flesh. Mack squirmed and whined. After she'd disinfected the places where the cougar's claws had ripped, she swabbed down the dog's sides around the wounds.

She reached for a needle already threaded with catgut. "Hold him still." As she inserted one hand into the gash, she pulled the edges of torn muscle together over the bone and took the first stitch.

Mack howled and tried to thrash, but the men leaned into their task and kept him pinned to the table.

The minutes ticked by while Daisy took meticulous stitches. She lost track of time. The room grew warm, and sweat dripped off her nose. She wiped her face on her sleeve, then returned to sewing the dog back together. Her back ached from bending over the table.

Mack whimpered with each thrust of the needle. Daisy closed her ears to his pitiful whines.

Periodically, she stopped to wash her hands again or to sterilize her instruments. At last, she snipped off the last stitch of the canvas thread and stepped back. She swiped the kerchief from her head and mopped her face with the cloth. "I think he'll make it."

The men released the dog, who now lay silent on the table. Jim Bentley unwrapped the cloth from around the animal's muzzle and gave Mack an awkward pat.

Daisy touched the rancher's shoulder. "When you take him home, keep him inside on a clean sheet or blanket. You must keep him clean, do you understand? If he gets dirt into the wounds, he'll get infection."

Mr. Bentley ducked his head in acknowledgement. "Yes, Doc Daisy."

"If you let him get infection and undo all my hard work, I'll come after you." She waved a finger beneath his nose in mock warning, and the rancher grinned at her. "You'll be sorry."

"If you'll excuse me, Doc Daisy, I'll head down to the livery to rent a buckboard. I can't tote Mack home slung over my saddle."

"You certainly can't. Go on, now." She gave him a gentle shove toward the door. "I'll clean up here."

When the rancher had departed with his dog and Daisy was alone with Rafe, she turned to look at her husband for the first time since she'd begun her surgery. He was staring at her with his head tipped, a thoughtful expression on his face.

"You make a fine doctor."

His praise meant more to her than the moment when she'd held her medical degree for the first time. At his tribute, her fatigue melted. She straightened. "Thank you." She tried to guard her emotions, but she knew some of the joy she felt at his compliment showed on her face.

Rafe paced around the table and came to a halt beside her. "This town could use a doctor like you."

Daisy shrugged. "I hope I can make a difference."

"And how is Benje doing?"

She cast him a sideways glance, gratified that he'd remembered her first patient.

Her husband sent her an intent look. "I haven't forgotten what you did for Benje. And the miners have been talking about the pretty woman doctor."

Her face turned warm as she shrugged away his backhanded compliment. "I'm thankful to report that Benje's foot is healing nicely."

"Tom was livid when he heard that a doctor had treated his son for a simple cut, but he calmed down when he found out that you didn't charge them."

Daisy gestured with her palms out. "Ada was worried about what her husband would say. She didn't think the cut called for a doctor's visit, but that wound would have festered until it really needed medical attention."

"I think you may get more business from the mining community after this."

"I hope so." Daisy sighed and glanced around her at the wreckage of the kitchen. She tossed her kerchief onto the table and bundled it up with the stained sheet, then pulled off her bloodied apron and added it to the pile. "I hope you don't mind that I used the kitchen as a surgery. I couldn't think of any place else that had what I needed, and I didn't have time to ask."

"I figured as much. When I looked out of my office window and saw the crowd around my porch, I knew you had to be involved." Rafe smiled at her for the first time since she'd returned to Summit.

Daisy paused with the dirty linens clutched to her bosom. Her insides melted, and she smiled back. Time hung suspended as they stared at each other. At last, Daisy turned away. "I have to clean up this mess, so I'd better get busy." She laid the soiled items on the table and gathered up her instruments.

"Let me help."

They worked together to clean up the kitchen. While she gathered her things together, Rafe pumped more water so Daisy could sterilize her instruments. She disinfected the red and white checked tablecloth and then attacked the floor with the broom.

"You'll need a new dress after this."

Daisy paused to find Rafe watching her from across the room.

He pointed to her frock. "You've got blood on your dress."

She glanced down at her pretty yellow and white gingham frock and grimaced. Blood and dog hair smeared the fabric in several places where the apron hadn't covered. "I didn't have time to change."

Rafe looked at her with an expression she couldn't interpret. "Yet you still saved a mutt's life."

"Doctors save lives, whenever we can." She shrugged. "My dress isn't important. What's important is that I saved a valuable working ranch dog."

"Who may never be able to work again."

"Mack may surprise us all."

Her rumbling stomach alerted Daisy to the fact that she'd missed lunch. "What time is it? I completely lost track of the time."

Rafe leaned over the sink to look out the window. "From the position of the sun, I'd say it was the middle of the afternoon." He straightened and swung toward her. "I'd wager that you're hungry. I know I am. Why don't I get us something to eat at Katie's place and bring it here?"

The suggestion of food made Daisy's mouth water. The prospect of a meal alone with Rafe made her heart sing. "That sounds good. I'll scrub the floor while you're gone."

When the door had banged shut behind her husband, Daisy poured hot water into a bucket. She found the scrub brush in a metal pail beneath the sink, right where it had been kept when she'd lived here. While she knelt on the floor swiping the scrub brush over the bloody stains, she thought about a private meal with Rafe. She tingled with anticipation. Hope that they might salvage their marriage blossomed. In her euphoria, she didn't notice how the pungent scent of disinfectant stung her nose.

She'd almost finished the floor when Rafe returned. When she heard his footsteps cross the veranda, she leaned sideways a little to peer through the kitchen door into the great room and sat back on her heels. A glad smile teased her lips as she anticipated the moment when her husband would step inside.

The outside door swung open, and Edith stepped into the house. Rafe followed and closed the portal behind them.

Daisy's smile died. Her gaze swung to Rafe.

He had the grace to look sheepish. He gave her an apologetic glance and shrugged.

Eying Daisy with a disdainful expression, Edith halted near the kitchen door. She wrinkled her nose at the strong disinfectant smell. "I happened to run into Rafe outside of Katie's Café and saw that he needed help, so I carried one of the plates for him." She lifted the covered plate as an excuse for her presence.

Daisy very much doubted Rafe had needed help carrying two plates, and she wished he'd declined Edith's offer of help. The amicable meal she'd hoped to enjoy with her husband now promised to be an awkward occasion presided over by the elegant Edith. Daisy's appetite vanished, and the fatigue that Rafe's attention had banished crashed over her again.

Edith frowned down at Daisy. "What evah have you done to your dress? And what are you doin' on the floor?"

Tossing the scrub brush into the bucket and splashing droplets of water over her clean floor, Daisy climbed to her feet. She paced into the great room. Her irritation over Edith's company escalated into hot anger. "I got blood on my dress during a surgery this afternoon. And I'm washing the floor because blood and other body fluids spilled during the surgery." She couldn't hold her tongue. "I'm sorry I don't meet your expectations, but a doctor can't be glamorous all the time."

As soon as the words left her mouth, she felt spiteful and petty. She snatched a deep breath and tried to rein in her temper. "I apologize. That was uncalled for."

Rafe stepped forward. "Ladies, we need to eat. Daisy's had a difficult day, and she skipped lunch. Edith, thank you for your help, but Daisy and I can manage now." He reached for the plate she held.

Edith danced out of his way. "Now, Rafe, what kind of a friend would I be if I left you to fend for yourself?" Not taking his hint that she leave, she brushed past Daisy into the kitchen.

Daisy ground her teeth. Perhaps she shouldn't blame Rafe for Edith's presence. The Southern belle seemed determined to stick closer to Rafe than a tick on a hound dog and appeared to have designs to thwart the private meal he'd planned for his wife.

When Rafe halted beside her and urged her into the kitchen, Daisy flounced into the room. She had no desire for lunch, but neither would she concede the field to Edith.

CHAPTER 11

As she stood beside Katie and her family during the first hymn, Daisy cast a discrete glance about the simple church. She didn't see Rafe. With a sigh, she turned her attention back to the song's words. Before the war, for him to miss a service would have been unthinkable. That he should cut his faith from his life grieved her.

She resolved to pray harder for her husband. Before Rafe could be a proper husband to her, he first had to mend his relationship with his Savior. The Lord could restore Rafe to fellowship and heal their marriage, and she refused to believe otherwise.

After the service, she made her way to the back of the church, greeting people as she went. The rancher, Jim Bentley, caught her attention just outside the door.

"Doc Daisy, I'd like you to meet my wife." He drew forward a sturdy, dark-haired woman whom Daisy guessed to be around her own age. Two youngsters hung by her side. "Doc Daisy, this is Meg, my wife. And Jim Bob and Ned." He dropped his hands to his sons' shoulders.

Meg greeted Daisy with a shy smile and ducked her head.

"I'm pleased to meet you, Doc Daisy. My husband has talked of nothing else except how you saved Mack."

Daisy acknowledged Meg's greeting. "And I'm pleased to meet you as well." The women shared a smile. "And how is Mack doing?"

"Mack is doing just fine." Meg went on to detail the dog's recovery.

While Meg talked, Daisy assessed her with a professional eye. Mrs. Bentley bloomed with pregnancy. Her rounded stomach filled out her simple dress. Daisy estimated that she should deliver before the end of the summer.

When his wife had finished detailing Mack's progress, Jim Bentley cleared his throat. "Doc Daisy, we'd like . . ." He cleared his throat again. "That is, Meg would like it if you could attend her when it comes time for her to deliver her child."

Daisy returned her attention to Mrs. Bentley. "Certainly, I can attend you. But will Doc Irby resent it if you don't call him? If you're his patient, I don't want to step on his professional toes."

"I'm not Doc Irby's patient. My husband delivered Jim Bob and Ned. We didn't have a doctor come." Meg cut a glance at her husband.

The noonday sun beat down on them while they stood near the church steps. The other parishioners had gone, leaving the Bentleys alone with Daisy. At Meg's words, Daisy forgot about the heat. She looked at Jim Bentley, who had reddened to his hairline.

"You delivered both boys?" Daisy asked, incredulous.

The rancher nodded and swiped his cowboy hat from his head, then settled it on again. He rolled his shoulders. "I've delivered calves before. I figured that pulling a baby couldn't be much different. And money is tight."

Daisy bit back a lecture on the risks of childbirth. She wouldn't waste her breath. The Bentleys' situation wasn't much different from many families in the mountains, who considered childbirth to be no different from a cow calving or a mare foaling. "Well, I'm glad you were able to deliver both boys safely, but please call me when Meg's time comes." Daisy squeezed Meg's arm. "Meg, if that husband of yours even thinks about changing his mind, you let me know. I don't want him to take such a risk with you again."

Jim Bentley shuffled his feet and looked sheepish. "Don't worry, Doc Daisy. Meg won't let me change my mind. She's set on having you there when the baby comes."

"I'll be there. And Meg, in the meantime, if you don't feel well or if you think anything might be wrong, send your husband to me. Don't worry about the money."

Jim Bentley spoke up for his wife. "Thank you, Doc Daisy. I'll keep an eye on her. After two other pregnancies, I know what to look for." The rancher took his wife's arm and turned her toward the buckboard at the edge of the church yard. He shepherded his sons ahead of him. Looking back over his shoulder, he tossed another comment to Daisy. "And you can call me Jim."

With her Bible clutched against her waist, Daisy watched the Bentleys' farm wagon rumble out of the yard, leaving her alone beside the church steps. At least she had another patient, and the chances of Meg's baby having a safe arrival were better with a doctor in attendance. Whether or not the Bentleys could pay for her services was another matter, but she shrugged away that concern. What mattered was that she'd be at their ranch to deliver Meg's baby.

As she trudged toward the hotel, her thoughts flew to her husband. Would Rafe be eating lunch with the Montgomerys again today? Even if he wasn't a luncheon guest in their home, he'd spend the evening playing chess with Edith's father. No doubt Edith would make the most of the time to work her wiles on him.

Daisy hadn't seen her husband since the day he'd helped with Mack's surgery earlier in the week. Each day she hoped to encounter him, but every day she'd been disappointed. She thought that in a town the size of Summit she'd see him more often, but running the mine occupied his days, and he never sought her company. He only took his meals at Katie's café on occasion, so she didn't see him at dinner. She wondered if Edith was feeding him on a regular basis. She wouldn't be surprised if the Southern beauty was taking him meals.

At that depressing possibility, Daisy set her jaw. Something had to be done, but no schemes for winning back her husband came to mind.

CHAPTER 12

Daisy stood with Katie and her children on the boardwalk watching the July Fourth parade pass. Excitement thrummed in the air. Cheering and music beat against her ears, and the hot July sun baked the town. A trickle of sweat ran down her spine.

Dust scented the air.

Her thoughts skipped to Rafe. Where he was this morning? She refused to let the possibility that he might be with Edith dampen her excitement. Rafe might not know it yet, but she had plans for them today.

The Summit band, comprised of men who played with more enthusiasm than skill, marched down the street from the direction of the train depot. With American flags held aloft, three teenaged girls wearing sashes made of red, white, and blue bunting followed. The crowd that lined both sides of the road cheered. Several cowboys mounted on their cowponies came next. They made a dashing sight with colorful bandanas tied about their necks and their six-shooters belted about their waists. They waved their hats at the bystanders, who whistled and cheered.

One of the cowboys pulled his spotted mount to a halt. He jabbed at his horse's sides with his spurs and pulled on the reins at the same time, making the horse rear. The cowboy jerked his six-shooter from its holster and fired several shots into the air before his horse dropped to the ground.

A pretty city girl, one of the tourists who'd arrived in Summit to see a mountain-style July Fourth celebration, stepped off the boardwalk into the road. She waved to the cowboy, who urged his gelding to the girl's side. While he held his restive mount in check, the cowboy untied his red bandana and thrust it into the girl's hand, then bent low over his saddle and stole a kiss from his admirer. His companions hooted, and the girl blushed.

When the girl had rejoined her friends and the cowboys had moved on, Daisy leaned closer to Katie to shout over the pandemonium. "I hope I don't have to dig a bullet out of anyone today."

Katie shrugged. "Today, anything is possible. People get frisky and careless."

Daisy couldn't help but savor the revelry. This July Fourth promised to be a festive occasion, very different from the last four holidays when she'd spent the day working the wards at the hospital where she'd been employed.

On this holiday, she intended to enjoy herself and spend time with Rafe. She refused to allow him to ignore her all day. Though he had to oversee the festivities and was obligated to take tourists up in his plane that afternoon, the celebrations wouldn't occupy him all day. At some point during the fete she'd corner her husband, if need be, to ensure that he made an opportunity for them to be together. Her heart beat faster at the prospect.

Clowns with painted faces followed the cowboys. They impressed onlookers with their tumbling and acrobatic stunts.

Children shrieked when one of the clowns tossed handfuls of penny candy at the crowd. A mad scramble ensued, with children searching for the sweets among the adults' feet.

When the parade ended, Daisy accompanied Katie and her brood to the lake in the middle of the meadow. With the mine and all businesses closed for the day, and the town's population swelled with tourists, a sizeable crowd thronged the reedy shore. Two of the local ranchers had donated a whole steer apiece, and now the delectable scent of barbequed beef roasting over an open pit gave off a mouthwatering aroma. Tables loaded with cakes, pies, and cookies tempted the hungry. A small three-sided tent that housed a stand on which rested pitchers of iced tea and glasses provided refreshment for the thirsty. Farther down the shore, away from the families, two sawhorses with boards slung across them held a large iron kettle. Daisy squinted at the young men who patronized the makeshift table. That kettle must hold something stronger than tea, despite the prohibition of liquor. When men wanted to drink, they'd find a way.

Daisy's blood quickened at the festive atmosphere that filled the air. With Katie's toddler parked on one hip, she scanned the fete's activities. Off to one side, men tossed horseshoes. Along the shoreline, colorful booths offered entertainment. Beneath a red, white, and blue banner, Edith told fortunes. A gypsy costume lent her fortune-telling act an air of mystery. A green canvas tent housed a ring toss game. Children grabbed bags of popcorn from another table.

"I'd better find a spot to spread out my blanket and feed my children. Then I can think about eating." Katie steered their group away from the crowd around the lake. She angled for a vacant spot behind the food tables.

"I'll help you." Daisy grabbed the hand of Katie's next-to-the youngest when the little girl wanted to dart away.

Although Katie's two oldest boys had disappeared into the crush with their friends and could fend for themselves, she still had her two youngest to wrestle into order.

"If you stay with the children, I can handle the food." Katie found a vacant spot to her liking and halted. With a flourish, she snapped out a gray wool blanket.

Daisy turned the two little girls loose and grabbed the quilt's other corners. Together she and Katie spread the blanket on the short mountain grass. While Katie went in search of food, she corralled her friend's two youngest and tried to entertain them until their mother returned with their food.

Katie's husband had been detailed to escort visitors into the mine shaft and to conduct tours of the areas where the public was allowed. When he completed his shift, he'd join Katie. Daisy tried to be patient and not to count the minutes until she'd be free to find Rafe.

After they'd finished eating, Daisy collected the tin plates and forks they'd used.

"I'll return these. You just rest."

Katie made a face. "You call lassoing these two resting? Ha!"

"George should be done with his shift before I get back. Then it will be his turn to deal with your hooligans." Daisy laughed and turned away. As she strolled past the booth where Edith had been telling fortunes, she noticed that the tent was abandoned. Edith must have gone to lunch.

Daisy threaded her way between revelers to where galvanized tin tubs had been placed for the collection of dirty dishes. After she'd dropped the eating utensils into the tubs, she paused and glanced around, hoping to locate Rafe.

Being taller than most men, her husband wasn't hard to spot. He stood off to one side, engaged in conversation with

Mr. Montgomery. Edith stood at Rafe's other side, close enough that her shoulder brushed his arm. Arrested by the sight, Daisy froze and watched the Southern beauty. Even in her gypsy costume with its bohemian, off-the-shoulder style, hoop earrings, and a kerchief that covered her bright hair, Edith possessed a classiness that provided a counterpoint to Rafe's innate sophistication.

Daisy wilted. Edith seemed a better match for Rafe than she herself. She'd been nothing more than a socialite's maid before Rafe married her.

Edith had been born to privilege. In different circumstances, Daisy might have been her maid. Perhaps Edith had been right when she'd said that Daisy would hold Rafe back. Perhaps Rafe would be better off without her as his wife. If she loved him, maybe she should she leave Summit and clear the way for her husband to be with Edith.

After several agonizing moments, Daisy shook off her doubts. No, she wouldn't slink away in defeat. Rafe was her husband. In spite of her background, he'd chosen her to be his wife. They'd been married in the sight of God and witnesses, a covenant they both believed should last for a lifetime. She'd fight for her husband and her marriage.

Edith had no right to cast her wiles at another woman's husband.

Daisy had chosen her outfit with Rafe in mind. She'd purchased a new skirt and blouse set in the hopes that she'd see him today. Her mirror told her that her slender figure showed to advantage in the ensemble's straight lines. The skirt's hem flared about her calves with a flirty air, and the blouse's dropped waist flattered her. The cheerful green and yellow plaid pattern gave the costume a jaunty appeal, and the fancy embroidery about the pockets and scooped neckline made it chic.

Lifting her chin, Daisy squirmed between two groups of tourists. The movement caught Rafe's eye. When their gazes connected, the contact seared her to her toes. She halted and waited to see what Rafe would do.

Rafe concluded his conversation with Mr. Montgomery, then excused himself and eased away from Edith.

Though she and Rafe still had eyes only for each other, Daisy caught Edith's frown when Rafe left her side. When the Charleston beauty realized that Rafe had abandoned her to join his wife, she propped both hands on her hips and narrowed her eyes. She tossed Daisy a glittering look of dislike.

Rafe came to a halt before his wife and shoved back his cowboy hat. He stared down his nose at her in silence.

Daisy waited for him to speak.

"Are you enjoying our July Fourth celebrations?" His tone revealed only the casual curiosity one might show to an acquaintance.

His offhand greeting dismayed her. She'd hoped for a warmer reception, but she refused to be daunted. "So far, I am. I just hope I don't have to dig a bullet out of anyone today. If those cowboys drink too much of whatever's in that kettle over there, they'll become a menace to the rest of us." A jerk of her head indicated the kettle where several miners and cowboys imbibed the pot's contents.

Rafe's glance followed her nod. "That's probably some locally made hooch. Today is a chance for them to let off a little steam. Tomorrow they'll be chasing cattle from dawn to dusk or working the mine."

"They can let off all the steam they want, as long as they don't shoot anyone."

Rafe continued to stare down at her.

Unnerved by his scrutiny, Daisy shifted her weight to her other foot. "When will you start giving plane rides?"

"Rides start soon. I should head over to my plane right now and get her ready."

Even as he spoke, the red-haired tourist who had accosted him in the café joined them. She shook her abundant curly hair over her shoulders and tossed Rafe a coquettish smile. "I'll be one of your passengers this afternoon, Mr. Wild Wind. I'm looking forward to the ride."

Rafe stared down at her without returning her smile and propped his fists on the gun belt slung about his hips. "Again? Your thirst for adventure hasn't been satisfied by two plane rides already this summer?"

Undeterred by Rafe's brusque response, the girl plowed on. "I could never get enough of flying with you. You're an ace, and I love going up." The redhead cast Daisy a curious look before she returned her charm to Rafe. She tousled her hair in a flirty manner and tossed him a come-hither smile. "You make me feel safe up there, yet daring, too."

Rafe didn't respond to her coquettishness. Instead, he hooked an arm about Daisy's waist. "Have you met my wife? This is Daisy, my wife."

The redhead couldn't hide her dismay. All flirtatiousness vanished. She managed a nod in Daisy's direction and whirled, disappearing into the crowd without a backward glance.

Rafe removed his arm.

Daisy exulted in Rafe's public acknowledgement of their married status, even though he'd only admitted to their relationship to fend off a troublesome female. She dared not comment about what he'd done, though she couldn't help but smile. "I don't think she'll be one of your passengers this afternoon."

"I hope not. She was becoming a nuisance, and apparently money's no object for her. The last time I took her up, I charged her double the fare."

"You should keep taking her up. After a while, she'd make you a fortune."

Rafe didn't respond to her teasing, as he would have done in the past. "I have to do my pre-flight check." He turned away as though to head for the hanger. After one step, he wheeled. "Would you like to go with me?"

His simple invitation thrilled her almost as much as his marriage proposal had done. For the first time since he'd left to go to war, he requested her company without some obligatory reason in mind. Then she remembered Katie, who waited for her to return after disposing of their dirty dishes. She hesitated.

When he saw her indecision, Rafe shrugged. "Don't feel as though you have to go with me. I just thought you might like to see my aeroplane."

And if she didn't accompany her husband, Edith undoubtedly would. Daisy made up her mind. "Yes, I'd love to. Can you give me a moment to tell Katie where I'm going? I'm supposed to be helping her with the children."

Rafe rested his weight on one hip and nodded. "I can wait."

Daisy darted away on her errand. When she returned, Rafe still stood where she'd left him. They fell into step together and wove their way through the revelers to the hanger beyond the mining families' homes.

When they reached the hanger, Daisy glanced once at her daughter's grave in the nearby cemetery, then turned away. Today was a day of possible new beginnings, not grief. She wouldn't think of Molly now, except to rejoice in the short years Molly had graced her life.

Rafe stepped into the three-sided hanger. Daisy trailed behind and watched while her husband began a meticulous check. He circled the aircraft, inspecting the tires, the engine cowling, and the machine's exterior. He ran his fingers down the cables and examined the connections. He checked the oil and other fluids, then stepped onto one wing and climbed into the open cockpit.

While he continued his pre-flight routine, she studied the craft, sheltered within the hanger. Its nose pointed outward toward the open wall and the meadow beyond. Rafe's aeroplane was a two-seater biplane painted a flashy red color. Lacquered canvas stretched over a wooden frame. She marveled that such a fragile machine could soar into the heavens and yet bring its passengers safely back to earth. When she thought of Rafe fighting the Hun in such a flimsy craft, she shuddered. The aeroplane's skin wouldn't have stopped bullets.

Unwilling to dwell on the war's memories, she sent a prayer of thanks heavenward for her husband's safe return. Through Divine providence, Rafe had been spared the fate of so many other flyboys. Her husband had come safely home.

Rafe's voice recalled her to the present. "Would you care to go up for a spin?"

Daisy's breath hitched. She'd never flown before. Just the prospect of leaving the ground and committing her life to the aircraft made her dizzy. She wasn't sure she wanted to trust her life to this machine.

He leaned out of the cockpit and stared down at her. "Edith goes up with me."

CHAPTER 13

Once she heard that Edith had flown with Rafe, Daisy determined she'd go up with her husband. She wouldn't cry craven while the other woman had been bold enough to fly. Though anxiety filled her, she nodded. "I'm sure it's safe. I've been told from a trustworthy source that you haven't lost a passenger yet."

"Do I detect a note of reservation in your voice, Mrs. Wild Wind?" Rafe still peered down at her from over the cockpit's rim.

Daisy gave him a searching glance. For the first time since he'd returned from the war, he showed a glimpse of the old Rafe. This was as close as he'd come to teasing her in the four years since the war's end. Humor gleamed in his dark eyes. And he'd called her Mrs. Wild Wind. To hear those words cross his lips stirred her heart. "I do believe you're correct, Mr. Wild Wind. I indeed have reservations about letting my feet leave the ground."

"And what must I do to convince you that you're perfectly safe with me?"

Daisy pretended to consider. She tapped one forefinger

against her chin. "I suppose that, other than having a friend vouch for you, I'll just have to trust you."

Rafe's humor vanished. For a moment, he simply stared at her. "A wise decision, Mrs. Wild Wind." Gripping the padded edges of the cockpit, he stood and swung a leg over the aeroplane's side. After stepping onto the wing, he leaped to the ground. "Let's gear up."

He strode to a wooden trunk in the hanger's back corner and lifted the lid. After he'd rummaged in the contents, he extricated a small brown leather jacket and thrust it at her. "Here, try this. It's probably too big, but it's the smallest one I have."

Daisy took the jacket and shrugged into it. She fumbled with the buttons until Rafe brushed her fingers aside and fastened them for her, then smoothed down the collar. For a moment, his palms rested on her shoulders before he dropped his hands and turned back to the trunk. He took out his own larger flyboy's jacket and slipped it on. Aviator patches decorated the front and sleeves.

Daisy would have liked to slip the buttons through their holes for him and to feel his muscled warmth beneath the leather, but she didn't dare. She thought it best to let him set the pace of wherever their relationship was going. At least today, he wasn't ignoring her.

When he turned away toward a shelf above the trunk, she saw the words, "The Lafayette Escadrille" emblazoned in a semicircle on the jacket's back. She ached to ask him about the war and his time with the flying unit, but any mention of the war shut him down. For the first year he'd been in France, he'd mailed her a letter every week, so she knew about that time of his life. He'd stopped writing after the first year, and the rest of the war remained a mystery. What had happened during those silent months to change him so?

Rafe grabbed two leather helmets and two pairs of aviator goggles from the shelf and pivoted. He took Daisy's arm and hustled her toward the plane. When they reached the wings, he pulled her to a stop and turned her to face him. Concern crinkled the corners of his eyes. "Are you sure about this?"

She longed to tell him how sharing this moment with him was the best thing that had happened to her since he'd left for France, but the uncertain state of their marriage prevented such complete honesty. She couldn't share that tidbit with him. She could only give him the answer he sought. "You didn't tip me into the water when you took me rowing, and you never let me fall when you were teaching me to skate, so I'll have to trust you with this."

"If you're sure . . ."

"I am."

"Let me roll this crate out of the hanger, and then I'll help you up." Rafe moved around to the craft's back. Lifting the tail off the ground with one hand and putting his other onto the fuselage, he wheeled the light machine into the open. He turned it toward the meadow's length, away from the town, and returned to Daisy's side.

With one hand on her elbow, he escorted her to the biplane. "In you go then." Rafe's big hands closed about her waist, and he boosted her up onto the bottom wing. "Just climb into the front cockpit and sit down."

Daisy scrambled over the cockpit's side and slid into the canvas seat. Rafe followed her onto the wing and leaned over the cockpit's rim, then fitted the snug leather helmet over her head. He secured the strap beneath her chin and handed her the goggles. "Put these on and strap yourself in."

She slipped the goggles over her helmet and fastened the strap over her lap.

When Daisy had secured herself, Rafe leaped off the wing and strode to the front of the plane.

She leaned to one side and peered around the plane's nose to watch her husband. He reached for the propeller. With both hands gripping the blade, he thrust his shoulder into the effort and heaved. The propeller came to life and spun in a blurring arc. The engine coughed and spit flame. Gray exhaust billowed from the cowling. The motor sputtered and then settled into a steady throb. The aeroplane vibrated as it strained against the brakes, fighting to break free and surge into the sky.

When her husband had settled himself in the rear cockpit and prepared to take off, Daisy held her breath. Her fingers turned icy, and her heart battered against her ribs. What momentary insanity had allowed her to accept his invitation? Was it too late to leap out? A vision of the chic Edith flying with Rafe banished her qualms. If Edith could fly, so could she.

The craft eased forward, trembling with eagerness to launch upward into the heavens. Daisy gripped the cockpit's rim as the biplane gained speed and surged ahead, bouncing a little over the grass. Wind whipped past her face and snatched at the hair which hung beneath her helmet. She closed her eyes, unable to look at the ground flashing by beneath them. Suddenly, the bouncing stopped, and her stomach lurched when the red plane lifted into the air.

She forced open her eyes as the craft continued to climb. After a moment, she dared to peer over the side. The earth had fallen away below them. The meadow spread out like a large bowl cradled within the encircling mountains. The lake appeared to be a small blue splotch in the center, and the July Fourth merrymakers seemed nothing more than dots. Above her spread the soft blue Colorado sky and the aircraft's top wing.

She remembered to breathe and relaxed her hold on the cockpit's rim. The cold wind rushing past and the engine's thrumming filled her head. The feeling of weightlessness she experienced seemed odd, but she thought she could accustom herself to the sensation.

Ahead, a wall of mountains rushed toward them, so close she could pick out individual evergreen trees growing on the slopes. When a collision with the granite peaks seemed inevitable, the aeroplane swooped upward and soared over the top, then dove down the other side. The move pinned Daisy against the seat and hurled her stomach into her throat. She swallowed a scream. The summit flashed past below. More mountains, like rumpled ocean waves, layered the earth's surface beneath them.

The right wings dipped, and the plane wheeled into a dive. Daisy's abdomen somersaulted, and she closed her eyes. She gripped the cockpit's rim again and hung on, convinced she'd tumble out or they'd smash into the ground. After several moments when she felt certain that imminent death waited, the craft leveled off and glided mere yards above a high mountain meadow. Just beneath them, a herd of white-faced cattle broke into a panicked, lumbering gallop.

By the time Rafe swung them into a wide loop and brought them in low over the lake's shoreline, Daisy had begun to enjoy herself. She looked down on the picnickers below her, people who tipped up their heads to watch the aeroplane's approach. Many of them waved.

The craft banked left and slowed. The engine's rhythmic cadence sputtered, then throbbed again. The miners' homes drifted past just below them as the plane sank lower. The engine sputtered once more, and the earth reached up to grasp them. Rafe cut the engine. Moments later, the wheels touched the ground. The plane bounced twice and came back to earth, then rolled to a stop just beyond the hanger.

Daisy leaned back in her seat. She'd done it. She'd flown with Rafe and hadn't even lost her lunch. She unclenched her clammy hands.

The plane dipped a bit when Rafe stepped out onto the wing. His big form loomed over her cockpit, and she tipped her head back to look at him. He reached in to unbuckle the strap that secured her. She took his hand when he offered his aid, and he helped her over the side. When her feet touched the ground, she pulled off the goggles and peeled the leather helmet from her head, then fluffed her hair.

The ground swayed beneath her, so she clutched at the plane's side to steady herself.

Rafe jumped down beside her and shucked off his own goggles and helmet. "Well, what do you think?"

Daisy took a cautious breath. Her stomach settled, and her heartbeat assumed its normal rhythm. She stared into her husband's earnest face. "I think I could learn to enjoy flying, once I get used to it."

"As long as you didn't hate it, you can learn to enjoy it."

"I thought for a minute I was going to fall right out when you swooped down over those cattle." She managed a grin.

"I'd never do anything that would endanger you."

"I know you wouldn't."

An invisible skein of emotion drew them together. Their gazes caught, and time hung suspended.

Their flight over the picnic area had signaled that the ace had begun to give plane rides, and the first eager customers swarmed toward them. The moment shattered, and they glanced toward the crowd.

Rafe tossed her a wry grin. "Now it's time for me to play aerial taxi driver."

"And I'm sure you'll have many satisfied customers."

From that moment through the rest of the afternoon, Rafe's aeroplane droned in repeated circles over the mountain rims and back. Daisy found Katie, and from their vantage point beside the lake, she watched his plane shuttle one passenger after another in looping circuits over the meadow.

"After the last passenger, Rafe will perform aerial stunts for our entertainment." With her sleeping toddler in her arms, Katie cocked her head toward the plane that had just touched down.

After having experienced her first flight, Daisy couldn't imagine the nerve it would take to perform aerial stunts. She closed her eyes. What if something should go wrong? What if the engine failed? Rafe would be killed, shattered into a thousand pieces and engulfed in an inferno of flaming canvas and wood.

She shook herself from the terrifying vision and tried to smile at Katie. "I'm sure Rafe is an excellent pilot, since he survived the Hun."

"I know he is. I've seen what he can do."

"I think he's about to begin. Let's get closer so we can see better."

With Katie's husband holding his daughter's hand, the trio strolled to the meadow. Onlookers already lined both sides of the makeshift runway. They found places halfway down the field.

As her heart hammered against her ribs, Daisy watched Rafe taxi his plane between the double row of bystanders. The craft gained speed and, bouncing twice, leaped into the air.

What followed turned her heart to ice. She watched, transfixed with terror, as Rafe pushed his aeroplane to the limits of its ability. She couldn't tear her gaze from the craft as it looped, rolled, and spun over the meadow in hair-raising maneuvers. She held her breath while her husband hammered the biplane straight upwards at the sun.

When the aircraft was a mere red speck in the sky, it rolled and dove downward toward the earth. The craft plummeted in a series of spins. The plane's engine whined at the strain. While the other spectators gasped, she closed her eyes, certain that her husband would perish. She couldn't watch while Rafe smashed into the ground. The crowd let out a collective sigh, and she peeked through half-closed lids.

Rafe had pulled his machine out of the dive and leveled off just above the meadow. Faintness made her vision dim, and she clutched Katie's arm.

Katie glanced at her. A frown puckered her forehead. "Are you all right? You look pale."

"I think I might faint."

Katie jostled her toddler to one shoulder and curved her free arm about Daisy's shoulders. "Do you need to sit down?"

Daisy considered the question and shook her head. The dizziness had passed. "I don't think so."

"Well, if you can stand to watch, Rafe is about to do his final stunt. He does this every year."

Daisy turned her attention to the plane. Rafe had flung the machine toward the mountain peaks at the meadow's far end. The craft raked the summit, then rolled and headed toward the lake. Just before it reached the water, the biplane flipped. Her husband was flying upside down. She goggled, unable to believe her eyes.

At the shore nearest town, Rafe righted his plane and wheeled it back over the meadow. He buzzed the crowd, wings waggling. After a final loop over the meadow, he brought his machine down onto the grass and cut the engine.

As Rafe climbed from the cockpit and leaped off the bottom wing, a cheer sounded from the onlookers. He was still pulling off his leather helmet when a bevy of young ladies rushed at him. When they reached the aeroplane, they clustered about him, all babbling at once. Some thrust pens and papers at him, hoping for an autograph.

Relieved that her husband had both feet planted on the ground, Daisy smiled at the beleaguered expression on his face, while women peppered him with comments and questions.

Katie cut her a sideways glance. "I told you he was popular with the girls."

Daisy propped one hand on her hip. "I can see that. I wonder how many of them have already gone up with him?"

"Probably most of them. Rafe tends to have repeat customers."

Daisy viewed the scene through narrowed eyes. "I imagine so. Do men ever fly with him?"

"Some do, but most of his customers are women."

"Hmm . . ." A movement to her right caught Daisy's eye. Edith, still clad in her gypsy costume, advanced on the plane with a purposeful stride.

Edith's determined impetus indicated that she didn't intend to share Rafe with his admirers. She cut a swath through his fans as the young ladies parted to let her pass. With her arm looped through his, she tossed a triumphant smile at the girls and towed him away.

Daisy tracked their progress toward the picnic area. Disheartenment clutched her by the throat. She should have been the woman to rescue Rafe from his followers. If she'd been more confident of how Rafe would have reacted, she would have hurried to his side. Instead, the brash Southern beauty had been the one to claim the advantage.

What did Rafe really think about Edith's boldness? Rafe had been capable of extricating himself from unwanted attention without anyone's help, but, with the whole crowd watching, he'd been gentleman enough not to spurn Edith's gesture. Now Edith would have his company throughout the evening meal and the fireworks display afterward.

Daisy sighed and turned away. The day had lost its luster.

CHAPTER 14

Daisy settled cross legged on the blanket beside Katie and took her friend's sleepy toddler in her lap. The day's events had worn out the child, who dozed while they waited in the darkness for the fireworks display to begin.

Excitement rippled through the crowd, while boys added to the festivities with their sparklers. Glittering wands held high, several youngsters stampeded past the blanket on which Daisy and Katie lounged.

Daisy frowned after them as they disappeared into the crowd. "I hope they're using store-bought sparklers. Homemade sparklers can be dangerous."

Katie watched the throng swallow the boys. "Those are miners' children. I doubt their parents have money to buy sparklers."

"I understand the boys wanting to have fun, but they don't realize how dangerous steel wool and accelerants can be. And if those boys made the sparklers themselves, who knows how much accelerant they used?" Daisy tried to slough away the concern that rode like a dark cloud at her back and resolved to enjoy the festivities. "Shouldn't the fireworks start soon?"

She'd no sooner determined to put thoughts of injury aside when a muffled bang sounded. A sharp outcry followed, and a stir in the crowd alerted her that a crisis had occurred.

She shifted the sleeping child to Katie's lap. "Something has happened. I think I should see if anyone is hurt."

Daisy scrambled to her feet and joined the stream of people already headed in the direction of the explosion. Down by the lakeshore, dim figures clustered about a form stretched out on the grass. She wriggled her way through the crowd to where the injured child lay and knelt beside him. The boy was one of the miner's sons who had just galloped past her and Katie. The child's weeping mother kneeled on the ground with her son's head cradled in her lap. Even through the darkness, Daisy could see that blood soaked the boy's right hand and arm. "What happened?"

"His sparkler went off." The mother managed to reply through her sobs.

Daisy glanced up at the woman's husband, who stood at her shoulder. "Was the sparkler homemade?"

The miner nodded.

Armed with the knowledge that the child's injury might be worse than it might have been had he been holding a professionally made sparkler, Daisy bent closer to peer at the boy's injured hand. Thankfully, he still possessed all his fingers, though in some places, bone and tendons showed through the skin. White bone gleamed in the darkness in the youngster's forearm. Merciful unconsciousness cloaked the boy, though he moaned through the black mists that enveloped him.

"We must get your son away from here." Daisy considered her options. The boy needed to be moved to a place where she could treat him. Would Rafe object to her using his kitchen table again? She'd just made the decision to instruct the father to take his son to the kitchen when Rafe appeared through the darkness.

Her husband squatted opposite her and looked at her across the prone child. "What can I do?"

Edith hovered at Rafe's shoulder.

"Do you mind if I use your kitchen again?"

He shook his head.

"Thank you. We'll take him there." Daisy spoke even as she bent closer to the injury. "I need to borrow your handkerchief."

Rafe fished in his jeans' back pocket and produced a large white cotton handkerchief, which he thrust into her hand. "I haven't used it."

Daisy nodded without taking time to reply and wrapped the cloth about the most damaged area in a makeshift bandage. She beckoned to Edith and concealed her surprise when the other woman approached without grumbling. Daisy grabbed Edith's hand and guided it to the bandage. "Hold your hand there and keep up the pressure. We need to slow the bleeding."

Still without protesting, Edith knelt beside the boy and pressed her hand against the handkerchief. Her colorful gypsy dress puddled about her on the grass.

Daisy rose, while a portion of her mind admitted that perhaps the socialite wasn't all fluff. She'd expected the other woman to faint, or at least object to lending her assistance.

Daisy addressed Rafe across the child's inert form. "I'll get my medical bag. Take this boy to your house and put him on the table. Make sure the table is clean."

In her hotel room, Daisy checked her medical bag and grabbed extra bandages before she squirmed out of her sunny yellow and green plaid outfit. She tossed the clothing in a crumpled heap on the bed. Pulling her functional dark skirt and white blouse from the wardrobe, she wriggled into the clothes. Her hasty fingers fumbled at the buttons, but at last she was dressed. With her skirt swirling about her calves, she snatched up her black leather bag and fled from the room.

When she burst into Rafe's kitchen minutes later, she saw the boy's parents huddled in one corner. At the sink, Rafe was pumping water into a large metal pot. Edith still held the handkerchief against the wound, though blood soaked the cotton. They all glanced at her when she swept through the door.

Daisy dropped her bag on the wooden sideboard and approached the boy's parents. In her most professional manner, she curled her fingers around the mother's cold hands and spoke in soothing tones. "What is your son's name?"

"Billy."

"And what is your name?" Daisy peered into the woman's teary eyes.

"Grace, Mrs. Wild Wind. Grace Jenks."

"Well, Grace. I'm going to take care of Billy and do my best to see that he can use his hand and arm again. While I'm working on him, would you and your husband wait in the other room? Just make yourselves comfortable until I come out to talk to you." With a hand on Grace's shoulder, she turned the woman about and nudged her out of the kitchen. Mr. Jenks followed his wife.

With the boy's parents dealt with, Daisy hurried to Billy's side. She glanced at Edith, who still pressed the cloth against the injury. "Thank you, Edith. I appreciate your help." Having Edith as an ally in this crisis, with both of them united in the struggle to save Billy's hand, gave Daisy an odd feeling. "After you wash up, could you keep the Jenks company?

Mrs. Jenks will need someone to keep her mind off what's happening in here."

Edith nodded. "I can talk to a brass post, so keepin' Mrs. Jenks occupied will be like takin' candy from a baby."

When Edith stepped away, Daisy made a quick visual examination of her patient. Soot from the explosion smudged the boy's face, and blisters had formed on his cheeks, but no further injury showed there. She turned her attention to his arm. After she'd peeled the handkerchief from the wound, she leaned closer to assay the damage. The injury would need a good bit of repair work, but Billy should be able to use his arm again once he'd healed.

She moved on to inspect his hand, where the explosion had done more harm. The repair here would be trickier, but she hoped she could restore some usage to the hand.

When she'd tied a kerchief about her hair and donned her medical apron, she and Rafe both scrubbed up.

Turning to her patient, she cleansed Billy's face and swabbed down the injured area with disinfectant. The boy moaned and stirred. She delved into her bag and extracted a bag of sterile cotton wool, followed by a brown bottle of chloroform. The anesthesia would keep Billy unconscious while she worked.

After she'd dealt with Billy, she plucked her portable torch from her bag and thrust it at Rafe, who waited for instructions on the other side of the table. "I'll need more light. Can you come around to this side and aim the torch where I'm working?"

Without commenting, he joined her on her side of the table. She tried not to let awareness of his big body looming beside her distract her.

He aimed the light where she pointed. She took a deep breath and said a silent prayer, then bent over her patient.

Daisy had been working for over an hour when a commotion outside the kitchen interrupted her. She straightened and eyed the closed kitchen door. As Rafe laid the torch on the table, she caught the tension that radiated from him.

The door burst open, and Doc Irby stood in the aperture. A couple of miners hovered behind him.

"What's going on here?" Doc Irby stalked into the room. He brushed past Rafe and came to a halt beside the unconscious Billy.

Daisy motioned to her patient. "Billy's hand was injured when his sparkler exploded. I'm repairing the damage."

Doc Irby leaned down to inspect her work, then glanced at her over his shoulder. "That arm will have to come off."

A gust of whiskey fumes hit Daisy in the face. The good doctor must have partaken of a liberal amount of his own Patent Medicine during the day's festivities. Either that, or he'd imbibed too much hooch. She shook her head. "There's no need to amputate. I can save his arm."

That she should disagree with his diagnosis seemed to infuriate the doctor. He straightened and thrust a plump finger beneath her nose. "Young lady, I'll have you know I've been a doctor since before you were born. Besides, you're a woman. Women don't make doctors, they're only nurses. Now, move over and let me get to work."

Behind the doctor, Rafe made a motion as if to forcibly remove their intruder from the premises. Daisy shook her head at her husband and addressed the physician. His attack rattled her, but anger overrode her nerves. She was no longer the timid girl who had worked for a New York socialite. Since those days, she'd faced down overbearing doctors who thought women had no place in the medical field and had stood up to despotic hospital ward matriarchs. She didn't intend to let an inebriated excuse for a doctor order her around.

Drawing herself up to her full petite height, she stared Doc Irby in the eye. "This is my patient. You won't touch him."

The doctor reared back as if he couldn't believe that she would address him in such a manner. His mustache quivered. "You'll kill him if you don't amputate. Now, get out of my way."

Daisy shook her head. "You're more likely to kill him if you do."

From what she guessed of his medical habits, the good doctor didn't bother to scrub before he treated his patients. The bacteria he'd introduce into Billy's wounds would fester into gangrene and turn septic. Besides that, his rumpled suit looked none too clean. The finger he'd thrust into her face had a rim of grime beneath the nail. He didn't look as if he'd bathed or changed his clothes during the last week.

"That arm needs to come off." Doc Irby huffed out the words on another gust of fumes, and his walrus mustache quivered.

"Surgery has advanced since you attended medical school. We don't amputate now unless there's no possible way to save a limb."

"I say, that arm should come off." Doc Irby looked fierce. His eyebrows beetled together over his nose.

"This isn't the Civil War. We don't amputate anymore just as a matter of course. Please leave and let me get on with my patient." Daisy injected a firm note into her voice.

"Now, see here, you can't talk to me that way."

Daisy raised her chin. "I asked you to leave, unless you want to stand back and watch."

Her suggestion that he should watch her perform a

surgery rendered the doctor speechless. His mouth worked, but no sound emerged.

Rafe stepped up to the doctor and gripped him by the scruff of the neck. "Unless you want to watch, you'll need to leave. Now."

Doc Irby seemed disinclined to challenge Rafe, who topped him by several inches. "You'll be sorry. When that boy dies, his blood will be on your hands."

While Rafe marched the doctor out of the kitchen and onto the porch, Daisy poured more hot water into the dishpan and scrubbed up to her elbows again. Just the doctor's presence made her feel dirty.

Rafe returned to the kitchen and joined her at the sink. He thrust his hands into the water and lathered with her soap. They remained silent, both occupied with their washing. When they'd finished, Rafe stepped away and shook droplets from his fingers. He looked down at her, a gleam of admiration in his eyes. "You've come a long way from the timid girl you were when we first met. You never could have taken on Doc Irby back then."

She met his look with a serious one of her own. "That girl doesn't exist anymore. Working alongside the doctors at the war's front changed me. Nursing at the front made me see myself in a different way and gave me the determination to be what I am today."

"I guess I'll have to get to know the new Daisy. She's someone I haven't really met."

"The new Daisy isn't so different from the old one. I'm still me in a lot of ways."

Rafe's lips curled in a small smile. "I'll have to find out. And the new Daisy had better get busy with saving Billy's hand."

CHAPTER 15

Daisy stepped into her former home and closed the door. Today was one of her scheduled days where Rafe had given her permission to sterilize her instruments in the kitchen two mornings a week.

Each time she entered the house, yearning filled her. The sensation that she still lived here overcame her, and the years when she'd been gone fell away. Being in the house felt so right. To fall into the trap of pretending that she and Rafe lived here together would be all too easy.

The home's quietness enveloped her. On the shelf above the coal stove in the great room, the Napoleon Hat style mantel clock's steady ticking marked the seconds. Otherwise, the house was silent. Daisy gripped her medical bag's handle and wheeled toward the kitchen. Indulging in fantasy, no matter how pleasant, wouldn't get her equipment sterilized.

While she worked, her thoughts drifted to last week's July Fourth celebration. Billy's progress gave her professional satisfaction. Despite Doc Irby's dire predictions, no infection had set in. Billy continued to heal, and Daisy had confidence he'd regain most of the use of his hand and arm.

With tongs in hand, Daisy lifted her tongue depressor from the boiling water and laid the instrument on a towel to dry. Next, she removed a scalpel and dropped it beside the tongue depressor. The routine activity of sterilizing her instruments allowed her mind to flit to her husband while she worked.

What had Rafe meant when he'd commented that he should get to know the "new" Daisy? Shouldn't he spend time with her if he wanted to know her better? He'd remained elusive since he'd assisted with Billy's surgery, and she'd only seen him once. One evening last week they'd bumped into each other at Katie's Café, and they'd shared a table. Daisy hugged the memory to her heart. Warmed by thoughts of her husband as he'd sat across the table from her, his gaze on her face as they shared the events of their day, she withdrew a pair of forceps with her tongs and laid it on the towel.

Hard on the heels of her elation, doubt intruded to spoil her euphoria. Rafe had walked her to the hotel after they'd eaten, but he'd made no plans to spend time with her. With a frown, Daisy nibbled on her lower lip. Should she track him down and force her presence on him? No. Her husband wouldn't appreciate being hunted. She tossed her tongs onto the sideboard and spun toward the kitchen door.

While her instruments dried, Daisy wandered to the foot of the stairs and stared at the landing where the staircase curved upward into the second floor's shadowed dimness. In all the times she'd been back in her home, she hadn't yet had the courage to visit the upstairs bedrooms. She needed to face her demons and conquer the distress that waited for her on the second floor.

Daisy curled her palm around the mahogany railing and put one foot on the bottom step. She took another step, and one more until she reached the landing where the staircase took a turn. A compulsion she couldn't deny drove her all the way to the hallway at the top.

The bedroom she and Rafe had shared lay straight ahead. The door stood open. On either side were two rooms, with one more at the back. Molly had occupied the room on the right.

Daisy turned toward her daughter's bedroom. At the closed door, she hesitated and steeled herself against the inevitable pain. She breathed deeply through her nose and opened the portal.

The sight of Molly's room hit her like a blow. She staggered and leaned against the door jamb for support. Nothing had changed since Molly's death. After the funeral, she'd been unable to put away her daughter's things, and apparently, neither had Rafe. Everything remained just as it had when Molly had been taken ill.

Ruffled pink gingham curtains framed the window on the opposite wall. The crib beneath the window still held the rumpled blankets that had been there during her final illness. A stuffed bear with one eye and a bent ear, Molly's favorite toy, still lay beside her pillow. Her toybox along the left-hand wall held her playthings. The blocks she'd been playing with when she fell ill were still scattered on the rug beside the dresser. A bookshelf near the door held the books that Molly had loved. A rocking chair with a pink blanket draped over the back stood in one corner. She'd sat in that rocker with Molly in her arms as her daughter had breathed her final gasping breaths.

Daisy choked. Grief ripped her into pieces, the jagged edges tearing at her soul. She staggered into the room and dropped into the rocker, unable to stand. Her arms ached to hold her daughter. Though she couldn't weep, her mother's heart felt the loss as if Molly had just died.

Time ceased to exist. She didn't know how long she sat in her daughter's room, overwhelmed by dry-eyed sorrow. At last, she pushed herself out of the rocker and tottered, like an old woman, across the room to the crib. She plucked up the stuffed bear and snuggled the toy beneath her chin. Closing her eyes, she stroked the teddy bear's fur. Finally, drained of grief, she laid the bear on the blankets and patted it once.

Daisy turned and made her way across the room. At the door, she swept the room with a final glance and closed the portal.

One more emotional journey remained. She took the few steps to the bedroom she'd shared with Rafe and stood in the open doorway. The spacious room stretched along the front of the house. A pair of windows framed a panoramic view of the whole valley. Sunlight spilled between the drapes and spangled the patterned Turkish carpet with glitter.

Rafe's presence stamped the room. His essence surrounded her. Daisy closed her eyes and let the sensation fill her. Even his scent, a mixture of leather and his own personal male substance, remained.

She lifted her lids and trailed a glance about the room. The large bed with its carved headboard hadn't been made, and the blankets had been shoved toward the foot. The pillow on Rafe's side still held the indentation of his head. He'd tossed a shirt and a pair of jeans over the Morris chair in the corner beside the stove. Riding boots rested beneath the chair, one of them tipped over onto its side. A pair of socks spilled from the boots' tops.

Daisy drifted into the room. Her clothes had once hung in the cedar wardrobe beside his. Her night rails and underthings had once shared space with his underwear in the dresser beside the door. Now, no trace of her ever having lived here remained.

She paused at the foot of the bed and turned in a slow circle while the room's atmosphere enveloped her. As she stood in the very heart of the house, memories tumbled over each other in frantic succession. In the Morris chair in that corner, Rafe had held her on his lap and comforted her anguish after Molly had died, though he, too, had been wracked with grief. They'd wept together. Here, in that bed, they'd loved and laughed and made plans. They'd prayed here and marveled at how God had brought them together as husband and wife.

Daisy made a fist of both hands and pressed her knuckles against her mouth to hold back the scream that choked her. Memories and emotions battered her, tearing her apart. She felt as though she'd burst into a thousand pieces. Closing her eyes, she struggled to compose herself. When she'd gathered all the jagged pieces of herself back into order and felt once more in control, she opened her eyes and lowered her hands to her sides.

She eased across the room toward the mirrored dresser that stood between the windows and halted. Her gaze dropped to the objects scattered across the surface. In a gilded frame, a sepia photo of herself and Rafe, with Molly on her lap, occupied a corner of the dresser's top. Daisy lifted the photo. Looking very much like a happily married couple, a much-younger Rafe and herself stared at the camera. Molly's cherubic face, with her dimpled cheeks and fair curls, smiled out of the frame. Pain stabbed Daisy again.

She traced Molly's visage with a forefinger and returned the picture to the dresser. Rafe's comb and brush lay beside a carved box made of golden wood. A stylized design of darker inlaid wood created an intricate pattern on the box's lid. Rafe must have acquired the coffer since he returned from the war. He hadn't owned it when they'd lived here together. Curiosity about what Rafe might keep in the box compelled Daisy to lift the lid.

Dark blue velvet lined the interior. Wooden dividers partitioned the inside into smaller sections. In a corner square nestled Rafe's wedding band. Daisy's heart clenched. To see his ring shut away in this box tore at her insides. The gesture told her how much he'd repudiated their marriage and made her question whether he'd ever wear the ring again.

She plucked the wedding band from its hiding place and held it on her open palm. The gold felt heavy and cool. The fingers of her other hand traced the ring's circular shape, a symbol of unending love. Did Rafe still love her? She didn't know. He'd shown no outward sign of that emotion during any of their encounters. Only during the brief moments when his composure had cracked had she caught a glimpse into his innermost being. She'd seen his misery, and that had to be enough to give her hope.

The rings Rafe had given her still adorned her left hand. She'd never taken them off, even after Rafe had left her. She envisioned her husband's left hand, bare of his wedding band, and she determined that whatever the future held, she'd never remove Rafe's rings.

With her fist closed around his wedding ring, she held the gold band against her heart for a moment before she returned it to the box.

Two other items caught her eye—medals Rafe had earned during the war. Her husband had received two medals for his exploits, yet he hadn't told her what he'd done to earn them. She hadn't dared to ask. The French Croix de Guerre and the United States Army Air Service's Military Aviator's Medal occupied two sections. Having seen Rafe's flying skills the week before, she didn't question his prowess in the air, but she wondered what bravery he'd shown to earn these awards. Curiosity about the lost months of his life consumed her.

She lifted the Army Air Service's bronze medal from the box. An eagle with wings outspread dangled from a straight bar boasting the words "Military Aviator." A clasp at the back would fasten the medal to his uniform, should Rafe ever choose to wear his regalia again.

Daisy stared at the object on her palm, wondering what lay behind the award. She drew the Croix de Guerre from the box and laid it beside the American medal. A stylized bronze cross bisected by crossed swords hung from a striped military ribbon. This token represented another act of courage, something else about which she knew nothing. That time of her husband's life remained blank.

The door slammed down below, and Rafe's footsteps thudded up the stairs. Panic clutched her. Would Rafe be angry that she'd invaded his domain, even though she had every moral and legal right to be here? Her fist closed around the medals, and she whirled toward the doorway.

Rafe came to an abrupt halt just over the threshold. Surprise at finding her in their bedroom crossed his face before his expression shuttered. He took another step into the room and swept off his cowboy hat. A flick of his wrist sent the headgear sailing onto the bed. "What are you doing here?"

In her haste to defuse the situation, Daisy almost stuttered. "I'm sorry. I didn't mean to intrude. I came up to look into Molly's room." She paused and swallowed. "I haven't been in her room since I came back."

Rafe propped his fists on his hips. "And you just happened to wander in here."

Daisy nodded.

"I didn't invite you in."

"I have a right to be here. I'm your wife."

Rafe said nothing to that. He continued to stare at her.

Daisy fidgeted. "I didn't expect you to come home now, or I wouldn't have come up."

At her words, Rafe yanked his shirttails from his jeans and began to slip the buttons from their holes. "I'm here because I got oil on my shirt when I was fixing some equipment at the refinery. I came to get a clean shirt."

Daisy watched, fascinated, as her husband shrugged out of his stained flannel work shirt and flung the garment at the Morris chair. The sleeveless white knit cotton undershirt he wore beneath the now-absent shirt molded his powerful chest. His shoulder muscles bunched, and his brawny arms flexed. She swallowed and wished she could run her hands over his warm flesh.

She might not even have been present. Rafe ignored her as he strode to the dresser and jerked open a drawer. He pulled out a clean, faded blue shirt. After shaking out the folds, he thrust his arms into the sleeves. Only when he'd buttoned the shirt and tucked the tails into his jeans did he look at her again.

"So, what are you doing in here?"

She shrugged. "I'm not sure. I guess I was curious."

"About what?"

"I don't know. I just wanted to see where we lived together, and what you'd done to the room since you got back." She didn't mention that she'd wanted to feel his presence, that perhaps being in their bedroom would make her feel closer to him.

"Well, you've seen it. I left it pretty much the same."

"I noticed."

She'd forgotten the war medals she clutched until Rafe frowned at her and glanced at her hands.

"What do you have there?"

Daisy stared at her fists in guilty silence. Her heart thudded. Rafe had caught her going through his things. He wouldn't be happy at the intrusion.

Rafe crossed the room with long strides and grabbed her hands, then pried open her fingers. His war medals scorched her skin as they both gazed down at his trophies.

After a long moment, Rafe scooped the awards off her palm. "You've been prying into my things. You had no right."

Daisy jerked her gaze to her husband's coldly furious face. "You're right, I shouldn't have poked into your things. I'm sorry, but there's so much about you I don't know anymore. I'm just trying to figure out what happened to change you so. If we're ever going to get back together, I have to understand you so I can help you."

Rafe turned toward the dresser. Lifting the box's lid, he flung his medals inside. He slammed the lid with a decisive *thunk*. "That part of my life is none of your business. You'd be wise to let it lie. I don't want you meddling in my war years." He pivoted toward her, his expression dark. "You still don't get it, do you? We're not going to get back together. Ever. Get used to it."

Daisy stared at him, wounded all over again. He sounded as though he didn't want to try to heal their marriage. He seemed not to care for her at all.

Rafe spun and stalked to the door. At the threshold, he tossed a glance at her over his shoulder. "You're still free to use the kitchen for sterilizing your things, but don't come up here again." He vanished down the hallway and took the stairs two at a time. Below, the door slammed behind him.

Daisy sagged against the dresser. Rafe had just shattered her world.

CHAPTER 16

A fist hammered against her hotel door. Daisy laid her Bible on the lamp stand and crossed the room, then flung open the portal.

The hotel receptionist stood just over the threshold. His spectacles glinted in the dim hallway light. Curiosity glittered in his eyes. "One of the miner's boys is asking for you downstairs. He said it was something about his mother."

Daisy closed her door and followed the clerk to the lobby. Benje stood in the middle of the room. His bony ankles protruded from beneath his too-short trousers, and his wheat-colored hair looked as though it hadn't been combed. Freckles stood out against his pale skin. "Doc Daisy, can you come quick? My ma has been took bad."

Kneeling, Daisy studied the youngster's distressed face. She curled her hands over his shoulders in a comforting gesture. "What happened to your mother, Benje?"

"Don't know, Doc Daisy. She was in the yard scrubbin' clothes when she just keeled over. I came for you as fast as I could."

Daisy squeezed Benje's shoulders. "Wait here while I get

my things. Then we'll see about your mother." She rose and patted his thin back. "I'll take good care of her."

Benje's anxious expression smoothed out, and relief almost made him smile. He nodded. "I know you can fix my ma."

Daisy hoped the boy was right. She hurried to her room and gathered up her medical bag.

At the Johnson home, Daisy followed Benje through the gate and up the walk. A black iron wash kettle stood in the side yard where Ada had been doing her laundry. The empty yard told Daisy that Ada had managed to make her way to the house.

Inside, Benje's younger siblings huddled together about the kitchen table.

"Where's your mother, Benje?" Daisy came to a stop in the middle of the room.

The boy pointed to an open door off the kitchen. "In there. I helped her to the bed."

Daisy swept into the small bedroom and laid her black leather bag on an upended fruit crate that served as a lamp table. She turned to the still figure lying on a worn blanket.

Ada lay with her eyes closed, her hands folded across her abdomen. The slight mound of her stomach told Daisy the miner's wife expected another child. She bent over the bed. "Ada."

Ada's lids lifted slowly as though the effort to open her eyes cost her more energy than she possessed. A tired smile curled her mouth. "Doc Daisy. You didn't have to come. I'll be fit as a fiddle after I've rested a bit."

"From the looks of you, you'll need more than a bit of rest."

Ada's smile vanished. "I don't know what's wrong with me. I'm tired all the time these days."

Daisy glanced again at Ada's abdomen. "What happened?"

"I was just bending over the wash tub scrubbin' Tom's shirts when all of a sudden everything went black. The next thing I knew, I was on the ground and Benje was tryin' to get me up."

"How far along are you?"

Ada sighed. "About four months."

"Maybe you shouldn't be scrubbing shirts in your condition. And hauling water or chopping wood."

Ada eyes flashed open, and she stared up at Daisy. "But Doc Daisy, if I don't do it, who will?"

Ada had voiced the dilemma the miners' wives faced.

By giving the medical advice Ada needed to help her through the rest of her pregnancy, Daisy would be meddling in an area that Ada's husband wouldn't appreciate. She hesitated before she decided to intrude in a delicate area. "Could Tom chop wood for you and carry the water, at least until the baby comes?"

Ada pushed herself up on one elbow. "Tom?" She pushed a strand of lank hair off her face. "He'd be more likely to backhand me if I even asked."

Daisy's opinion of Tom Johnson sank even lower, but she kept her thoughts to herself. Any man who raised a hand against his wife and wasn't willing to help her when she was pregnant didn't deserve the title of husband. "Perhaps if I asked him . . ."

Ada clutched Daisy's arm. "No, Doc Daisy. You stay away from Tom." She flopped back onto the pillow, and her hand dropped onto the blanket. "Tom's a good man. He just works so hard, and we have a hard time keepin' body and soul together. And with another baby on the way . . ." Ada sighed.

Daisy clamped her lips shut to keep back the retort that struggled to burst free. Tom spent too much of his wages on local illegal hooch. Perhaps if he didn't drink so much and stayed home to help his wife more, she wouldn't be lying on their bed suffering from exhaustion, but to rail against Tom wouldn't help his wife.

"Well, let me check you over to make sure nothing else is wrong." She reached into her bag for her thermometer. When Daisy had completed her examination, she sat on the edge of the bed. "Ada, all that's wrong with you is too much hard work and not enough good food."

"I never had this trouble with my other babies." Ada covered her eyes with one work-worn hand.

"This is baby number six. Your body isn't what it used to be, and you have the care of your family, as well. You need to rest. Perhaps Benje can help with some of the chores?"

Ada nodded behind her hand.

"You rest today. I'll have Katie send a nice supper down from her café, so you won't have to cook tonight."

Ada peeked out from beneath her hand. "I thank you, Doc Daisy, but we can't afford to pay you for the meal, and Tom's too proud to accept charity."

Once more, Daisy bit back a pithy comment about Tom's character. "Don't worry about the meal. It will be my treat. Tom can't turn down a surprise like that, can he?"

Ada looked doubtful, but she didn't protest further.

"And you tell Tom I won't charge you for coming down here today. I just want to look after you."

Ada nodded again.

Daisy packed her medical bag and returned to the kitchen. Five pairs of blue eyes stared at her out of five anxious, freckled faces. She gathered the brood about her and smiled down at Ada's youngsters. "Children, your mama will be fine. She's going to have another baby, and that's made her very tired. She'll need you to help her with the chores. Can you do that?"

They nodded in solemn agreement.

Daisy addressed Ada's eldest. "Benje, your mama will need a lot of help with the heavy work. You're getting to be a big boy, so maybe you could help her carry the wood and get the water."

Benje's chest puffed out. "I can do that. I don't like my mama to work so hard."

"That's right. We don't want her to lose this baby, so you'll need to be a big man for her."

Daisy left the house confident that between Benje and the younger children, Ada would at least have some help. Benje seemed older than his years and responsible enough to see that the younger siblings helped where they could.

Daisy dropped her medical bag in her room before she went to Katie's café to order a meal for the Johnsons. She returned to the hotel lobby and was just about to step onto the boardwalk when two people strolling toward her caught her eye through the hotel's etched glass door. Rafe and Edith sauntered along the walkway in the direction of Katie's Café.

Edith wore another chic outfit that flattered her figure, and her burnished hair glinted in the sun. She'd tucked one hand into Rafe's arm and walked closer to him than propriety allowed. She smiled up at him, her face alight, and Rafe grinned down at her.

Daisy ducked away from the lobby door and froze, hoping they wouldn't see her. The sight of them together bruised her heart. Several days had passed since Rafe had found her in their bedroom, and Daisy hadn't caught so much as a glimpse of her husband since. The fact that he seemed willing to spend time with Edith yet never sought out his own wife hurt her more than she wanted to admit.

Perhaps the time had come to admit her move to Summit had been a mistake. She couldn't continue to watch Rafe with Edith. The pain of seeing them together took too great a toll. Rafe had warned her he'd never again be a husband to her, but she'd been so sure she could win him over. Seeing him with Edith, whom he was no doubt escorting to lunch, speared her heart. To admit defeat and to return to Denver would remove her to a place where she wouldn't be wounded each time she saw them together.

Conscious of the receptionist's curious gaze, Daisy squared her shoulders and stepped onto the boardwalk. She turned in the other direction to avoid an awkward encounter with her husband and Edith. After she crossed the dusty street, she entered the post office to check her mail. At least on this side of the road she shouldn't suffer an embarrassing meeting.

At the end of the week, Daisy had just settled at a table in Katie's café when the door burst open and slammed against the wall. A tall, burly man stood in the aperture with his booted feet planted wide and his hands fisted at his sides. Bearded stubble darkened his cheeks. His gaze raked the dining room and came to rest on her.

Her heart stuttered when the man stalked toward her, weaving his way between tables. The man's dress identified him as a miner, and although she'd never met him, Daisy guessed his identity.

The man halted at her table and glared down at her. Daisy rose, feeling intimidated by his height. Even though he still towered over her, she felt better able to deal with him on her feet.

He leaned toward her and glared down at her. An ugly

expression darkened his features. "You mind your own business, missy. Stay away from my wife. How dare you tell her she shouldn't chop wood? Chopping wood and hauling water is woman's work. My wife don't have time to be layin' around the house. Laziness, that's all it is."

His words confirmed Daisy's suspicions. This man was Tom Johnson, Ada's husband. Apparently, he hadn't appreciated the advice Daisy had given his wife. "Your wife is pregnant, Mr. Johnson. She needs to take it easy, or she may lose the baby."

"What do you know? You're just a woman who's been meddlin' in other people's lives."

Tom breathed hard, and his chest heaved.

The other diners froze in their seats. Conversation ceased. Not even the clink of cutlery on glass plates disturbed the silence.

The scrutiny of the other patrons made Daisy want to sink into a corner, but she struggled to remain calm, though Tom's disparagement of her professional skills rankled. "I'm a certified doctor, Mr. Johnson. I'm fully qualified to give your wife medical advice."

"You call tellin' Ada to lay about in bed during the day medical advice? She's bein' pure lazy is what she's doin'. Some of Doc Irby's tonic will fix her right up."

"No, don't give Ada any of Doc Irby's patent medicine!" The thought of what the tonic would do to Ada and her baby horrified Daisy.

"Why not? It made my back ache go away."

"A backache and a pregnancy are two different things. A pregnant woman shouldn't partake of alcohol."

Tom shrugged as if dismissing Daisy's comment. "I won't have it, do you hear me?" He angled toward her again, his face close to hers.

Daisy refused to back down, though her legs quivered.

Anger gleamed in his dark eyes. "Stop meddling in my family life. Stay away from my wife." Without giving Daisy an opportunity to speak, he spun and stomped from the café.

Daisy dropped into her seat and stared at her plate. Her appetite had fled. She'd just been taken to task by an irate husband and had her professional skills disparaged in front of a room full of people. Her husband wasn't speaking to her and had taken a meal with another woman. The prospect of them repairing their marriage appeared dim. What could she hope to accomplish by staying in Summit? In that moment, she almost admitted defeat.

CHAPTER 17

After the service on the following Sunday, Daisy trudged across the church yard. When she reached the road, she glanced toward the two imposing houses that dominated the street's head. Just then, Rafe clattered down the porch steps of his home and crossed the lane to where Edith and her father lived. Daisy halted and watched her husband, unaware of the other church goers who cast pitying looks her way as they plowed around her.

Rafe jogged up the steps and onto the veranda of Cole's house. Before he could rap on the door, Edith swung the portal wide. With a bright smile, she curved her hand about his arm and drew him inside. The door shut, cutting them from Daisy's sight.

Her shoulders slumped. Once again, Rafe had been invited to Sunday dinner with the Montgomerys and would spend the afternoon in Edith's company. He'd play chess with her father. Images of the three of them in cozy companionship tortured her.

She turned toward the town. Her lonely hotel room held no appeal, but Katie's café full of Sunday diners held less allure. She couldn't face sitting alone at a table, while the whole town knew where her husband was spending his afternoon. Eating at the other diner would present the same dilemma. No matter where she went, Summit's citizens knew her husband spent his Sunday afternoon in the company of another woman.

Daisy spent the darkest hours since she'd returned to Summit alone in her room.

* * *

Shouts in the street beneath her room woke Daisy from a sound sleep. She flung back the covers and slipped out of bed. Crossing to one of the windows, she swept aside the curtain and peered into the darkness. Torches carried by dim figures who scurried down the street in the direction of the livery stable and the train depot bobbed like miniature stars in the night.

Daisy tracked their progress until the window frame blocked the procession from view. Something serious enough to warrant the assistance of half the town's male population had roused men from their beds. Her medical expertise might be needed.

Letting the curtain drop, she wheeled and hurried to the wardrobe. After she'd grabbed a plain white blouse and dark skirt from its depths, she wriggled into her clothes and joined the throng jostling down the road.

The crowd reached the livery stable. Flames engulfed the livery's roof and licked along the outside walls. The terrified neighs of horses could be heard above the inferno's rumble. When Daisy reached the fire, most of the horses had already been taken to safety and were being held at the end of the lane near the train depot's platform. Although the men had fought to douse the blaze, the conflagration roared out of control. Now the firefighters stood beaten back by the heat, empty buckets dangling from their hands.

Orange sparks shot skyward, spiraling into the dark sky. Oily black smoke rolled upward. Fumes coated the back of Daisy's throat and layered on her tongue.

Jeb Harte stood with an empty water bucket hanging from his fingers and stared at the inferno, an island of dejection amidst a sea of people about him. His shoulders drooped.

Daisy squirmed through the throng to the front and halted. Everyone stared expectantly at the livery's door, and she tracked the crowd's gaze. Someone must still be within the building.

She caught her breath. The roof could collapse at any moment, trapping whoever was inside. She gripped her hands together and prayed that the person would reach safety in time.

A hush descended over the onlookers. After interminable moments, a dim form emerged through the dark smoke that poured from the stable door. The figure led a terrified sorrel horse who fought the man's hold on the lead rope. The man clutched the rope with one hand and gripped the shank up at the gelding's halter with the other as the sorrel plunged about in panic. The man's shirt wrapped about the horse's head and covered its eyes.

He led the frightened gelding toward the depot. They'd just reached the place where the other horses were being held when the roof collapsed with a whoosh and a roar. Sparks corkscrewed skyward into the darkness, whirling in the updraft. The fire seemed to be a living thing. Flames licked the walls and interior stalls with greedy tongues, lighting up the night.

Daisy forgot the inferno. Without conscious thought, she

headed in the direction of the horses. The man who had just escaped death was Rafe.

When she reached the men who held the terrified horses beside the depot, she located her husband. He'd turned the horse he'd just rescued over to another man and now stood off to one side, staring at the blaze. His white undershirt gleamed in the flickering darkness. As if he'd forgotten it, he held his work shirt down alongside one thigh.

Daisy halted before him. "You could have been killed."

Rafe dragged his gaze from the fire and stared down at her. He shrugged.

She supposed her husband had come to terms with death during the Great War, so dying now held no terrors for him, yet the possibility that he could have been killed tonight made her shake.

"That was the last one. We got all the horses out." His rasping tone held a note of satisfaction. He coughed and cleared his throat.

Daisy ran a professional eye over her spouse. Soot dusted his hair and clothing. Large blisters had begun to form along his shoulders and arms where his sleeveless undershirt hadn't protected him, but she forgot about the blisters as she noticed the fine tremors that shook his frame. She laid a hand on his upper arm. Beneath her fingers, a rhythmic trembling quivered. Rafe displayed symptoms of going into shock. The possibility of shock hadn't occurred to her. He'd never shown fear before in all the years she'd known him.

She tugged at his arm. "Rafe, you've been burned. Let me treat you."

He balked. "Daisy, don't fuss. I'm fine."

She didn't loosen her hold. "You need to be treated."

"I'm not going to make a big deal over a few blisters. They'll heal."

"They could get infected."

He glared down at her. "A man doesn't run to the doctor over a few blisters."

She planted her fists on her hips and glared back. "How do you know it's only a few blisters? You probably inhaled a lot of smoke."

Narrowing her eyes and taking a closer look, she saw that his breathing seemed too fast. She slid her hand down to the inside of his wrist and pressed where his pulse beat, fast and irregular, beneath her fingertips. Before he could protest, she laid her other palm against the side of his face. His skin felt clammy.

Rafe jerked his head back. "What are you doing?"

Her hand slipped from his face to her side. "You look like you're going into shock."

"Why would I do that?"

"I don't know. You tell me."

His expression shuttered, and he turned his attention once more to the blaze.

Daisy tugged at him again. "There's nothing more to be done here. Come with me."

"I need to stay until the fire is out."

"Jeb Harte will take care of that. It's his property. You're not needed here now."

Rafe swung his head toward her and sliced her with a look that would have shriveled her had he given her that look in the early days of their courtship. For her to tell him he wasn't needed ran counter to everything he'd been taught from boyhood.

"You wouldn't have said what you just did when we first met." His disgruntled tone betrayed his resentment.

"When we first met, I wasn't in the habit of expressing my opinion. I've changed."

"So I've noticed."

Their gazes clashed, but Daisy refused to back down. "I know men hate to see a doctor, but I won't let you get away with that excuse tonight. Come with me."

"You've turned into a bossy little thing." Rafe took a reluctant step.

"It's time someone took you in hand. You don't know what's good for you." She pulled on his arm again, and he took another step.

"Humpf." Rafe made a noise in his throat, but he kept moving.

When they reached the hotel, Daisy drew him inside. A single lamp on the reservation desk cast a dim light over the lobby.

"You wait right here while I get my medical bag. Don't move." She fixed him with a stern look.

He tossed her a mock salute. She shook her head at him and fled up the stairs to her room. Not bothering to shut her door, Daisy sped to where she kept her doctor's bag in a dresser drawer and yanked it out. She dropped the bag on the bed and ran her fingers through her blonde bob, then tucked her blouse into her skirt. When she'd made herself presentable, she grabbed her bag and hurried downstairs.

Rafe waited in the middle of the lobby, a resigned expression on his face. When she reached him, he took the bag from her. His other hand rode the small of her back as they left the hotel and turned toward his home.

A bloated moon hung in the night sky and sprinkled the world in sliver. Daisy shivered in her thin blouse.

They didn't speak while they walked. Just as they neared the house, Edith stepped onto the porch of the home across the road. Wearing pajamas and a robe, her father followed.

With one hand gripped on the railing, Edith glided down

the steps and halted on the last tread. She gathered a silky robe about her nightgown. Curling papers decorated her hair. "What happened?"

Rafe slid his hand from Daisy's back to her arm and hauled her to a standstill, but he didn't cross the road. "The livery caught fire."

The moonlight revealed Edith's yearning expression as she cast an attentive eye over the man at Daisy's side. She flicked a glance at Daisy, then returned her stare to Rafe. "You've been hurt." She stepped onto the street. "Let me help."

Daisy froze. If Rafe capitulated to Edith's request and allowed the Southerner into his house, she vowed she'd hit him with her medical bag and leave him to Edith's tender mercies. She wouldn't share her husband's care with the other woman.

"Daisy's here to fix me up, so we'll manage." Rafe's tone was mild. "Thanks for the offer."

Edith took another step. "Rafe, I want to help."

"Edith, go back inside. Daisy's a doctor. She knows what to do." Rafe's voice, satin over steel, acquired an edge that brooked no argument.

Edith sniffed and spun. She flounced up the steps and across the porch. Her father shrugged at Rafe and followed his daughter into the house.

Rafe hauled Daisy along, up onto the veranda and inside. "I don't need two women fussing over me. One is bad enough."

Daisy let him grouse and didn't bother to comment. "I'll work in the kitchen."

They angled into the kitchen. Rafe turned a knob on the wall beside the door, and light from the overhead lamp illumined the room. He paced to the table and dropped her bag onto the red and white gingham oilskin cloth, while Daisy pulled out a ladder-backed chair. She patted the chair's back. "Sit here."

Arms crossed, Rafe stalled long enough to make the point that he still ruled in his own home. He sent her a grumpy look. "Bossy. You're bossy."

"So you've said. Sit down."

He dropped his length into the chair. Daisy eyed her husband. He'd stopped shaking, but a sallow tint bleached his face. His normal ruddy coloring had vanished. Something about the fire had affected him, but she couldn't begin to guess what. Fire had never bothered him before. This was one more puzzle to add to the enigma of Rafe's changed behavior.

She decided not to pursue his reaction to the fire and focused instead on the blisters that had formed along his shoulders and bare arms. The heat in the stable had reddened his skin, and more blisters might form, but he'd avoided serious injury.

With a feather-light touch, she laid her fingertips where his undershirt's sleeveless style left his shoulders bare. The sensation of touching his warm skin for the first time since they'd parted before the Great War sent a shock through her system, though she struggled to maintain her professionalism and not allow her female reaction to show.

Rafe looked askance at her over his shoulder as if he sensed how he affected her.

Daisy bent closer for a better look at the blisters, then straightened and stepped away. "While I pump water, why don't you go upstairs and change that undershirt? And you should get the ash out of your hair before I work on you." She crossed the kitchen to the sink and began pumping water into the pot that waited there.

Rafe materialized at her side. He laid his hands on her

shoulders and drew her away from the sink. "I'll do this." With her out of the way, he took over the task of pumping water. When the pot was full, he transferred the pan to the stove and set about lighting the kindling that waited in the firebox.

Daisy scrutinized her husband and savored the simple pleasure of observing his economy of movement. Every motion was a minuet of graceful strength, and she derived a guilty pleasure from watching him. She resented each moment she'd been cheated of his company, time when she could have been storing up memories such as these. She'd been deprived of a myriad of the little occasions that make up a lifetime, the mundane occurrences that, over the years, unite two married people into one entity. Her whole being yearned for a lifetime with Rafe, of sharing precious moments with him.

Rafe returned to the sink. Ducking his head beneath the spigot, he pumped water over his head and shoulders with one hand. With his other, he ruffled his fingers through his hair. Cinders and ash rained downward.

Daisy hurried to the sideboard and pulled a towel from one of the drawers. She reached her husband's side just as he straightened and thrust out a hand, dripping water. She handed him the towel, and he scrubbed his hair with the cloth.

Their choreographed motions reminded Daisy of the countless times they'd enacted this very scenario in the three years they'd lived together. After a day's work, he'd scrub up at the sink, and she'd hand him a towel. Usually, he'd kissed her on his way out of the kitchen to change his clothes.

If Rafe remembered the ritual, he gave no sign. "I'll change and will be back down."

He brushed past her and left the room.

With a firm grip on the sink's edge, Daisy dropped her

head and closed her eyes. To be with Rafe and remember their past brought exquisite pain, yet she wouldn't deprive herself of one moment in his company. No matter the heartache, she still hungered to be with him.

She reined in her heartrending emotions and turned toward the table to rummage in her medical bag for a length of torn sheet. After she dropped the fabric into the boiling water, she left it there for several minutes while she scoured up to her elbows. By the time Rafe returned to the kitchen, the sheet was cooling on a towel on the sideboard.

He padded barefoot into the kitchen, wearing a clean pair of jeans and another sleeveless undershirt tucked into his trousers. At the sight of him, Daisy gulped and turned away, terrified she'd betray her unruly feelings. Behind her, Rafe dropped into the chair without speaking.

She plucked up the sheet and paced to Rafe's side. "This may hurt."

He glanced up. "It's already hurting. I can stand it."

She knew he spoke the truth. As she draped the fabric over his shoulders, she tried to be gentle. "I'll leave the sheet on for a few minutes. The cool water will take some of the heat out of the blisters."

Rafe didn't reply.

After she removed the sheet, she cleansed the area and applied hypochlorite solution to the cankers. Her husband remained stoic beneath her ministrations.

While she worked, she recalled the last time they'd been together in this house. Rafe had found her with his war medals and forbidden her to go upstairs again. They'd parted with anger on his side and heartbreak on hers. He'd avoided her since their altercation. Tonight was the first time they'd been together since that encounter. Like a dark fog, the memory hung between them now. Daisy's tongue stuck to the roof of her mouth. Rafe seemed equally disinclined to bring up the argument.

She finished applying gauze to the blisters and stepped back. "You'll need to be careful to keep the blisters clean. They mustn't get infected. I'll come every evening to cleanse the burns and apply hypochlorite solution."

Rafe rose from the chair and rolled his shoulders. "No need. I can handle it."

Daisy curled her hands into fists. "Don't be a ninny. You can't manage this alone. I'll take care of you. Besides, I don't trust you to apply your own medicine." She narrowed her eyes at him. "You'd be just like a man and think you don't need the ointment."

He met her glare with a bland look and shrugged. "Tend to my injuries if you insist."

She gritted her teeth. "Men always are my most difficult patients. They just can't admit they need a doctor. There are times when a man needs help, and this is one of them."

They stared at each other while the air sizzled between them. When he curled his lips into an unexpected grin, Rafe broke the tension. The creases in his cheeks deepened. He affected a broad Western drawl and doffed an imaginary cowboy hat. "Well, shucks, ma'am. If I'd known you were in such need to practice your skills on me, I'd have offered my body on the altar of medical science a long time ago." He pantomimed a courtly bow and pressed one hand to his chest. "With such a pretty doctor to attend to my wounds, I'll die a happy man."

His raillery reminded Daisy so much of the old Rafe that she gaped at him. His humor defused the conflict between them but introduced a new type of tension, one that hadn't been present since the war. For the first time, the knowledge that they were alone in his house in the middle of the night, and that they were married, brought to life desires that for years had lain dormant. Their emotions hummed between them like a fine wire strung taut. At last Daisy stumbled back, breaking the connection.

"It's late. I'd better go." Her voice sounded jerky and breathless to her own ears. Without looking at him, she eased around him and began stuffing her things back into her satchel.

Rafe watched her in silence.

Snapping her bag shut, she lifted her gaze to his face. "Good night, Rafe." She stepped past him.

With a tender grip on her arm, he brought her to a standstill. He stared down at her, his expression enigmatic. "Good night, Daisy. And thank you."

She nodded. His hand dropped to his side, and she fled.

CHAPTER 18

Summit, Colorado
Late Summer, 1922

Dust boiled from beneath the buckboard's wheels as the wagon rolled down the street. As she stepped from the hotel that morning, Daisy eyed the equipage barreling toward her. She recognized the driver as one of the cowboys who worked for Jim Bentley.

The driver sawed on the reins and brought his lathered team to a halt before the hotel. Daisy crossed the boardwalk and peered down at the cowboy. "What is it? Is it Mrs. Bentley's time?"

The cowboy nodded. "Mrs. Bentley was taken during the night. The boss told me to fetch you as fast as I could."

Daisy calculated the timing of Meg Bentley's labor. If her pains had started during the night, she'd already been laboring for several hours. This baby was her third child, so the birthing could go quickly. Unless, of course, complications arose. Daisy tried not to think of possible complications. "Let me get my things. I'll be right down."

In her room, Daisy made sure her medical bag contained everything she might need, including forceps. She packed extra clothes and some underwear and night things in a satchel. With her attending a delivery on a remote ranch, anything might happen. She could be sequestered at the homestead for days, and she wanted to be prepared.

She hurried down the stairs. With each step, both bags bumped against her legs. The hotel clerk watched her cross the lobby, his eyes alight with curiosity. Daisy thought him to be as nosy as a gossipy old maid. She ignored his unspoken questions as she slammed the door shut behind her.

The cowboy waited in anxious silence beside his rig. He leaped onto the boardwalk when Daisy emerged from the hotel and reached for her bags. "I'll take those, ma'am."

She surrendered her luggage to the cowboy, who jumped into the street and slung her bags into the buckboard's bed. Pivoting, he reached up for her as she leaned down. With his hands gripping her waist and her hands braced on his shoulders, the cowboy plucked her from the boardwalk and lifted her onto the wagon's seat. He jogged around the vehicle's tail and clambered up beside her.

He turned the team back in the direction it had come and slapped the reins against the horses' rumps. The sorrels broke into a smart trot.

They'd almost reached the end of the street by the mine's head, where the road degenerated into a rutted track that led to outlying ranches, when Rafe stepped into the road from his porch and flagged them down.

The cowboy brought the team to a halt, and Rafe approached the equipage. He directed his first comment to the cowboy. "I understand that Meg Bentley has need of a doctor."

The younger man tipped his hat farther back on his head and nodded. "Yes, sir. Her baby's comin'."

"Then she'll need a doctor right away. I'll fly Mrs. Wild Wind to the ranch. That will get her there much faster than this buckboard."

"I think the boss would like that." The cowboy looked relieved.

"It's settled, then. I'll take my wife with me."

Dazed, Daisy listened to the men make their plans. Without so much as a by-your-leave from her, Rafe reached up and hauled her off the buckboard's seat. Once her feet hit the dirt, he leaned over the wagon's side and hefted her bags from the bed. He tucked her medical bag beneath one arm and picked up her satchel. With his free hand, he gripped her elbow and turned her toward the hanger.

Daisy trotted along beside his lengthy strides. This time, she didn't try to slow him down. She shared his urgency.

When they reached the hanger, Rafe dumped her luggage on the ground beside his red biplane and began his pre-flight check. Daisy watched him but didn't distract him with conversation. He appeared focused on his task and tackled each item with a thoroughness that reassured her of his attention to safety, though he went through the steps with a speed that told her he'd done this countless times during the war.

Since Rafe's blisters had healed, she had no reason to see him. She hadn't laid eyes on him in over a week. He hadn't sought her out, though Daisy had noticed her husband hadn't been seen with Edith since the night of the fire. That fact offered her some slight comfort.

Rafe finished his check and approached. "Let's gear up."

He outfitted her in record time and got her settled in the

front cockpit. When he'd arranged her luggage by her feet, she spoke for the first time since he'd dragged her from the buckboard. "How did you know that Meg is my patient, and that Jim had sent for me?" She flung her husband a curious glance.

He paused in the act of stepping off the wing. "I know everything that happens in this town."

Rafe wheeled the aeroplane out of the hanger and pointed its nose down the runway, then jogged to the front. He gave the propeller a mighty heave.

As it had during her first flight, Daisy's stomach quivered when the engine caught, coughed, and spit flame. Exhaust swirled around the cowling. The familiar trembling throughout the aircraft's frame reminded Daisy of her first flight. She tried to quiet her heart's hammering with the reassurance of Rafe's skill as a pilot.

Her husband climbed into the rear cockpit. The plane rolled forward, lumbering a bit over grassy tufts and bouncing before it lifted into the air. Once aloft, the craft became one with the sky and soared with a graceful sweep toward the heavens. Its engine settled into a steady throbbing rumble.

Rafe banked the craft toward the mountains. Beneath their wings, the earth unfolded in a patchwork of high sere parkland dotted with cattle, interspersed with dark verdant evergreens and quaking aspens that thrust up from the Rockies' granite shoulders. They hadn't been flying long when several wooden buildings and corrals appeared in a meadow below them. The plane swooped down and leveled out just above the buildings. Rafe circled once, then brought his crate in with a low glide over the grass, just above the meadow's surface. He cut the engine moments before the wheels touched down. The aircraft bounced and rolled to a stop.

Mack, tongue lolling, loped from the ranch yard to greet them. A measure of professional satisfaction filled Daisy's chest as she watched the dog gambol toward them. Mack seemed a little stiff, but he looked as though he'd still be able to chase cattle. The cougar hadn't maimed him.

Jim Bentley waited for them on the porch. "Thank you for coming so quickly, Doc Daisy. Meg's in a bad way. It's a good thing your husband flew you here."

Daisy tossed a grateful smile at Rafe over her shoulder and climbed the steps, then followed Jim into the house.

Jim Bob and Ned sat at the table, empty breakfast dishes before them, and watched with solemn expressions as Daisy came to a standstill in the middle of the room. She put down her medical bag and knelt before the boys. "Don't worry. I'll take good care of your mama." She patted their shoulders and rose.

"I have water heating, Doc Daisy. I remembered how you cleaned everything when you took care of Mack, so I knew you'd want water. And Meg has clean sheets and blankets ready, just as you told her to do." Jim Bentley seemed anxious to please.

"Thank you, Jim. Now, I'll scrub up, and then you can take me to Meg. I'll have a look at her."

Before she scrubbed, Daisy donned her surgeon's long white apron and tied a scarf about her hair. She then began to wash in the hot water Jim had prepared. While she scrubbed, Rafe conferred in low tones with the rancher and clapped him once on the shoulder in male camaraderie. Perhaps her husband was sharing his own anxieties while she labored to bring Molly into the world.

When she'd finished her cleaning ritual, she turned to the men and looked Jim in the eye. "I'm ready to see Meg now."

Jim led her into a bedroom off the kitchen. Meg lay in the

double bed, propped up against the pillows. Her hair had come loose from its nighttime braid and lay in a dark nimbus about her head, matted now with sweat.

Meg reached out a hand toward Daisy. "Doc Daisy, I'm so glad you're here. This baby's takin' a long time comin'."

Daisy gripped Meg's hand and perched on the mattress's edge. "I'll take a look at you and see what's causing that little one to take so long. When did your pains first start?"

Before Meg could reply, another pain wracked her. She caught her breath and curled into a ball, her knees drawn up to her chest. She squeezed Daisy's hand in a tight grip. Daisy winced but didn't withdraw her hand from Meg's. When the pain passed, Meg relaxed and rolled onto her back.

Jim leaned over the other side of the bed and wiped his wife's sweaty face with a cotton cloth. "You just take it easy, Meggie. Doc Daisy and I will take good care of you."

Jim meant well, but Daisy doubted Meg appreciated her husband telling her to take it easy when labor pains were tearing her body apart. "Jim, I'll need a better light than what's here. Why don't you get some lanterns from the barn?"

Relief at being released from attending his wife's discomfort crossed Jim's face, and he tossed the cloth onto a table beside the bed. "I'll do that." He wheeled. Moments later, the men's voices sounded from the kitchen, and then a door slammed.

With the men out of the way, Daisy leaned over Meg. "How long have you been in labor?"

"The first pain came just as I was puttin' the boys to bed. It didn't seem too bad, and it was a while before the next one came, so Jim decided to wait until morning to fetch you. He didn't want to take the team out in the dark."

Daisy kept an attentive expression on her face while Meg

poured out the details of her labor, but if she hadn't sent Jim away, she'd have given him a stern lecture on behalf of his wife. That the rancher had put his wife at risk over the safety of his horses didn't set well with her. She tried to keep an edge from her voice and not take her ire out on Meg. "So you've been in labor for at least twelve hours."

Meg nodded. "And my water broke this morning while Jim was feedin' the boys breakfast."

Daisy sat in thoughtful silence, while Meg closed her eyes. Twelve hours wasn't unusual, even for third babies. Meg could labor for much longer, but something about this one didn't seem right.

"Meg, I'm going to take a look at you."

Meg opened her eyes and gave Daisy a trusting look. "Whatever you need, Doc Daisy."

Daisy pulled the covers down. Beneath a white cotton nightgown, Meg's belly thrust up in the rounded bloom of full pregnancy. Daisy closed her eyes to help her focus and let her experienced fingers travel across Meg's stomach. She pressed against the uterus, feeling the baby's shape. As she suspected, the baby was in a breech position and not engaged in the birth canal. She'd have to turn the little one, since she doubted Meg was large enough to deliver a successful breech birth. She straightened and pulled the covers back up around Meg's shoulders.

Settling on the mattress's edge, Daisy took Meg's hand. "Meg, your baby isn't in the right position for you to deliver it. I'll have to turn it, and it's going to hurt. I'm sorry."

Meg's face paled, but she lifted her chin. "Do whatever you need to do. I'm just glad you're here to help." She cast a knowing look at Daisy. "Jim wouldn't have known what to do, would he?"

Daisy shook her head. "No, he wouldn't have known

what was wrong. You just wouldn't have been able to birth the baby."

Meg shivered. "I'm glad I made him get you." Another pain hit her, and she gasped.

When the men's voices in the kitchen told Daisy they'd returned, she left Meg's side and joined them. Jim was setting the lanterns on the table when she entered. He looked up with a questioning expression. "How is Meg?"

Daisy walked up to him and looked him in the eye. "The baby is in a breech position, and I'll have to turn it. I'll need your help."

For a moment, Jim looked as though Daisy had hit him between the eyes with a sledgehammer, but then he shook his head as if to clear it and squared his shoulders. "I'll do anything. Just don't let Meggie die."

"First, take those lanterns into the bedroom and place them where the light will shine on Meg, even if you have to move furniture. Then scrub up."

Rafe stood motionless just inside the door, a barn lantern in one hand. Daisy caught the look he sent her and shook her head. While Daisy gave instructions to Jim, her husband strolled to the table and offered the lamp to Jim.

Jim took the lamp and vanished into the bedroom.

Rafe drew Daisy away from the table, where the boys still sat, ears tuned to adult conversation. He turned his back to the table and spoke in a low tone. "Is Meg in trouble?"

Daisy replied in a voice pitched just above a whisper. "The baby is breech, and Meg is too small to deliver that way. She would have died if Jim hadn't asked me to come."

Rafe's lips tightened. "Can you turn the baby?"

"I should be able to. It will be uncomfortable for Meg, though."

"Better that than dying."

Daisy nodded, then swallowed her next words when Jim emerged from the bedroom and crossed to the sink. After much splashing, he approached. Water droplets dripped from his hands.

"I'm ready, Doc Daisy."

Daisy addressed her husband and tipped her head at the boys. "Perhaps you could take Jim Bob and Ned outside."

For the next couple of hours, Daisy forgot everything except getting Meg's baby safely into the world. With Meg propped against Jim's chest and her legs braced against the footboard, Daisy worked to reposition the little one.

Finally, Daisy had the baby in the correct position. She looked at Meg. "The baby is head down now. It shouldn't be long."

Meg's contractions came fast and hard. She gripped her husband's hand and swallowed her screams.

When the baby's head crowned, Daisy said, "Push, Meg. Push hard."

Meg grunted and pushed.

"Again."

Meg pushed again, and again.

"The baby's coming. Push."

After a last mighty heave, Meg's baby slipped out into Daisy's hands.

Daisy held the wet, slippery body in both hands. For several moments, the child looked blue and lifeless while she cleared mucus from the infant's throat. The little chest expanded with a breath as the baby sucked in oxygen. Its skin turned a rosy pink, and a wail filled the bedroom.

While the baby cried, Daisy checked the infant over. The child looked perfect. She glanced up at the new mother. "Meg, your boys have a baby sister."

Meg, who had been drooping against the pillows with her eyes closed, roused. Her lids flashed open. "A girl!"

Daisy nodded. "Yes, you have a little girl."

Jim came around to the foot of the bed and gazed at his daughter. "She's awfully small, but she has a good set of lungs."

"She'll surely let you know when she's hungry."

While Daisy wiped the baby dry, her own arms felt Molly's loss. Would she ever again hold a child of her own? The prospect seemed dim, yet despite her personal bereavement, she couldn't help but experience the wonder she always felt when she assisted at a birth. A new life provided a counterpoint to death, something Daisy encountered all too often. Birth and death, the cycle of life continuing through the ages, as ordained by an Almighty Providence.

With the baby cleaned, Daisy wrapped the infant in a soft blanket and placed her in Jim's arms. "Take the baby out to your boys and let them see their new sister. I'll clean up Meg."

With Meg washed and dressed in a new nightgown, and the soiled bed linens replaced with fresh sheets, Daisy wandered into the empty kitchen. She sighed and pulled the kerchief from her head. After tossing the handkerchief onto the table, she untied her apron and draped it over a chair. She rolled her shoulders to loosen tired muscles, then cleaned her hands at the sink.

Daisy wiped her hands and turned toward the door. Now, she had to face her husband.

CHAPTER 19

She found Rafe with Jim and the boys in the meadow beside the biplane. The brothers gazed down at their swaddled sister as if she were a species of animal they hadn't before encountered.

"What do you think of your new sister?" She came to a standstill beside the boys.

Jim Bob scrunched up his freckled face. "She looks like a baby chicken, all red and wrinkly."

Daisy laughed. "She does, but soon she'll fill out and be pretty, like your mama."

Ned poked a finger at his sister's cheek. The baby screwed up her face and screeched. Ned jumped back. "She's loud."

"She's probably hungry. Your daddy should take her back inside and let your mama feed her."

With Jim holding his daughter and shepherding his sons toward the house, Daisy turned to her husband.

Rafe had propped his length against the plane's fuselage, one booted foot cocked. He'd hooked his thumbs in his jeans' front pockets, and his cowboy hat rode low over his brow. He looked her over with a knowing air. "You're tired."

His words reminded Daisy of how exhausted she felt. "I am. Meg's a good patient, but the birth was hard on her. It took a lot out of both of us."

"We can stay here as long as you like. The mine will run without me."

"If it's no imposition, I'd like to stay here for most of the afternoon. I want to be sure Meg doesn't hemorrhage, and Jim will need someone to feed the boys. I can fix something for us all to eat."

Rafe motioned to the nearest of the biplane's wings. "Sit down and rest before you launch into fixing a meal."

Daisy legs wobbled when her husband mentioned sitting, and she perched on the aeroplane's nearest bottom wing. For several moments, neither of them spoke, though they maintained an amicable silence. The wind ruffled Daisy's hair, and a breeze fingered her cheeks. She tilted her face to the sun and closed her eyes, luxuriating in nature's tranquility and a sense of satisfaction from the achievement of a successful birth.

"Daisy."

When Rafe's voice broke the stillness, Daisy lifted her lids and slanted a glance at her husband. He pushed away from the plane and squatted before her, perusing her face with an intent expression.

She returned his stare. Lines radiated from the corners of his eyes. Grooves slashed his lean cheeks and reminded her that her husband was no callow boy. The years he'd lived had marked him.

"Daisy, I must ask you to forgive me."

His words caught her unawares. She sharpened her gaze on his face. "What . . ."

"Hear me out." Rafe shoved to his feet and turned his back to her. He halted and fisted both hands on his hips, then spun to face her. With a deep breath, he launched into speech. "Ever since you returned to Summit, I've been fighting against what you made me feel. You made me come alive." He swept the air with one hand. "You made me experience things I was afraid to feel."

She listened while Rafe poured out his heart, something he found difficult to do. She sat motionless on the plane's red wing while the sun's rays drenched her with their warmth as her husband unburdened himself.

"Before you came back into my life, I was a walking dead man. Nothing touched me. I figured I'd get through the rest of my days as a numbed shell. That way I didn't have to remember the war. I put the war in a box and shut the lid."

He glanced once at her and looked away over the meadow. "I'm still a damaged man, Daisy. I don't know if I'll ever be able to put the pieces of myself back together. I may never be able to be a husband to you, but I hope you'll give me the chance to try."

Daisy heard him out in stupefaction. Although she'd prayed to hear those words pass his lips, the opportunity poleaxed her when the Lord offered her a second chance with her husband. She gathered her wits and thanked God for this new beginning. Perhaps what Rafe tendered wasn't a complete reconciliation, but at least now he was willing to try to mend their marriage. They could build on whatever he offered her today.

She slipped from the aeroplane's wing and closed the gap between them. Curving her hands about his shoulders, she tipped her face up to his. "Of course, Rafe. We'll take this one day at a time."

He took a breath, and his shoulders lifted and fell beneath her palms. "Perhaps I could court you, as I did before we married. We could start there."

"That would be a fine starting point." She wanted to ask him about Edith, but she held her tongue. His tangle with Edith would sort itself out later.

"First of all, I apologize for that scene in the bedroom when you found my war medals. I had no right to take my war trauma out on you. The house is yours, too. Feel free to go into any of the rooms."

Daisy ran her hands down his shoulders to his arms and then his hands. She curled her fingers around his and nodded. "I feel at home there, as if I never left."

"The house is waiting for you, but I'm not ready for you to move in yet." Rafe squeezed her hands. "I must ask you to forgive me for leaving you after the war. I know I hurt you badly."

"Of course, I forgive you." She brought one of his hands to her mouth and dropped kisses on each knuckle. "Our separation taught me to trust God more. And if you'd stayed with me, I wouldn't have gone to medical school. In those things at least, something good came of our separation." Daisy's mixed emotions about that part of her marriage churned in her breast.

Rafe gave a jerky nod. "I wasn't in any position to be a husband to you then, but I still regret it." He paused and pinned his intent gaze on her face. "Thank you for continuing to love me even when I didn't show you love. These past few months haven't been easy for you, living in Summit and me not being a husband to you."

Daisy nodded but didn't comment, unwilling to halt the flow of his confession.

"And I must ask you to forgive my relationship with Edith."

Daisy met his gaze, unsure about how to respond. Perhaps his relationship with Edith was more than she'd thought. What was he admitting? "Why don't you tell me about Edith?"

"At first, Edith was just there, dangling in front of me. I was lonely for female companionship, and her father was my friend. Since I was married, I convinced myself that nothing could come of my friendship with her. I felt safe within that boundary."

Daisy waited for him to continue. A mixture of chagrin and shame marked his expression.

Rafe pulled his hands from hers and ran a forefinger down the bridge of his nose, then propped both hands on his hips again, feet planted wide. "I didn't have to make any commitments with her. I had nothing to offer her, so it suited me to just drift along in a half-romantic relationship with her."

She ought to feel sorry for her husband for getting himself into such a coil, but she couldn't rouse the pity.

"Then things started to get complicated. Edith wasn't satisfied with a simple friendship. She wanted a commitment and marriage. She made that plain enough."

"Yes, I noticed."

"And she's not an easy woman to refuse."

"I noticed that, too."

"I tried to back off, but the more I cooled, the more she pursued me."

"Why didn't you tell her you were married?"

He shrugged. "I don't know. I'd gone so long behaving as though I didn't have a wife that I just couldn't admit it to her.

I know I lied by omission, but after being separated from you for so long, I didn't really feel married anymore. At least, not until you came back to Summit and upended my life."

"It's a good thing I came back when I did. There's no telling what would have happened."

"Once you were back, I had to acknowledge you as my wife and admit I was married. I did Edith a grave disservice by not telling her the truth early on and letting her hope for more than was possible. I'll have to mend my fences with her, too."

Daisy guessed that conversation wouldn't go well.

Rafe pivoted away from her and fell silent.

Daisy eyed his back and waited for him to continue. Apprehension about any further revelations made her heart thud against her ribs.

He tossed his next words over his shoulder as if he couldn't bear to look at her. "I'm ashamed to admit that after I got so angry with you the day I found you with my medals, I deliberately went out with Edith in an effort to prove to myself that you had no hold on me, and that I was a free man." Rafe dropped his chin onto his chest for a moment, then turned in a slow arc toward her. Contrition marked his face. "All I did was to entrench Edith in the belief that we had a future together and to hurt you. And I made myself miserable in the process, as well."

Even with the knowledge that her husband was trying to repair their relationship, his last admission touched raw wounds. Daisy could only nod. His confession left her speechless.

"By playing around with Edith, I made you an object of gossip in the town. I regret that more than I can say. You didn't deserve my betrayal. Will you forgive me?"

Daisy stared into his face. His revelation that he'd deliberately gone out with Edith to prove himself free of his wife was harder to forgive than his other disclosures. She swallowed. He met her gaze with pleading eyes. She hesitated, hurting and wondering if she could really forgive him for his most recent offense.

A reminder of all the sins her Savior had forgiven her convicted her of her reluctance to acquit Rafe of his sin against her. She must be willing to forgive her husband for even this last injury. Daisy caught her breath and nurtured the pain a few heartbeats longer. Silence stretched between them while the bright Colorado sun poured over them, and Rafe stood mute and motionless while he waited for her verdict.

Finally, she laid one palm against his cheek, content to put even his guilt regarding Edith behind them. "Yes, I forgive you, although Edith should take some of the blame. Once she knew you were married, she should have stopped chasing you. Especially in front of me." She dropped her hand.

Rafe grimaced. "In light of my recent behavior toward her, I think she's been trying to force me to choose between the two of you. She must have felt confident I'd choose her."

"She seems very sure of herself. She even told me I should leave Summit because I wasn't good enough for you."

His expression turned stony. "I'm glad Edith isn't here now, or I'd be tempted to forget I'm a gentleman. She had no right to say such a thing to you. I'm the one who's not good enough for you."

"That's not true, either. We were good for each other before the war, and we can be again."

Silence fell as they regarded each other without touching. The wind stirred his hair and fluttered Daisy's bob away from her face. At last, Rafe launched into his final confession.

"I must apologize to Edith's father for the way I treated his daughter. If Edith were my daughter, I'd be tempted to meet the blackguard with pistols at dawn."

Daisy couldn't help but grin at Rafe's exaggerated sense of chivalry.

He wasn't done. "And I must ask you to forgive me for letting my brokenness turn me away from the Lord. I want to get things right with God. That will go a long way toward helping me be a husband to you again."

"I haven't stopped praying for you all these years. The Lord can heal you and our marriage."

He nodded. "I have confidence about that." Rafe slid his gaze to Daisy's face. "I'll start attending church again. I'll pick you up at the hotel before the service this Sunday."

Daisy smiled. "I'll be waiting."

Rafe rested his hands on her waist and drew her toward him. "As much as is possible for a broken man to love, I love you. I never stopped, even though after the war I thought myself incapable of love, and I shut you away in the same box as the war."

"I never stopped loving you, either." She waggled her left hand beneath his nose, then wound her arms about his neck. "I'm still wearing your rings. I never took them off." She snuggled close and dropped her forehead against his chest. "It feels so good to be in your arms again."

Rafe's chest rumbled beneath her as he chuckled. "I'm enjoying holding you, too, but I think we're providing entertainment for the whole ranch."

Daisy peeked toward the house. Jim Bentley and his boys stood on the porch, staring their way. Down at the barn, several ranch hands loitered around the entrance and cast amused looks in their direction.

Daisy sprang out of her husband's arms. Her cheeks heated. "Well, now we've caused gossip of another kind."

Rafe took her hand and turned her toward the house. "I'd rather have gossip about me embracing my wife than what's been making the rounds lately. And did I hear you mention something about a meal?"

CHAPTER 20

"Well, bless mah heart! Do I see Rafe Wild Wind in church?" Edith's hand, with its scarlet nails, splayed across her bosom. She flicked a glance at Daisy, then returned her attention to Rafe. A coy smile curled her crimson lips. "I nevah thought to see you in church."

Edith and her father approached from a row of pews near the front of the sanctuary. Edith came to a standstill, unmindful of the fact that she blocked the aisle.

Daisy and Rafe lingered at the end of their row, waiting until the crowd thinned enough for them to leave. Rafe's presence behind her warmed Daisy's back. All during the service she'd been aware of him sitting beside her. His muscled length along her side had distracted her from the preaching.

In a possessive move, Rafe curled a hand about Daisy's waist. "I thought it was time for me to attend services with my wife."

Both Edith and her father caught Rafe's gesture and the message he conveyed. Edith's smile faltered, then returned to its former brightness. "Can we expect you for dinner today? Cook has fixed your favorite meal."

Daisy recognized a dig when she heard one, but she refused to let the jab puncture her joy. Rafe would spend the day with her, and that knowledge filled her with happiness.

Rafe's fingers tightened on her waist. "Thank you, but no. I should have told you sooner, but I'll eat dinner with Daisy today." He tipped his head toward Mr. Montgomery. "And I won't be there for our chess game tonight. Perhaps another time."

"Certainly, my boy." Mr. Montgomery acknowledged Rafe with a nod. "Another time. You know our door is always open to you."

"But Rafe, you always spend Sundays with us." Edith pouted. "I'll be so lonely without you at the house."

"Edith, Rafe has a wife. He's spending the day with her." Mr. Montgomery grasped his daughter's elbow and pointed her at the door. "Come along, now."

Daisy watched the Montgomerys exit the church.

When the pair had passed through the door, Rafe tugged at her. "We can leave now."

Neither spoke until they left the church yard and turned toward the town.

"I gather from that exchange you haven't spoken to Edith." Daisy tried to keep her tone expressionless, though she'd hoped Rafe would have settled his situation with Edith before now.

"Not yet. I've been busy, and to tell the truth, that's one conversation I've been putting off." Rafe expelled an explosive sigh. "I'll have to meet with her, though. I can't play the coward any longer."

Daisy giggled and cut a sideways look at her husband. "She's not going to like what you're going to tell her."

"Not one bit." Rafe looked hunted.

They stepped onto the boardwalk.

Daisy thought back to the encounter in the church. "She's got brass, inviting you to dinner right in front of me."

"She was very rude, but more than that, she was rubbing my relationship with her in your face. I won't let her get away with that again. Whatever relationship we had is over, and I need to make the fact clear to her." Rafe took two more strides before he continued. "I should have set her straight before this."

"And to think of the juicy tidbit that scene caused with the gossip hounds."

Daisy felt her husband's glance. She turned her head and met his look.

"We'll have dinner together at Katie's Café, where half the town can see us. That should make tongues wag." Rafe curled up one corner of his mouth in a lopsided grin, and his eyes twinkled.

Daisy laughed, one of the first genuine laughs to pass her lips since Rafe had left her. Surprise at the sound of her own laughter flowed through her, yet since their conversation at the Bentley ranch, happiness had bubbled through her veins like champagne. She felt young again, a rebirth of the Daisy she'd been when Rafe had first courted her.

Rafe caught her mood and chuckled. "I hope that us being together will counter some of the gossip I've caused."

"Or it will stir up more gossip. I can hear the rumors now. People will say you've got two women on a string."

They exchanged smiles as they reached Katie's Café, and Rafe held the door for her to enter.

By unspoken consent, they strolled to the cemetery after they'd eaten. The hinges squealed when Rafe pushed open the gate. Daisy knelt at Molly's resting place by the back fence. She pulled dead flowers from the tin can and tossed them aside. "I'll have to bring fresh flowers."

"I tried to keep flowers on her grave every summer." Rafe came to a halt behind her.

Daisy craned her neck to look at her husband over her shoulder. "The first time I came here, I saw you'd put flowers on her grave. That told me you weren't a lost cause, no matter what you said."

A solemn expression firmed Rafe's face. "Putting flowers on her grave made it seem less lonely. And I didn't want to forget her."

Daisy twisted around to the front and laid one hand on the grass that covered her daughter's resting place. Green blades poked up between her splayed fingers. "I love you, Molly. Nothing will ever make me forget you." Her voice cracked.

Rafe hooked his hands about her shoulders and drew Daisy to her feet. With her back to him, he enclosed her in his arms and crossed his hands over her stomach, then nestled his chin in the curve of her neck. "We'll remember her together." His breath ruffled the hair at her ear and warmed her skin.

Daisy nodded. After a few moments, while she struggled against her tears, she curled her fingers about his forearms. "Rafe."

"Hmm . . ."

"One of these days, when I'm stronger, I should do something about Molly's room. It hurts too much to see it exactly the way it was when she was alive."

"I'll help you. Whatever we decide to do, we'll do it together."

"Taking her things out will make her death seem so final."

Rafe turned Daisy to face him and linked his hands at the small of her back, pulling her against him. "Her death is final. Making her room a shrine won't bring her back."

She rested her palms on his chest. "I know, but . . ."

"We don't have to make a decision right now. There's plenty of time. Now, how about I take you up in my plane?"

His fingers linked with hers, Rafe led Daisy from the cemetery, and they sauntered the short distance to the hanger. When they entered the structure, the now-familiar scent of oil and aeroplane fuel filled Daisy's nostrils. Somehow, the smells had gotten mixed up with Rafe, and she associated those odors with her husband.

After they'd gone through the pre-flight ritual and were airborne, Daisy tried to relax. She told herself Rafe was an excellent pilot and that he'd flown thousands of hours without mishap, yet the craft's flimsy construction terrified her. Since she and Rafe had reconciled and she'd be flying with him in the future, she should come to terms with her fear and learn to love flying the way he did.

To take her mind off her fears, she peered at the Rocky Mountain beauty beneath them. She marveled that the plane could travel such far-flung distances in much shorter times than locomotives. They could probably reach Denver in a couple of hours.

After taking the plane through steep passes and over granite peaks, Rafe brought the machine down in a long glide above a high meadow and cut the engine just above the short mountain grass. The craft drifted earthward. The ground rose up to meet them, and the wheels touched down. The aeroplane bounced and rolled to a stop.

Before Daisy could climb from the front cockpit, Rafe appeared. He extended a hand to her and assisted her onto the wing, then leaped to the ground. He reached up and gripped her about the waist. She clung to his shoulders as he swung her off the wing. When her feet touched the ground, he didn't release her, but stood with his hands resting on her hipbones.

Her palms clung to his shoulders. She delighted in the solid feel of him beneath her hands.

The air hummed between them as they stared at each other. Rafe twitched the goggles from her face and unbuckled her leather helmet's strap, then jerked the headgear free and flicked it upwards into the cockpit. He did the same for his own goggles and helmet before his arms closed about her. He yanked her against him and rested his forehead against hers.

"Daisy, may I kiss you?" His roughened voice rasped out the words.

The smooth brown leather of his flying jacket molded his muscled shoulders beneath her fingers. "I'd love for you to kiss me."

He angled his head as he bent to take her mouth. When his lips closed over hers, Daisy forgot the lonely years they'd been apart. The empty months might never have been. Their bodies remembered this passion. She responded with hungry abandon and wound her arms around his neck. Her grip tightened when he pulled her closer. This first kiss since he'd left to fight in the Great War sealed their reunion.

Finally, Rafe broke off the kiss and buried his face in the curve of her neck. As they savored the physical nearness, his heart pounded against hers. For a moment, neither of them spoke while their ragged breathing slowed, and their pulses returned to normal.

Rafe broke the silence when he muttered into her neck, "I must keep a tight rein on myself. I don't want to let my hunger for you override my ability to be a true husband to you. Until I know I can handle being a husband, my needs will have to wait."

Daisy leaned back against his arms and looked up at him. "You're being very noble."

"I want to do things right. I don't want to take you in selfishness and then realize I can't be a husband to you."

"I don't doubt your ability to be a husband. It just may take you a while to realize you'll be fine."

"I'm glad you have so much faith in me."

"In you, and the Lord."

Rafe nodded down at her. "Let's walk."

With hands linked, they sauntered across the meadow toward the evergreens that ringed the valley. Though bright sunlight shimmered in the clear mountain air, autumn had already touched the range. Snow dusted the craggy peaks, and the aspens, which grew along the meadow's edges and the mountains' shoulders, blazed with gold. Brown grasses crunched beneath their feet. Daisy shivered in her leather jacket, grateful for its warmth.

They reached the woods. Rafe lowered himself to the ground and tugged Daisy to a sitting position beneath the trees. Leaning against the smooth, gray-white bole of an aspen tree, she stretched out her legs and tucked her blue and white striped skirt about her knees. Rafe laid his head in her lap and closed his eyes, his long-fingered hands lax on his stomach.

While her husband dozed, her greedy gaze roved over his face. His dark eyelashes fanned his cheeks. His straight blade of a nose thrust up from his strong features, a legacy from his half-Cheyenne father. She smiled to herself. All of the Wild Wind men sported a bold nose.

Daisy slumped against the tree trunk with lids closed and let nature's peace envelope her. The aspen's coin-shaped leaves rattled. Birdcalls filled the air with music.

After a time, Daisy opened her eyes and looked down at her husband, who still rested with his head in her lap. She couldn't resist the urge to touch him. She traced the bridge of his nose with one forefinger, then ruffled her hands through his curls. She ran a finger along the curve of his ear.

When he tipped up the corners of his lips, he betrayed the fact that he no longer slept. His eyes crinkled.

"I know you're awake." Daisy leaned down to plant a kiss on his lips.

His hand cupped the back of her head, and his mouth took hers. After a leisurely kiss, he murmured, "Mmm . . . I'm just enjoying being with you again." He feathered light kisses on the edges of her lips and along her jawline.

Rafe slid his hand from the back of her neck to her shoulder, then draped his forearm across his stomach. "Do you remember the first time we met?" His intent gaze roved over her face.

"Yes. Our first meeting was when Garnet dragged me along with her when she'd found out where you and Cole attended church. She wanted to meet Cole at church and make it look like an accident. I was scandalized."

Rafe chuckled. "Cole played along with her, since he was as interested in her as she was in him."

"And you got roped into playing escort to me so we could make up a foursome."

"I didn't mind."

"I was so shy. I could hardly talk to you. And you were so handsome, I was tongue-tied." Daisy laid a hand alongside his cheek. "I knew you were just being kind. I was only Garnet's maid."

"At first, that was true—I was being kind. But as I got to know you, I liked what I saw. It didn't matter to me that you didn't come from money."

"That's what Garnet said when I told her you were only being a gentleman."

Rafe ran his fingers through her short hair and sifted the

silken strands through his fingers. "You were so innocent, so unsure of yourself, that I wanted to protect you from all life's difficulties. And you looked at me as though I'd hung the moon. You made me feel like a hero."

"You were a hero to me." Daisy dropped a peck on his lips. "You still are."

A moment of silence followed while Rafe stared up at her. "And that puppy Trystan flirted with you when we were at the Slash L for Christmas. I was worried you thought I was too old for you and that you'd fall for him instead."

Daisy smiled as Rafe confessed previous fears. "Trystan was a nice boy, but he was just that—a boy. Compared to you, he didn't measure up. No one did." She traced the lines of his face with tender fingers. "No one ever has."

CHAPTER 21

An aeroplane droned overhead and lured Daisy from the kitchen where she'd been sterilizing her medical instruments. She stepped onto the veranda and let the door slam behind her. Hurrying to the steps, she shaded her eyes with one hand. A mountain breeze fluttered her pink and green plaid dress with its dropped waist against her body.

Rafe had spent the day in his office, so whoever now flew over Summit wasn't him.

A white biplane with a red nose buzzed the valley and circled once, then dropped lower and drifted over the meadow before it touched down and taxied toward the field's upper end. As the areoplane rolled to a stop near the hanger, its engine coughed and died.

Rafe appeared on the mine's porch and descended the steps. When he reached the road, his booted feet sent up puffs of dust with each stride.

Daisy skimmed down the stairs and joined her husband in the street. "Are you expecting anyone?"

He shook his head and kept walking. "It may be that the pilot needs help."

Together, they made the trek past the cemetery to where the white biplane waited in front of Rafe's hanger. The pilot had climbed from the cockpit and was peeling off his leather helmet when they came to a halt beside the plane's wings.

The man tucked his helmet in his jacket pocket and turned toward them. He appeared to be a few years younger than Rafe. A shock of auburn hair fell over his brow, and a smile lit his hazel eyes when he saw them. "Well, old buddy. Don't stand there like you've seen a ghost. It's me, Will."

Rafe took a stride forward, and then the men engaged in a male greeting ritual, with much backslapping and grins. When they'd stepped apart, Rafe looked his friend up and down. "What are you doing here? We're rather out of the way."

"I came to see you. And I have mail for Summit. I've been flying for the US Mail Service since the war, and I've just been assigned this leg. Aerial mail delivery is moving West."

Daisy studied the biplane. A red mailbag with the letters "US Mail" decorated the fuselage just behind the wings.

"Don't tell me that Summit rates having its own mail drop." Rafe sounded doubtful.

Will chuckled and slapped his leather gloves against his thigh. "Nope, but after I tracked you down, I wanted to stop by and see you. I thought I'd leave the town's mail while I'm here."

"Can you stay for lunch? And do you need fuel?" Rafe motioned toward his own plane, parked within the hanger, and a tall metal barrel where he kept his supply of fuel. "I have my own tank."

"I'm a little ahead of schedule, so I have time to eat lunch with you. And I'm good on fuel, but thanks for the offer." Will eyed the hanger and Rafe's red biplane. "I knew you wouldn't be able to give up flying after the war. You were too good a pilot."

Rafe shrugged. "Flying got under my skin, and I use the plane for business." He motioned toward Daisy. "You must meet my wife. This is Daisy." He moved to her side and touched her shoulder. "Daisy, meet Will Blake. He was the wingman in my squadron during the war."

Daisy recalled Rafe mentioning Will Blake in the letters he'd sent before he stopped writing. Rafe and Will must have flown together all during their Lafayette Escadrille days and into the time after the group had been absorbed by the Army Air Service when the United States had entered the war. She regarded the other man with interest and held out her hand. "I'm pleased to meet you." She thought him to be handsome in a quiet, thin-faced way. His lanky height equaled her husband's.

Will took her hand and gave it a hearty shake. "So, you're Daisy. I'd have recognized you from your photo. Rafe kept a picture of you taped to the instrument panel of his plane. He wouldn't go up without your picture."

Daisy cast a sideways look at her husband, a look Rafe ignored, then turned her attention to her husband's former wingman. Will might be a source of other tidbits she could glean about Rafe's war years. "Rafe never told me that."

"Rafe's not one to talk about himself."

"No. I have to pry information out of him."

Rafe cleared his throat. "If you'll give me the Summit mailbag, I'll drop it off at the post office on our way to lunch. There's a good café here where we can eat."

Will strode to his plane. Stepping onto the wing, he reached into the mail compartment in front of the cockpit and drew out a white canvas drawstring bag. He leaped to the ground and tossed the bag at Rafe. "Here you go, compliments of the US Mail."

When they reached the town, Rafe veered off across the street to the post office with the mailbag in hand while Daisy took Will to Katie's Café to secure a table.

Inside the café, Will drew out a chair and seated Daisy, then dropped into a seat opposite her. He grinned at her across the checkered red and white oilskin napery. "Well, now that I've met you in the flesh, I can see why Rafe was closed mouthed about you."

Daisy blushed and wished again that her fair skin didn't color so easily. "You're very kind."

Will snorted. "I'm not being kind, I'm being truthful. Rafe always was a lucky dog."

"You both were fortunate to survive the war."

Will sobered and nodded. "So many others didn't."

A brief silence fell between them. Pans clattered in the kitchen, and tantalizing scents drifted from that direction. The murmuring voices of other customers filled the dining room with a low rumble.

Daisy jumped into the conversational gap. "Rafe never talks about the war. If I mention anything about it, he shuts down."

With one forefinger, Will traced circles on the oiled tablecloth. He seemed absorbed in the activity before he flattened his hand and smoothed out the creases his finger had made. He looked up at her from beneath lowered brows. "It wasn't an easy time for any of us. After the war, those of us who lived wanted to forget what happened over there."

"Rafe hasn't forgotten. He's just bottled it up inside him."

Will turned his head away from her and stared off into nothingness. With his head in profile, Daisy saw the faint scar that traced a line across his temple. The scar must be a souvenir of the war.

Will swung his head toward her again. His intent expression reflected his own emotion. "It's his way of coping. He went through a lot in France."

"I'm sure, but I could better help him if he'd open up to me."

"Give him time."

The café door opened on a shaft of sunlight, and Rafe stood silhouetted in the dazzle. He shoved the door shut and crossed the dining room toward their table.

Unaware of the longing on her face or of the fact that Will watched her, Daisy eyed her husband as he approached with his usual graceful stride. When Rafe reached them, he pulled out the chair next to hers and lowered himself into the seat. He swiped his cowboy hat from his head and laid it in the middle of the table, brim up.

"Have you ordered?"

"Not yet," Daisy replied for both her and Will.

"I recommend the antelope stew." Rafe settled his shoulders into the chair's back and stretched out his long legs.

After they'd ordered and their meal had been placed before them, they applied themselves to the food. For several minutes no one talked, but after Rafe had scraped his bowl clean, he rested his elbows on the table's edge and crossed his arms.

"So, Will, what have you been up to besides delivering mail?"

Will laid down his spoon and shrugged. "Not much. Delivering mail keeps me busy."

"From what I hear, flying for the Postal Service is almost as dangerous as flying for the War Department."

"It can be." Will shrugged. "We've lost a lot of pilots and

planes to bad weather or mechanical failure." Will grinned and tossed Rafe a conspiratorial look. "At least now I have a parachute."

Rafe pinned his buddy with a penetrating stare. "If delivering the mail is so dangerous, why do you keep flying?"

Will spread his hands wide. "I'm like you. I've been bitten by the flying bug and don't want to do anything else."

"I see that you're flying a Jenny."

"Yes, but I hope to soon be issued one of those new Standard JRs. Those crates are larger and stronger than the Jenny and can carry heavier mail loads. They're safer, too."

Rafe's gaze sharpened. "I'd be interested in seeing one of those Standards."

"When I get one, I'll fly it in, and you can have a look. I'll even let you take it up."

"I'd like that."

"You may like it so well that you'll decide to fly the mail with me."

Rafe cast a look at his wife and shook his head. "I doubt that. I have enough to keep me grounded right here."

The men launched into a discussion of the flying merits of both aircraft. Daisy listened in silence, content to watch her husband. She hadn't seen him so animated since before the war.

With the topic of planes exhausted, Rafe brought up another subject. "Did you get married, Will?"

"No. I haven't found the woman yet who will put up with the long hours I'm away from home. I spend more time in the air than on the ground."

Rafe turned solemn. "It's hard to love a woman and to love flying, too."

Will grinned. "Both flying and women are demanding mistresses. They usually can't coexist."

Daisy knew that Will teased, yet she felt the need to defend her sex. "I can see you've been associating with the wrong women."

"I'm sure I have. I guess I just haven't met anyone like you."

"When you meet the right one, you may not want to spend so much time in the air."

"She'd have to be a special lady to make me not want to fly so much, although I can see why Rafe doesn't want to fly the mail."

Daisy wasn't sure how to answer. When Rafe turned the conversation to another topic, she fell silent, grateful she'd been spared the necessity of replying to Will's back-handed compliment.

"Why don't you come for a visit at the end of the month? We'll have our annual end of the summer festival then. A couple of the local ranchers donate steers for barbequing, I give plane rides, and we end the evening with music and dancing."

"Maybe I will come. I have some vacation time due me. Your shindig sounds like a treat too good to pass up."

"If you own a private plane, you could give rides and make some money on the side. The girls really go for it."

"Girls, did you say?"

Rafe clapped his buddy on the shoulder. "Yes. The town is flooded with tourists. It's the last time visitors can kick up their heels before going back to the city and their boring jobs, and the children start school again."

"Did I hear you mention girls?"

Daisy hid a smile behind her hand. "Women love a pilot, so most of your customers will be girls. Rafe is mobbed with girls after he does his stunts."

Will turned an eager face to his war buddy. "You do

stunts?"

"The tourists love it."

"And I'm terrified just watching him." Daisy recalled her alarm when Rafe had performed his aerial acrobatics on July Fourth.

Will her tossed a quick glance. "Don't be frightened. Rafe is the best pilot I ever saw climb into a cockpit."

"But anything could go wrong with the plane." Rafe had grown silent, and Daisy knew the conversation had taken him back to the war.

"Unless Rafe has gotten lazy, I know he keeps his plane in tiptop working order. He'll check out every screw in that crate before he goes up, so safety shouldn't be an issue." Will turned to Rafe. "I have my own private plane. I'll fly in here for your bash and give plane rides with you. I'll take some of those girls off your hands."

Rafe roused from wherever his thoughts had taken him and tousled his hair with his fingers. He gave a gusty sigh. "That would be a relief."

Will had warmed to the idea of stunt flying. "We can do stunts together. It will be just like old times, just like what we did during the war."

"It won't be anything like what we did during the war. The Hun won't be shooting at us." Rafe's harsh voice ground out the words. He snatched his cowboy hat off the table and jammed it onto his head, then shoved his chair back and rose. Curling his hand about Daisy's upper arm, he pulled her to her feet. "Don't let us keep you from your mail schedule. We'll see you around the end of the month."

With Daisy in tow, Rafe thrust his way between tables to the door. Before they reached the exit, Daisy glanced over her shoulder. Will stood beside the table and stared after them, frowning.

CHAPTER 22

Daisy paused at the bottom step of her former home. As she stared up at the closed front door, she gripped the porch handrail and put a foot on the first tread. Rafe must be inside. He hadn't shown up for dinner at Katie's Café, and she hadn't found him at the mine office or the hanger. If she didn't run him to ground at the house, she didn't know where else to look.

After they left Will Blake in the diner, Rafe had escorted her to the hotel and then stalked to the mine. He'd been white-faced and silent, and she hadn't dared question him. She hadn't seen him since. Now, with darkness pressing on the earth and no word from her husband, uneasiness prompted her to seek him out.

She placed her other foot on the next tread, and the next, until she stood on the veranda. What would she do if she found Rafe inside? She didn't know. She knew only that her husband was alone and hurting, and she couldn't leave him to suffer in solitude. Will Blake's appearance had seemingly brought the war back to Rafe, and this time, she didn't intend to let her husband shut her out.

She crossed the planked porch floor to the door and turned the ornate brass knob. The door swung open, and she eased over the threshold. An oppressive silence weighed on the house. Closing the door behind her, she paused and scanned the great room. A single lamp on a table beside the leather sofa cast a dim pool of light. Shadows shrouded the rest of the area.

Daisy took another step. Beyond the stairway, a pale oblong of light spilled onto the carpet runner from the open door of Rafe's home office. She padded in that direction.

Just past the stairs, she paused at the office door and poked her head into the room. Rafe sat at his desk, his chin sunk onto his chest. His forearms rested on the chair's wooden arms. The banker's lamp on the desk's oak surface cast his face into a portraiture of light and shadow and emphasized the strong planes of his face. Behind him, the corner windows that framed his desk on two sides stared with blank, dark eyes into the room. Heavy tomes rubbed shoulders with mystery novels on the bookshelves at the right-hand wall, reflecting Rafe's wide reading tastes.

Daisy waited for her husband to acknowledge her. He didn't move, though he must have been aware of her presence. When he didn't speak, she paced across the room and circled the desk. She came to a standstill beside his chair and laid one hand on his shoulder. The muscles beneath her palm felt rock hard. "Rafe."

Rafe continued to ignore her.

Daisy massaged his shoulder, pressing her fingers into his tight muscles. "Rafe, talk to me."

"Go away, Daisy. I'm not fit company." His low growl aimed to intimidate. He flung off her hand.

She wouldn't allow him to chase her away. "Where in our wedding vows did we agree to support each other only when we're happy? I vowed to have and to hold, for better and for worse, until death parts us."

Rafe only grunted a response.

"You'll not get rid of me so easily." She circled his chair and perched on a corner of his desk. While she waited for Rafe to break his silence, she swung one leg back and forth as if she could wait all night.

They sat without speaking for several minutes, until Daisy had had enough. If Rafe wouldn't talk to her, she'd talk to him. "I thought you were glad to see Will today."

Rafe stonewalled her with more silence.

"I liked him. I think he was a loyal friend to you during the war."

At the word "war," waves of hostility radiated from her husband. Daisy plowed on. "You might as well face it. The war was a part of your life, a part of both of our lives, and you can't pretend it didn't happen."

Rafe hunched his shoulders but otherwise continued to sit without moving or speaking.

"You have to open the door on the war if you're going to heal."

Daisy scooted off the desk and slipped behind his chair. She framed his shoulders with both hands. "You're tense. Relax." She dug her fingers into the tight muscles beneath his flannel shirt, and this time, he didn't shrug her off. She worked on his shoulders and up the back of his neck until his muscles loosened beneath her ministrations. "That's better." Giving his shoulders a final pat, she circled to the front of his chair and knelt before him. She laid her hands on his knees. "Don't shut me out, Rafe."

They stared at each other until, with a groan, Rafe scooped her up and sat her crosswise on his lap. He tucked her head beneath his chin and encircled her within his arms with desperate strength.

"Stay with me for a little while, Daisy. Just stay here. I need you right now."

She curled one palm about the back of his neck. "Of course, I'll stay. I'll stay as long as you need me."

Rafe buried his face in the curve of her shoulder. His breath warmed her skin. "I can't sleep tonight." Desperation tinged his voice. "I can't sleep."

She buried her fingers in his thick curls and combed his hair with her hands. "Why not?"

He shuddered. "I can't talk about it, but I mustn't sleep."

"All right. We'll stay awake. I'll listen if you want to tell me about it."

"Not now. Perhaps someday . . ."

"Then we'll just sit here. Later, I'll fix us some coffee."

He nodded into her shoulder, and they sat in silence. Daisy wrapped one arm about him and rubbed soothing circles on his back.

A while later, he spoke into her neck. "Seeing Will today brought the war back."

Daisy stroked down the back of his head and rested her hand on his shoulder. "I thought so. Do you still want him to come to the barbeque?"

The seconds ticked by before Rafe replied, "Yes. The next time I see him, I'll be prepared." He clutched her again. "Hold me, Daisy. Hold me tight."

* * *

The bell over the shop door announced her arrival. Daisy paused and swept the Denver boutique with a glance. Drop-waisted gowns made of satin or velvet and decorated with sequins, beads, and glitz greeted her eyes. Tall mirrors that reflected the muted overhead lamps lined the walls. A display of headbands, tiaras, and jewelry glittered from a glass display case to her right. Whatever purchases she made in this store would cost Rafe a pretty penny. Even the air smelled expensive.

Last night during supper she'd mentioned her misgivings to Rafe. At the end of the meal, she'd laid down her fork and cast him an imploring look across the table. "About that dinner you're planning while Will is here . . ." She'd paused and perused his face.

Rafe swallowed the last bite of bread and washed it down with a swig of tea. "What about it?" He met her gaze.

"I don't have anything to wear."

"I just bought you two new dresses."

Daisy leaned toward him. "Yes, and I appreciate the new clothes, but your dinner will be a dressy affair."

His eyes lit as comprehension dawned. "Edith will be there."

"Exactly. I'm glad you've made your peace with her and her father and am happy to entertain them, but . . ."

"No doubt she'll be dressed to the cat's meow."

Daisy heaved a sigh. "I know I shouldn't be jealous, but she'll look like a Hollywood starlet, and I don't even have an evening dress."

Rafe reached for her hand and curled his larger one about hers. "You're beautiful to me no matter what you wear, but I don't want Edith to outshine you." His gaze warmed. "Why don't you take the train to Denver tomorrow and go shopping? Buy something that will be all the glam."

Daisy squeezed his hand. "You don't mind? An evening dress won't be cheap."

"No matter. I want you to be comfortable at our dinner, so

buy something that will show Edith she's not the only one who can dress."

Now, a blonde saleswoman who reminded Daisy of Edith swayed toward her. She halted and ran a discerning eye over Daisy's figure. "Is madam looking for an evening gown? Perhaps for dinner or the theater? Or the clubs?"

Armed with the knowledge that sales ladies judged potential customers by their clothing, Daisy had dressed with care for her shopping expedition. She wore the *chic* green frock with pink polka dots she'd worn the day she arrived in Summit, and her long pearl necklace. No saleswoman would dismiss her when this dress clad her body. "I need a gown for a dinner party." She tipped up her chin and met the clerk's gaze.

The other woman cast another look over her person. "We have several gowns that might be suitable. Please come with me."

Daisy followed the saleswoman to the back of the boutique, past mannequins dressed in beaded and sequined sleeveless costumes. She frowned. If fashion decreed that sleeveless evening dresses were in vogue, she'd need a shawl to ward off the mountains' nighttime chill.

The saleswoman stopped before a rack from which several gowns hung. She pulled one from the rod and held it out for Daisy's inspection. "Madam would shine in this."

Daisy inspected the dress. Layers of peacock blue chiffon decorated with beading dazzled her eyes. She'd freeze in chiffon. "That's beautiful, but I'll need something warmer. What do you have in velvet or satin?"

A search for velvet and satin gowns followed. Daisy tried on several dresses, determined to find one which suited her own style yet would reflect well on Rafe. She couldn't compete with Edith in glamour, but she had her own fashion sense that would make a statement.

When she saw her reflection in the dressing room mirror wearing a wine-colored velvet outfit, Daisy sucked in her breath. She had to purchase this dress. The rich color complemented her fair skin, while the square neckline and straight lines flattered her figure. Crystal beading glittered over the soft fabric, and a band of satin roses girdled her hips. Rafe would look twice at her when he saw her wearing this gown, and she smiled.

Before she left the boutique, Daisy included a burgundy silk shawl, diamond eardrops that swung below her jawline, and a diamond tassel necklace as accessories to complete her costume. On a final impulse, she added a diamond tiara to the pile on the counter and ignored her conscience when the saleswoman rang up the total. Edith wouldn't be the only lady with glitz at Rafe's dinner party.

CHAPTER 23

Will Blake clattered down the hotel stairs, wearing a pilot's brown leather jacket over his shirt. Camel-colored jodhpurs, tucked into high boots, clad his long legs.

Daisy halted her pacing and waited for Will to notice her. He'd flown in the day before in his personal biplane. Rafe had shown him about the mine, and the men had spent the day together.

Will grinned when he spied her. He crossed the lobby and halted before her. "Good morning. I see Rafe has entrusted me into your care."

"Yes. He has business at the refinery, so he asked me to show you around Summit. There's not much to see, so a tour shouldn't take long."

Will shoved his chestnut hair off his forehead. "We'll manage, I'm sure."

"Rafe would like you to come to dinner at the house tonight. We'll have a couple of other guests, as well. It will be a party."

"That sounds like a good deal, if you don't mind that I didn't pack my fancy togs."

"Whatever you brought with you will be fine." Daisy cast him a sideways glance. "Anyway, you strike me as the type of person who is as comfortable wearing jeans as you are in tux and tails."

"You've got me pegged." Will grinned down at her and took her arm. "Let's begin our tour of Summit's high spots."

They ambled across the lobby to the door. When they stepped onto the boardwalk, Daisy turned them in the direction of the train depot. "Do you like to fish?"

"I've been known to catch a fish or two."

"There's good fishing in the lake, and in Big Bear Creek, if you want to hike that far."

"I'll leave the hiking to the athletic chaps. The farthest I want to walk is to the hanger."

Daisy laughed. "Then you'd better fish in the lake. Big Bear Creek is quite a hike."

When they reached Montgomery's Emporium, Edith popped out of the shop and blocked their way, looking chic in a camel-colored, drapey wool jersey suit. She cast a flirty look at Will. "So, this is Rafe's flyin' buddy."

Will and Daisy halted. Daisy tried not to sigh. She'd hoped to get through town without encountering Edith. "Yes, this is Will Blake. He flew with Rafe during the war. Will, meet Edith Montgomery. She and her father will be our guests at dinner tonight."

Edith's Southern drawl broadened. "I'm charmed to meet one of Rafe's war buddies. Are you a hero, too?"

Will grinned down at Edith and took her hand. "I'm not sure I qualify as a hero, but yes, I flew with Rafe during the war."

Edith patted her brass-colored curls and cast him an arch look. "Well, if you flew with Rafe, I'm sure you're a hero."

"Thank you for thinking so, but I must be modest. My kill score doesn't measure up to Rafe's."

Daisy made an attempt to extricate them from Edith's clutches. "We need to be moving along, Edith. We'll see you tonight at dinner."

"I'd love to show Mr. Blake around town." Edith tightened her fingers about Will's. "Daisy, I'm sure you must be busy with your doctorin'. I can show this war hero around town while you do whatever doctahs do."

Will smiled down at Edith with easy charm and freed his hand. "Rafe has turned me over to his wife, so I have an excellent guide. I'll look forward to seeing you again at dinner."

As she and Will continued their stroll, Daisy tried not to grin at Edith's crestfallen expression. "That was smooth."

Will didn't try to hide his own smile. "I've had experience with her type."

"I can imagine." Daisy's dry tone made Will's grin broaden.

They reached the train depot. "During the summer, the train comes up here every day of the week. During the off season, it only makes the run three days a week. In the winter, the tracks are often snowbound, so the schedule is irregular."

Will eyed the depot with disdain. "As long as I have wings, I have no need to take the train."

They crossed the street and continued back along the other side. When they reached the last building, Will said, "Let's walk down to the lake. I'd like to check out the fishing possibilities."

They reached the shore and stood together staring over the water.

Daisy turned to face Will and cast him a speculative look. This might be a good opportunity to pump him for information. Here they could be private, unlikely to be disturbed. "Will, tell me about the war. About Rafe. He won't open up to me, and there's so much I don't know." She hesitated. "If you don't mind talking about the war, that is."

"I don't mind. Where should I start?"

"Rafe stopped writing me after the first year, so I don't know what happened after that. But tell me anything that might help me understand how the war changed him."

Will shifted a step closer. The late-summer sun drenched him in its light. He hesitated. "I'll tell you anything you want to know, but first, clarify something for me. Why aren't you and Rafe living together?"

The unexpected question smacked her like a blow. Daisy caught her breath and almost told him the topic was none of his business, but the information might help him better understand Rafe. She met his curious gaze and spilled her story.

When she finished, he nodded. "I thought it very odd when you spent last night at the hotel instead of with Rafe."

She spread her hands in a beseeching gesture. "He's only recently begun to accept the fact that we might have a future together. He thinks he's too damaged to be a husband to me."

"He's not alone. We were all walking wounded. None of us went through the war unscathed." Will turned an intent stare on her, as though he could see into her head. "Not all of us wear our scars on the outside. Many of us are scarred inside. Your husband is one of those." He rested his hands on his hipbones, elbows jutting, and turned his gaze over the water.

Daisy eyed his profile. "Many of the patients I had during the war had symptoms like Rafe's, only worse. Shell shock, we called it. Some of those men had to be shipped back to the States because they weren't capable of fighting anymore. Often, they were committed to an asylum." She paused as her memories took her back to her nursing days on the front lines and the mental conditions some of her patients had displayed. "I'm sorry to say those men were often ridiculed for being weak-minded, but they suffered from trauma, not a weak mind."

Daisy lapsed into silence while she waited for Will to continue. Talking about the war couldn't be easy for him, either.

At last, he swiveled his head toward her. "I have a lot to tell you if you want to understand your husband. We should sit, though. This could take a while."

They settled themselves at a nearby picnic table and stared over the water. Wavelets lapped at the shore. Neither spoke for long moments, though Daisy felt comfortable with the silence.

With his attention on the lake, Will squinted against the bright morning glare. "It's very peaceful here."

"Yes."

A bird's trill punctuated the quiet. Insects chirruped in the grass.

Will leaned back against the table behind him and rested both elbows on its planked surface, an introspective expression on his face. "When all of us American volunteers who joined the Lafayette Escadrille arrived in France, none of us had any flying experience."

"Did you and Rafe get to France at the same time?"

"We did."

"He mentioned you in his letters."

Will gave her a long look. "All of us homesick volunteers talked about our families. Except for Rafe. He didn't offer much information, only to admit he was married."

"Did he tell you about Molly?"

Will shook his head.

"Molly was our daughter. We lost her to whooping cough when she was two. Right after Molly died, Rafe left for France." Sharing Molly's story with Will helped ease some of the heartache over her daughter's death.

"That explains some things I wondered about." Will returned to his contemplation of the water. Silent seconds ticked past before he picked up the thread of his tale. "Right from the beginning, it was obvious Rafe was a natural pilot."

"Rafe wrote to me that anyone who could ride a horse could fly a plane."

Will grinned. "Rafe had an advantage over the rest of us there."

"He's a very skilled horseman. It's because of his Cheyenne background."

"Rafe has Cheyenne blood?"

"Yes. His father is half Cheyenne and in his younger days was a feared Dog Soldier."

Will nodded as if her statement answered a puzzle. "That explains something else I've wondered about."

Daisy waited while Will sat with his eyes half closed. When he didn't speak, she prompted him. "Well? What does that explain?"

Will cut her a questioning look, one eyebrow arched. "Are you sure you want to hear this?"

"Of course." As she tucked her feet beneath the bench, she twisted toward Will to better watch his face while he unveiled the mystery of what war experiences had changed her husband.

Will leaned forward and braced his elbows on his thighs, his hands clasped between his knees. "Rafe used to go up alone hunting the Hun. He had an uncanny ability to find them. He'd come in high and from behind, then swoop down and hit them before they even knew he was there. I don't know how many Hun planes he downed when he was flying by himself. Those kills weren't verified, so he didn't get credit for them, and Rafe never told us how many he shot down that way."

Daisy listened in silence. She could well imagine Rafe doing such a thing, though she shivered at the risks he'd taken.

"You have to understand one thing. Rafe was about twelve years older than the average pilot. Except for me, of course." Will turned his head and grinned at her over his shoulder. "Another thing that was obvious from the start was that he was a leader. The French made him an NCO and put him in charge of a squadron."

"He never told me that."

"Rafe's not one to brag."

"No."

Will paused before he collected himself and continued. "Rafe took his squadron leadership seriously. He painted his plane red so that the other flyboys could keep track of him during a dogfight."

"So that's why he painted his personal plane red."

"I caught that when I saw his plane the first time I came to Summit." Will took a breath. "Of course, his red plane made him a target for the Hun. After an engagement, he often came back with his plane shot full of holes, but he was never injured."

Daisy closed her eyes as she imagined her husband being shot from the sky. Only the Lord's protection had spared him. "I'm glad I didn't know that."

"The life expectancy of a flyboy was three weeks."

Daisy caught her breath. She hadn't known that fact, either.

"Rafe developed his own strategies for aerial warfare. He

trained his pilots in those tactics, so our squadron lost fewer planes than others, but he still had to write a lot of letters to grieving parents."

Daisy gripped her hands until her knuckles whitened. She began to get a glimpse of what Rafe suffered.

"Losing men was hard on him. I think that was one of the things that messed with his head. He took each loss personally." Will ploughed both hands through his hair. "We'd get new pilots to replace the ones we lost. Most of those boys had only fifteen hours of flying time when they came to us. Rafe took those young men who hardly knew how to fly a plane and made fighter pilots out of them. He nursed them along until he had them trained, and they could make a fighting unit. If they lasted long enough, that is."

Daisy couldn't speak. She could only listen and let Will's words paint a picture of the war.

"We went up without parachutes. We all knew being downed was a death sentence, one way or another. Unless a pilot could bring his crate in without crashing. That's supposing he was still alive to fly."

A pause punctuated Will's narrative. He took another breath and continued.

"We were flying in combustible deathtraps. If a plane caught fire, there was no hope for the pilot's survival."

Daisy stared at him in horror, unable to imagine such an eventuality.

"Those of us who survived all saw other pilots burn." Will dropped his head and stared at the ground before he continued his tale of death.

Daisy bent closer to hear his low-voiced words.

"Once Rafe came back with his plane shot full of holes. The canvas on his wings was shredded. I don't know how he managed to bring that crate in, but he did. Only a pilot with

Rafe's skill could have kept that plane in the air. Right after he landed, the plane caught fire."

Will tossed her a crooked grin. "He managed to grab your picture off the instrument panel before he got out."

Daisy pressed both hands to her mouth, aghast at her husband's close brush with death. "Now I understand why Rafe is afraid of fire."

Will straightened and got to his feet. He stared down at her. "What do you mean?"

She lowered her hands to her lap and related how Rafe had seemed to go into shock during the livery stable fire. "He'd never been afraid of fire before."

"Yet he still went in and rescued horses." Will shook his head. "That's so like Rafe."

Daisy thought she might be ill. Her vision darkened and blurred at the edges. The world spun. From a vast distance she heard Will say her name and felt his fingers tighten on the back of her neck as he pushed her head between her knees.

"Breathe. Take deep breaths. Don't you faint on me."

Daisy breathed in through her nose and out through her mouth. The blackness receded, and the world came back into focus. Embarrassed and wanting to sit up, she strained against the pressure of Will's hand. "I'm all right now. I won't faint."

Will stepped away while she sat up, though he watched her with narrowed eyes as if to be sure she wouldn't pitch off the bench.

"I'm not a fainter."

"I can believe that, but you never heard about Rafe nearly being killed in the war before, either."

Daisy gripped her arms and rubbed, trying to bring warmth to her flesh. "Thank you for sharing the war with me. I can see why Rafe doesn't want to talk about it. I understand so much better now."

"He has to face his demons, though."

"I feel more helpless than ever, now that I know what he went through."

Will stepped close. With a forefinger curled beneath her chin, he lifted her face. "Rafe is fortunate to have you to help him through this. If I could find someone like you, I'd almost be willing to give up flying." He seared her with a look. "Just be there for him. He needs you, though he doesn't know it. Be there for him until he figures it out."

CHAPTER 24

"Get the door, will you, Daisy? That's probably Will." Rafe cocked his head toward the front door at the knock that sounded. He stood at the sideboard cutting an apple pie into wedges.

With a platter of antelope steaks in one hand, Daisy left the kitchen and hurried to the front door. With her free hand, she swung the portal wide. Will stood on the veranda.

"Come on in. Rafe and I are putting the food on the table."

His auburn hair still damp from a washing and dressed in clean jeans and a fresh shirt, Will stepped inside. He grinned down at her. "I'm not late, then?"

"No. You're the first to arrive."

"That's good." He reached for the meat platter and plucked it from her hand. "Let me help. Where shall I put this?"

"The dining room is back here." Daisy led the way to the room behind the kitchen, opposite the staircase. "Set the platter there, near Rafe's place." She stood behind Rafe's chair at the table's head and indicated a spot near his plate.

Will set the platter down and sent a roving glance about the dining room, taking in the mahogany china cabinet, the matching table and chairs, and the long mirror above the sideboard. Daisy had put her personal touches to the room, with pictures and bric-a-brac. "Very nice."

"Rafe left everything as it was when we lived here together."

Will turned his attention to her. "Rafe had a good thing here to come home to. I hope he appreciates it."

"I'm sure he does."

"I meant you."

"We're working on that." Daisy blushed. Will's words made her aware of how she must look. After her shopping spree in Denver, Edith wouldn't outshine her this evening.

Conscious of Will's intent look, Daisy glanced at her outfit. The deep rose gown with its beading, complemented by her jewelry and tiara, made her feel like a princess. On a daring impulse, she'd added a touch of color to her lips.

"As I mentioned once before, Rafe's a lucky dog." A warm expression lit his face, and a smile tugged at his mouth.

"Thank you for the compliment." Daisy met Will's look. "I think he's beginning to come around."

"It's taking him long enough."

They made their way to the kitchen. Serving dishes heaped with mashed potatoes, vegetables, and a platter of biscuits waited to be transferred to the dining room. Daisy had just reached for a bowl of green beans when another knock sounded at the front door. "That must be the Montgomerys."

Will tossed them a rakish grin. "Ah, the delectable Edith and her father. I'll get the door." He left the kitchen, and moments later, voices sounded from the great room.

From his place beside the table, Rafe cast an inquiring look at Daisy. "What does he mean by that?"

"We met Edith today when I was showing him around Summit."

"Ah." They shared a smile.

From the great room, Edith's tinkling laughter followed by Will's deep chuckle told them that the two had already begun a flirtation.

"I think Will intends to charm Edith tonight, which might make up for the fact she may not talk to you since you've made it clear she has no future with you." Daisy skirted the table and came to a stop beside her husband. Stretching up on her tiptoes and curling her hand about his neck, she tugged him down so she could peck him on the lips.

"I don't care if Edith doesn't talk to me. I only care that you talk to me." Rafe hooked an arm about her waist and pulled her against him. He nuzzled her neck and murmured in her ear. "You're looking very fetching in your new gown, Mrs. Wild Wind. It was worth every penny, and I'm sure your costume cost a considerable amount of pennies."

"You have no idea how many pennies this outfit cost you, and you may not think it worth the price when you get the bill." She snuggled close. "I hoped you'd notice how I look."

"I noticed." He placed a kiss beneath her ear, then his mouth strayed to her lips before he put her away. "We have company."

"Yes, which means we have host and hostess duties."

He dropped another kiss on her lips before they joined their friends in the great room.

Edith sparkled in a spangled silver gown that left her slender arms bare. Diamond drops swung from her ears. A headband glittering with tiny silver sequins hugged her forehead and tied about the back of her head. Its long tails dangled over one shoulder. She greeted Daisy with cool politeness and acknowledged Rafe in an offhand manner at odds with her previous flirtatiousness.

Mr. Montgomery thrust out a hand for Rafe to shake.

After some brief conversation, they made their way to the dining room.

"Mr. Montgomery, you and Edith may sit here." Daisy motioned to the two chairs on her right. "Will, you sit over here." She indicated a chair on her left, while she and Rafe took their host and hostesses places at either end.

When their plates had been filled, Daisy announced, "I can't take credit for any of this meal. Rafe had the food brought over from Katie's Café." She turned to Will. "Katie is the best cook in town."

He swallowed a bite of biscuit. "I see what you mean. The food is delicious."

"It's much better than what I could have fixed. My talents don't run to cooking."

Edith chimed in. "We had the best cook in all of Charleston. She wouldn't come West with us, though. I've had to learn how to make coffee."

Her quip earned chuckles from the men.

Over apple pie, Edith laid down her fork and aimed a beguiling smile at Will. "You must tell us some war stories. I'd love to hear about your exploits. And Rafe must have stories, too."

Edith might have tossed a bomb into the room. Freezing with her fork halfway to her mouth, Daisy glanced along the table's length to her husband. Rafe sat unmoving, as if carved from marble.

Will shifted in his chair, his pie forgotten. "I'm not sure the war is a proper dinner party topic."

"Why evah not?" Edith persisted, her chin resting on her

linked hands. "All of our brave soldiers and flyboys saved us from the Hun. We should celebrate their bravery." She lifted her water glass in a toast. "To all of you war heroes."

No one joined her. Rafe continued to sit in frozen silence.

"What's the matter with y'all?" Edith pouted and returned her glass to the table. "The war is ovah, but we shouldn't forget your bravery. And Rafe will nevah talk about the war. We have two war heroes sittin' right here with us. I want to know what happened."

Her father patted her arm. "Edith, I don't think the men want to discuss the war. Mr. Blake can tell us about his mail service, instead."

"What an excellent idea." Daisy couldn't move. She didn't want Rafe's dinner party to be ruined with war talk. Having heard from Will something of what the men had experienced, she didn't think the topic suitable dinner table conversation. "Will loves flying the mail. I'm sure he has some exciting adventures to share. And perhaps he'll take you up in his plane tomorrow, Edith."

Edith cast her a stormy look.

Will glanced at Daisy, an enigmatic look in his hazel eyes. He then turned to Rafe. "No. Perhaps Edith is right. Maybe it is time for some war talk."

Rafe met his friend's gaze. A stony expression closed his face.

"Will. Not now. Please." Daisy implored him as she gripped his forearm.

Will gave her a look she couldn't interpret and returned his attention to Rafe. The men stared at each other for a moment. Tension twanged the air. "I think Edith's right. Rafe, your wife has a right to know how you earned those medals. I think it's time to bring everything out into the open."

Rafe continued to sit unmoving in frozen silence. His coloring had turned ashen.

"You want to hear about war heroes?" Will swept a glance at each of his companions. He pointed a finger at Rafe. "That man is a true war hero. Did you know he earned two medals for bravery?"

Edith's kohled eyes turned to Rafe, shining with new interest. "No, he nevah told me that. What did he do to earn those medals?"

"The first one was the French Croix de Guerre."

Will's words recalled to Daisy's mind the medal stashed in the wooden box upstairs. She sat transfixed. Despite her better judgment, she wanted to learn how Rafe had earned his medals. She couldn't tear her gaze from her husband's expressionless face.

"Rafe earned the Croix de Guerre for rescuing a downed American pilot under heavy enemy fire."

Silence heightened the tension. Each person at the table sat as if caught in some fairy tale witch's spell, silent and unmoving. Every eye focused on Rafe.

"Our squadron had been flying over the front, getting a look at German positions when we encountered Hun fighters. In the dogfight, one of the pilots got separated from the squadron. His plane was shot down, but he managed to land his crate safely between the German and Allied lines. The aeroplane was a loss, but the pilot survived. While he was trying to crawl to the safety of the British trenches, who should bring his plane down to rescue him but Rafe Wild Wind. What Rafe did seemed like a suicide mission."

Daisy couldn't look away from her husband. Only his burning eyes betrayed his emotion. He continued to stare at Will. His mouth clamped tight in a straight line.

"Bullets whizzed around us. The Brits were providing

cover for us, while the Hun were trying to blast us to eternity. The pilot had broken a leg when his plane crash-landed, so all he could do was crawl. Rafe got out of his plane and reached the pilot safely. He got the pilot up on his one good leg, put the pilot's arm about his shoulders, and half-dragged him to his plane. Rafe managed to take off without getting blown to smithereens and got them safely back to Allied lines."

Daisy transferred her attention to Will. "How do you know all this? I'm sure Rafe never talked about it."

Will flung her a look. "I was that pilot."

Will's admission broke the spell that had held everyone in thrall. Daisy slumped against her chair's carved back. Mr. Montgomery shuffled his feet.

Edith wriggled. Her gaze darted back and forth between Will and Rafe. "Why, Rafe, you saved your friend's life. I don't see why you can't talk about that."

Rafe ignored her. He still didn't look away from Will's face.

"What did he do to earn the other medal?" Edith persisted. Her avid expression betrayed her eagerness to hear the details.

"It was in the last year of the war, after the United States had entered the fighting."

"That's enough, Will." Rafe's voice grated with harsh intensity.

"No, it all needs to come out. It's for your own good." Will continued as though Rafe hadn't spoken. "Our squadron was one of several that had been detailed to escort some of our bombers over Germany who were on a mission to take out enemy fuel depots. We were intercepted by Hun fighters. One of our bombers got crippled by the Germans. Rafe took on three Hun fighters when they closed in to finish off our bomber. He prevented the Hun from shooting down the bomber and then escorted it home."

Rafe shoved to his feet. The backs of his knees hit his chair and sent it skittering backwards. His eyes glittered. "I said that's enough." He flung his napkin onto the table and stalked from the room. A moment later, the back door slammed behind him.

Stunned silence followed his departure. Edith made a motion as if to rise, but Daisy forestalled her. "Stay here with your father, Edith. I'll see to my husband." She rose and turned to leave without looking at Will.

His voice sounded behind her as she reached the dining room doorway. "Rafe needs you, Daisy. Go to him. I'll see your guests out."

She paused and nodded, then turned toward the rear of the house and followed her husband onto the back porch.

Rafe stood at the railing, both hands braced on the banister. His form made a black silhouette against the moon-silvered yard. Daisy paced toward him and laid one palm against his rigid back. They stood without speaking for long moments. When Rafe didn't break the silence, Daisy eased closer. She wrapped her arms about his waist and leaned her head against his spine. "I know you didn't like it, but I'm glad Will told us about your medals."

Rafe exhaled on an explosive breath. "I used my pilot's skills to kill. I shouldn't get rewarded for that."

"You were at war. You did what you did to save your men's lives and to protect our homeland."

"I was filled with hatred toward the Hun. I hated them and hunted them because they killed my men. For every pilot I got, that was one less German who would shoot down my men."

Sensing he wasn't finished, Daisy waited for him to

continue. His confession might finally cleanse him of the wounds that had festered since the war.

"Even as I hated them, I hated what I was doing more. By the end of the war, the Hun were sending up teenagers who should still have been in school. They were just boys. I killed boys, Daisy. *Boys.*"

Daisy wriggled around to his front and burrowed close. After a slight hesitation, he closed his arms around her. Rafe clutched her against him, one large hand curled about the back of her head. He rested his cheek on her hair.

"I killed boys."

"It was war, Rafe. The only other alternative would have been to let them shoot you down. You had no choice but to do what you did. And I'm so thankful you lived to come back to me."

They stood entwined, while the rigidity left Rafe's body.

Daisy spoke into his shirt. "The Lord doesn't hold it against you. You have to forgive yourself."

"You're a wise woman, Daisy Wild Wind."

"I don't know about that, but I do know what my husband needs to hear."

A gust of passion engulfed them. Rafe shifted and bent Daisy back over his arm. His mouth closed over hers. She curled one arm about his neck and pulled him closer, while his other hand roamed her body.

At last, he broke off the kiss and stared down at his wife. He spoke with ragged breaths. "Stay with me tonight, Daisy. I need you. I need you so much."

She returned his stare through the moonlight. "If I stay with you tonight, Rafe, I'll be moving back into the house in the morning. I won't spend tonight with you and then go back to live at the hotel."

He didn't reply. His breathing gusted against her cheek.

"We'll live together as husband and wife. Can you be a husband to me?"

In answer, he scooped her up, one arm beneath her knees and the other around her shoulders. With her held tight against his chest, he strode into the house.

Darkness and silence greeted them. Someone had turned off all the lights except for a lamp in the great room. Daisy gripped Rafe's neck with both hands as he took the stairs two at time. In the upstairs hallway, he shouldered open their bedroom door, swung her through, and kicked the portal shut with his boot.

CHAPTER 25

She was alone in their bed. Daisy stretched out a hand to Rafe's side and encountered empty sheets.

Sunlight pressed warm fingers against her closed eyelids. Must be morning. She cracked open her eyes and rolled her head toward the windows. An expanse of blue sky showed through the glass.

Rafe leaned against a window frame, fully dressed. He stood with his thumbs tucked into his front jeans pocket and one foot cocked. When she stirred, he swung his head in her direction.

"You're awake." His tone sounded solemn and set off alarm bells in Daisy's head.

"Barely." Daisy scooted up against the headboard and hitched the pillow up behind her. Feeling unexpectedly shy, she pulled the sheet up beneath her chin.

Rafe pushed off the window frame and strolled toward her. A somber expression touched his features, tightening his mouth. He reached the bed and sat down.

The mattress dipped beneath his weight. Daisy eyed her husband, not liking the look on his face or the tone he'd used.

Something had soured his mood. Perhaps he'd changed his mind about them living together. "Is something wrong?"

Rafe stared at her until Daisy squirmed.

"Rafe, tell me what's wrong. You're upset about something."

He leaned toward her, caging her between his thigh and a hand braced on the mattress beyond her waist. He rested his other hand on the sheet over her stomach, fingers splayed.

Her heart stuttered, guessing where this conversation would lead them. She caught his intent gaze and waited for him to speak.

"Tell me about the scar. You didn't have that scar when I left."

Feeling like a cornered rabbit, Daisy couldn't think of where to begin.

He narrowed his eyes at her. "I've been trying to imagine what could have caused that scar, and none of the possibilities I've considered is good."

"I would have told you about the scar when you first got back from the war, but you didn't touch me then, so you didn't see it. And we had other problems at the time."

"I've seen it now. Suppose you tell me how you got it."

Daisy gulped. Telling him about the child they'd lost whom her husband had never known existed could threaten the fragile reconciliation they'd just shared. "When you left for France, I was pregnant, but I didn't know it then. I left Summit right after you did to offer my nursing skills to the war effort." She closed her eyes for a moment and snatched a breath before she continued. "I was still in the States when I began to feel sick, but with losing Molly, and worrying about you, and going through nursing training, I didn't pay much attention to how I felt. I was too busy, anyway, to think of myself. Then I started having pain on one side and abdominal cramps. And I was dizzy."

Daisy looked down at Rafe's long fingers splayed over her abdomen, cradling the place where their child had lain. She gripped the sheet as she recalled the loss of a second child. "I passed out one day on the ward, and when I came to, I was in a hospital bed."

Rafe's nostrils flared, but he didn't interrupt her narrative.

"I needed immediate surgery." Daisy lifted her gaze to her husband's face. "After the surgery, the doctor told me that I'd had an ectopic pregnancy."

"Why didn't you let me know?"

Daisy shrugged. "I didn't want you to worry about me. With your flight training, you had enough on your mind. Soon after that you were in France fighting the Hun. And once I recovered, I shipped out to France and worked on the front lines. All of us doctors and nurses at the front were overwhelmed with wounded, so I barely had time to write at all." She paused. "And then you stopped writing to me."

Rafe gathered Daisy in his arms and cradled her against his heart. He nestled her face into the curve of his neck. "My poor darling, going through that crisis alone. And losing another child so soon after Molly. I don't know how you stood it."

His sympathy and comforting arms proved to be her undoing. Hot tears seeped from between her lids. Rafe stroked her back while she cried and tangled his fingers in her hair.

He murmured in her ear, "I can't bring back your baby, Daisy, but I can give you another one. We'll have more children."

His words only made her weep harder. She hiccoughed

and shook her head. "Th-the doctor told me I probably couldn't have more children."

Rafe said nothing. Instead, he gathered her up, sheet and all, and deposited her on his lap. He held her close and rested his cheek on her hair until the storm passed. When her sobs had subsided into sniffles, he leaned back and peered into her face. He stroked her hair away from her damp cheeks. "Better now?"

The weeping bout had left her feeling drained but cleansed. She nodded.

Rafe gave her a tender kiss and dried her tears with a corner of the sheet. "You're more important to me than children. I'm grateful that I didn't lose you, too. Instead, we both survived the war. We'll have a good life, just the two of us."

Daisy thought he only tried to make her feel better, but she allowed herself to be convinced. She remembered how much Rafe had desired children. Her inability to give him a family must be a blow, although he did a good job convincing her that he didn't care if she couldn't have more children.

"Now, I'm going downstairs to heat some water for your bath. While you're soaking, I'll get your things from the hotel and cancel your room there. We can move you back into the bedroom after breakfast."

He rose and let Daisy slide down his length. When her feet touched the floor, she wrapped the sheet about her, toga style, and stretched up on tiptoe to kiss her husband. "Thank you, Rafe. I love you."

He gave her another squeeze. "Let's play hooky today. I'll fly us off somewhere so we can be alone. We'll take a picnic lunch."

"What about your supervising the preparations for the barbeque? That's coming up in just a couple of days."

"We do the same thing every year, so the men know what

to do without me. Now, I'm going to get your bath ready, and then I'll go to the hotel."

Daisy reached for his hand when he turned away to leave the room. He halted and raised an eyebrow. "When you see Will at the hotel, don't be too hard on him. What he did last night, he did for your own good."

* * *

Daisy halted beside the wooden dancing platform that was under construction at the lake's edge. Will Blake had joined the other men who pounded boards for the floor and had stripped down to his undershirt. Sweat glistened along his shoulders and arms. He pounded a final nail into the floorboard and stood, stretching the kinks from his back.

Daisy waited until he saw her. A welcoming grin lit his face when he noticed her standing at the dance floor's edge. Hooking the hammer's handle into his belt, he sauntered toward her and came to a standstill beside her, his feet braced wide, arms crossed.

"Seeing you here is a surprise. I figured Rafe would keep you tethered close to him today."

"He's busy at the mine this afternoon, so I thought I'd come down here to check on you. I hope you and Rafe are still friends."

Will scuffed the toe of one boot through the brown grass and glanced away, then swung his attention back to Daisy's face. "We exchanged some hard words yesterday morning when he came to the hotel to get your things, but . . ." He shrugged. "Men can't go through war together, looking out for each other the way we did, to let an argument like that end our friendship."

"I told him not to be too hard on you."

"I suppose I deserved his anger, but what I said needed to be said."

"I told him that, too."

"How is he?" Will peered into Daisy's face.

"Better. I think he's healing."

Will gave a nod. "I hoped making him face his issues would help." He looked her up and down. "I see you've moved out of the hotel."

Daisy blushed. "Rafe and I are back together. He's ready to tackle being a husband again, so I have you to thank for that."

"Rafe would have come around, soon or later. I just helped him along a bit."

"I'm glad it was sooner. And thank you for getting our guests out of the house after that dinner. I couldn't have faced questions from Edith when Rafe and I came back inside."

Will shifted his weight to one leg, and the corners of his mouth tipped up. "I promised to take Edith up in my plane during the barbeque if she'd leave quietly. A specialized flight just for her. Something that would make the other girls envious. And I promised her the first dance tomorrow night."

Daisy grinned back. "You bribed her?"

"I'm not ashamed to say that I did. I have Edith pegged as a woman who can cause a scene if she's thwarted. I figured we'd had enough scenes for one night."

"You're right on both counts."

"And I'd consider it an honor if you'd save a dance for me. Rafe will just have to turn you loose for one dance. I won't let him monopolize you for the whole evening."

"I doubt that Rafe will monopolize me. Both of you will have your hands full dancing with those girls who love pilots. Those tourists we told you about."

"Ah, those girls. I noticed Summit's population is

swelling, and the hotel is filling up."

"By tomorrow, Summit will be bursting."

Will touched Daisy's arm. "I'll still save one dance for you. The other girls will just have to stand on the sidelines and watch."

"They won't stand on the sidelines. There will be plenty of cowboys and single miners who will dance those girls' feet off."

"But you'll promise me one dance?"

"Of course. I consider it an honor to dance with the man who helped keep my husband alive during the war. Downplay it all you want, but I know the two of you worked together as a team to look out for each other during aerial battles."

Will glanced away again. "We did."

"Having you around has been good for Rafe. I'm glad you reconnected with him."

"It took me a while to track him down. Flying this leg of mail delivery made it possible to drop in on him. And I'm glad I met you, Daisy. I saw your picture when Rafe and I were in France, and I wondered what kind of woman Rafe had married. Like I told you, he didn't talk about you."

Daisy stared at him, unable to reply.

"You're everything I hoped you'd be, for Rafe's sake." Will's expression turned earnest.

"Thank you. I hope I'm worthy of him."

"He'd better hope he's worthy of you." Will pulled the hammer from his belt. "I'd best get back to work, if we want to have this platform done in time for the dance tomorrow night."

Bemused, Daisy watched him walk away. Will Blake had been trying to tell her something without coming right out and saying it, but she wasn't sure what. Of one thing, she was sure. Will might joke and flirt, but he was a complicated man.

CHAPTER 26

Rafe's red biplane and Will's white one trembled in anticipation of taking to the sky. The aircrafts sat side by side on the meadow, their props spinning and their engines rumbling. Daisy checked the leather strap that secured her in the front cockpit. The buckled belt reassured her that she wouldn't fall out.

She glanced across at Will's aeroplane. Edith sat in the front cockpit like a queen receiving her due. Just as Will had confided to her yesterday, Edith held the coveted privilege of being Will's first passenger on this afternoon's autumn gala. Rafe had insisted that Daisy be his first passenger. At this fete, she had no doubts about where she stood in her husband's affections, no matter how many women he took up today.

From the back cockpit, Rafe must have signaled to Will, because Will nodded and sent Rafe a thumbs up sign. Rafe's plane surged forward, vibrating with eagerness to take flight, and Daisy clutched the cockpit's padded rim. Taking off always frightened her, although she'd never admit as much to Rafe.

She looked at Will's plane again. The white biplane kept pace with Rafe's. In unison, both planes lifted into the sky and soared upward toward the mountain rims that encircled the valley. The two planes flew as one, their maneuvers choreographed as though the pilots had rehearsed their moves hundreds of times. Daisy supposed that they had. The two men had flown like this on countless sorties during the Great War. What did Rafe think about flying with Will once more?

When the planes touched down in the meadow and taxied toward the hanger, dozens of hopeful young women hovered at the runway's edge. The word must have spread that today two war aces would be taking up passengers. The number of girls crowding the field had almost doubled from the July Fourth celebration.

Rafe's plane halted at the hanger. He cut the engine, and before Daisy could climb out, he appeared on the wing beside her. Reaching into her cockpit, he unbuckled her safety strap. With a tight grip on her arm, he helped her out of the aircraft and swung her to the ground. He leaped off the wing and hauled her against his chest. Despite dozens of onlookers watching them, he bent his head and kissed her.

His possessiveness gratified her. This was the Rafe she remembered, free with his kisses and generous with his love. She couldn't help but feel a bit of triumph that he'd claimed her in front of all the young women who'd hoped to score with the handsome ace. His kiss had made the statement that he wasn't available for a flirtation.

When Rafe let her go, she jerked off her goggles and helmet and smiled into his eyes. The intimate moment they shared warmed her to her toes.

During the afternoon while the planes droned overhead, returning only to exchange passengers and to refuel, Daisy basked in a contented glow. Rafe would return to her side in time for the barbeque dinner and the dancing. Unlike the July Fourth gala, she didn't have to scheme for a few minutes of his time.

Katie found her during the middle of the afternoon. With her toddler on her hip and her four-year old daughter by the hand, she bumped Daisy's arm with a shoulder to get her attention.

Daisy looked away from the sky, where the planes had just disappeared over the jagged mountain peaks, and saw her friend. "Katie! I'm sorry I've neglected you lately."

Katie looked her over with a shrewd eye. "You're glowing. I guess the gossip is true, then. You and Rafe are back together."

"Yes, thanks to his friend. Will did something that Rafe would never have tolerated from me, and it got us together."

"That's what I'd heard. Apparently, Edith has found consolation elsewhere."

Daisy laughed. "Will is serving as a stand-in for Rafe. I'm not sure what will happen when Will leaves."

"Rafe will keep her at a distance." Katie gave her friend a knowing look.

Daisy basked in the security of her husband's love. She recalled the moment on the day they'd moved her things back into their bedroom. He'd removed his wedding band from the wooden box on the dresser and crossed the room to the chest of drawers where she'd been storing her underthings. She'd looked up at him when he'd halted beside her.

He held his wedding band on his open palm. "Here. I'd like you to put my ring back on."

She plucked up the ring, and he held out his left hand, fingers spread wide. With trembling solemnity, she pushed the golden circlet onto his ring finger. He closed his hand about hers and drew her toward him, then kissed her with a husband's passion. Daisy curled her arms about Rafe's neck, and they forgot about unpacking her things. Much later they returned to the task of moving her into their room.

Now, she smiled at Katie. "Rafe can handle Edith."

At the afternoon's end, when the last passenger had been flown, Rafe and Will took off once more to entertain the crowd with their stunt flying. Daisy and Katie joined the throng in the meadow to watch.

"I think I'm more nervous now than I was on July Fourth," Daisy confessed. "This time I know what chances he'll take, and with him and Will flying together, I'm afraid the two of them will do something even more dangerous."

Katie sympathized. "I'd worry myself to pieces if that were my husband up there."

In spite of her anxiety, Daisy couldn't help but watch the two pilots display their skills. After hearing Will's account of their dogfights during the war, she understood how the stunts they performed had their origins in the aerial maneuvers they'd employed while fighting the Hun. The loops, spins, screaming dives, and their climbs upward at the sun, had all been evasive tactics they'd used when German planes had tried to shoot them from the sky. She looked on with new appreciation as she envisioned their battles with the enemy.

When they both flew over the lake upside down in the grand finale and then buzzed the onlookers, pride filled her chest. The planes circled the meadow once more before they touched down and taxied to the hanger. This time, when eager young women besieged both planes, Daisy didn't hesitate. She thrust her way through the crowd of females to her husband's side.

Rafe had peeled off his leather helmet and goggles and had tucked them in his jacket pocket by the time she reached him. He was signing his name to a young woman's dance card. Another female with short blonde curls pushed her Brownie camera into Daisy's hand.

"Could you please take my picture with the ace?" The girl didn't wait for a reply. She darted to Rafe's side and positioned herself at his shoulder.

Rafe shrugged and sent Daisy a pained look.

Daisy bit back a smile and aimed the camera. "Smile, you two."

The young woman beamed into the camera, while Rafe held himself stiffly erect. After Daisy had snapped the shot, the girl flashed Rafe a radiant grin. "Thank you ever so much, Mr. Wild Wind. My friends will be so jealous."

Before Rafe could move, a redhead sashayed to his side. She presented him with a bouquet of long-stemmed white roses. "These roses show my appreciation for what you did for our country during the war. I know you risked your life for us." The girl's tone expressed her sincerity.

Rafe accepted the roses with a resigned air. "Thank you. I'd do it all over again."

A tall brunette waved to get Rafe's attention. "Mr. Wild Wind. Will you save me a dance?"

Rafe apparently had had enough. He reached for Daisy and pulled her against him. "I'll try to work you in, but most of the evening, I'll be dancing with my wife."

The brunette's crestfallen expression warmed Daisy's heart. Rafe belonged to her, and the other women's hopes of scoring with the ace had been dashed. Rafe had declared himself to be off limits.

Her husband worked his way through the group with Daisy tucked under his arm and the roses clenched in his other hand.

"Being a flying ace sure has its benefits." She cast a teasing look at him as they left his fans behind.

"It would serve you right if I went back there and let those women fawn all over me. I could dance every dance with them and leave you watching on the sidelines." His dark eyes laughed down at her, though his mouth maintained a solemn line.

"Go right ahead. I wouldn't want to monopolize the attention of such a popular war hero and deprive those hopeful girls of your company." Daisy's voice quivered with mirth.

Rafe's arm tightened around her, and he growled into her ear. "Don't you dare."

She relaxed against him and wrapped her arm about his waist. That he could tease again showed her how much he'd healed.

The spectators who'd gathered to watch the aerial display had dispersed. People headed toward the picnic area by the lake, where the tantalizing scents of barbequed beef beckoned.

Rafe and Daisy followed in their wake. Daisy cast a final glance at Will's plane, parked beside Rafe's. A crowd of females still encircled him. All smiles and male charm, Will soaked up their attention, while Edith fumed at his side. Will accepted the accolades of his fans and let the Southern beauty stew. Daisy decided Will was too smooth an operator to let Edith railroad him. Watching those two during the evening might provide some extra entertainment.

Rafe and Daisy filled their plates with barbeque, potato salad, and rolls, then found a secluded spot at the edge of the lake. Daisy settled herself on the grass, taking care not to stain her plaid, drop-waisted dress. She tucked her legs beneath her and waited while Rafe lowered himself, cross legged, to the ground beside her.

Rafe balanced his plate on one knee and leaned over to plant a lingering kiss on Daisy's lips.

She closed her eyes and returned the kiss, then cast him a curious look when he drew back. "What was that for?"

"I have six years to make up for. That's a lot of kisses."

"You don't mind that the whole town is watching?"

His eyes smiled. "They're already gossiping about us. What's a little more scandal for the gossip mill?"

"I suppose you kissing me at supper in front of a crowd of people is better gossip than you socializing with Edith."

"There won't be any more gossip of that sort. And besides, me kissing you may discourage certain young ladies from stampeding me on the dance floor."

"Let them stampede Will instead. I think he's up to the challenge."

Rafe chuckled and dug into his barbeque. "Will does enjoy the ladies."

Later, after everyone had eaten, Mr. Montgomery stood at one side of the dancing platform with his tabletop Victrola, situated on a wooden stand beside the dance floor. Edith's father placed a record of popular dance tunes on the phonograph's turntable and rotated the crank that made music burst from the machine. The tinny notes announced that dancing had begun.

A ring of flickering torches on poles that encircled the dance floor illuminated the area. When the music started, a rush of couples filled the platform.

As they stood near the edge of the crowd, Rafe curled an arm about his wife. "We'll take our turn in the next dance. The floor is full, anyway."

Daisy rose on tiptoe to peer around the people in front of them. "Look, there's Will dancing with Edith. He promised her the first dance."

"He'll dance more than the first one with her. I know from experience she's difficult to dislodge."

"Will is more than a match for Edith. I predict he'll dance with all those hopeful young misses, and Edith will have to find other partners."

Rafe's arm tightened about Daisy's waist, and he nuzzled her hair. "To be honest, I'm relieved to be out of Edith's clutches. I should have made up with you long before now."

She leaned her head against his shoulder. "I'd just about given up hope of us getting back together. You didn't seem interested in me or in fixing our marriage."

Rafe snorted. "That just goes to show you how little I know. To be honest, I had a hard time staying away from you."

Daisy tipped back her head to peruse his face. "I never would have guessed. You did a marvelous job of convincing me otherwise."

"It was really myself I was trying to convince. Once you came back to town, you got under my skin, and I couldn't get free of you. It took a while for me to admit that I still loved you and wanted to get us back together. I'd been alone for so long I was terrified that I couldn't handle a relationship."

With Daisy's hand linked in his, Rafe eased them away from the people encircling the dance floor. He led her to a spot in the semi-darkness where they could have a private conversation. "Now that we're back together, I feel whole. You're the other half of me, Daisy. Without you, I'm not a whole person."

She linked her hands behind his neck. "It's the same for me. Without you, I'm incomplete."

He crossed his arms around the small of her back and drew her against him. The Victrola blared its music, and laughter and conversation filled the night, but the two of them might have been alone beside the dark water. Rafe kissed her thoroughly and touched his forehead to hers. "We don't have to stay here long, do we?"

"Of course not, but I can't leave until I dance with Will. I promised him one dance."

"I don't know why I should let that rascal dance with my wife, but if you promised, I won't make you break it. A promise is a promise, after all."

"And you have dance partners waiting for you. You wouldn't want to disappoint all those young ladies, would you?"

Rafe straightened and made a face. "Huh. I don't want to dance with them, but I suppose I should keep my word."

The music wound down, and the dance ended. Couples exited the platform.

Rafe reached for Daisy's hand. "It's our turn. Let's go before the floor fills up again."

Daisy danced the next two dances with her husband before Will claimed her. She and Rafe were standing on the sidelines when Will strolled up to them.

He came to a standstill and gave Rafe a good-natured punch to the shoulder. "If you don't mind me borrowing your wife for a few minutes, she promised me a dance."

"Daisy warned me you'd asked her. Behave yourself, you flirt. Don't forget that's my wife you're dancing with."

Will chuckled and escorted Daisy onto the dancing platform.

She smiled up at him. "Are you enjoying yourself?"

"Very much. It was a pleasure to fly with Rafe without having any Huns shooting at us."

"I'm sure. You two were incredible, and I could see how you used those moves in your dogfights."

Will nodded but didn't pursue that conversational bait.

Daisy threw out another line. "And then there are the girls . . ."

He tipped his head back and looked down at her through laughing eyes. "I haven't seen so many girls since high school."

The music started then, so conversation ceased, and Daisy gave her attention to the dance steps. On one circuit around the floor, they passed Edith dancing with a young man who wasn't a local. He must be a tourist who'd come to Summit for the barbeque. When she whirled around again, Daisy saw that a pretty young woman had engaged Rafe in conversation. Her husband might have a more difficult time avoiding the young things than he anticipated.

When the dance ended, Will and Daisy stepped off the platform onto the ground. With a hand at her elbow, he guided her away from the crowd. Daisy glanced around for Rafe.

"Never mind your husband. He's got a dance partner." With a nod in the direction of the platform, Will drew her attention to Rafe and the girl with whom he'd been talking. Rafe indeed had a partner.

"Hmm . . . Rafe was hoping to avoid the girls. He's a very reluctant partner tonight."

"So would I be, if you were my wife. I'd have no desire to dance with other women."

Daisy didn't comment, and Will said no more. They halted at the edge of the lake. A cool night breeze sighed off the water, and Daisy shivered. She clasped her arms about her waist in an effort to find warmth. "I thought Edith would have you stuck to her side for every dance tonight."

Will propped his hands on his hips. "I thought it best if I let Edith know she has no claim on me."

Daisy couldn't suppress her giggle. "I'm surprised we

didn't hear the fallout from that conversation. She must not have taken it well."

"She didn't." Will smiled down at Daisy. "Having a lot of male visitors today helped. She can still dance every dance without me."

Silence fell between them, with the Victrola providing a backdrop.

"Daisy."

She forgot to wonder if Rafe was still dancing and turned her attention to her companion. "Yes, Will?"

"I wanted to say a private goodbye to you tonight. I'm leaving in the morning."

"So soon? You can't stay longer? Rafe has enjoyed having you here."

"I've used up my vacation time and must get back to flying the mail."

"Now that you've found Rafe, you must come visit again."

"I will. I won't stay away." Will dropped his hands to his sides and stepped closer. "Daisy, I want you to know I'm glad Rafe took that step to get back together with you. You're a special lady. He's a lucky dog to have you, and I must admit to being a bit jealous."

"I'm the lucky one to have Rafe."

Will shrugged, his expression serious. "All that aside, if something happens, if you ever need help, please let me know."

Daisy couldn't keep the doubt from her voice. "What do you mean?"

"You'll know if the time comes. Just promise me that you'll contact me if you need anything. Anything at all."

"All right, I promise."

"Now, the dance is over, and Rafe is looking for you. We'd better go back."

Rafe met them near the dance floor. "There you are. Dance with me, Daisy."

Will turned her over to her husband, and the next time Daisy saw her husband's former wingman, he was dancing with a brunette.

When the music stopped, Rafe pulled Daisy off the platform. He linked his fingers through hers and drew her against his side. "Let's leave. I have a hunger for my wife."

CHAPTER 27

With a jolt, Daisy came wide awake and stared at the ceiling, wondering what had roused her. Beside her, Rafe muttered in his sleep. He thrashed and tossed off the blankets, then muttered again. She rolled onto her side and stared at her husband. Rafe must be having a nightmare.

He shouted, a hoarse sound that ripped through the darkness, and kicked the blankets to the foot of the bed.

Alarmed, Daisy sat up and curled her legs beneath her. She leaned toward her husband and laid a hand on his forehead. His skin felt clammy.

At her touch, he shouted and came upright in a rush. He knocked her hand away and whirled toward her, pinning her to the mattress with his big body. His strong hands clenched about her throat and tightened.

Daisy couldn't breathe. Rafe's hands clamped like a vise around her neck, and her throat burned. She kicked and flailed, while her vision darkened at the edges. With waning strength and consciousness, she pounded on Rafe's chest with both fists and shoved against his shoulders. She might as well have been trying to move a mountain. He didn't budge. She clawed at his hands in a desperate attempt to free herself.

With a gasp, Rafe wrenched his hands from her neck and launched off the bed. He came to a halt beside one window. His shoulders shuddered as deep breaths convulsed his body.

Daisy sucked in life-giving air. Her lungs heaved, while her vision cleared. She lay motionless as she struggled to regain her strength. Finally, she turned her head and peered at her husband. Rafe stood in rigid silence by one window, his back to her. After several more breaths, she crawled across the mattress and swung her feet to the floor, then wobbled across the room. Not daring to touch him, she stopped just out of arm's reach. When she tried to talk, she could only manage a squeak.

For a moment, he didn't respond. At last, he spoke without turning around. "Are you all right?"

"Yes." Her words rasped over her bruised vocal cords.

"I'm sorry. I never intended to hurt you."

They stood in a frozen tableau, neither speaking, until Rafe pivoted to face her. He didn't touch her.

"You were having a nightmare." Daisy's hoarse words seemed to free him from the trance that ensnared him.

"From time to time I still have nightmares of the war. Not often, but whenever something reminds me of the fighting."

Enlightenment clarified a question she'd wondered about but hadn't dared to ask. She cleared her throat and tried to speak past the soreness. "The night after you first saw Will when you told me you couldn't sleep, it was because you were afraid you'd have a nightmare."

"Yes. I knew that if I slept, I'd have one of my nightmares. I had to stay awake."

They stood in silence, staring at each other.

"What did you dream about this time?"

Rafe took another deep breath. "Fire. I was in a burning plane, and I couldn't get out. The Hun were shooting at me, and I was going down. These nightmares always take me back to the war. I relive the fighting."

Daisy's heart contracted. "I'm so sorry. When the livery stable burned, I realized you were afraid of fire, but I didn't know why."

"I saw too many of my boys go down in flames. It's something I'll never forget. It's with me still."

Daisy eyed her husband, wondering if she could touch him now. He needed comforting. Before she could decide, he continued.

"This is one reason why I hesitated to bring us back together. No husband wants his wife to see him screaming like a baby because he's had a nightmare. It's unmanning."

Daisy abandoned her inner debate about whether or not she should touch him and flung herself at his chest. Her arms closed about his waist, and she burrowed against him. She breathed in his scent.

He hesitated, then encircled her in a desperate embrace. He buried his face in the curve of her neck. "Daisy, Daisy, hold me tight."

They stood locked together, Rafe's heart thudding beneath her ear. His skin still felt clammy. When at last his heartbeat returned to normal and he'd stopped shaking, she pushed against his arms and looked into his face. "Don't ever hesitate to share your fears with me. I don't think less of you because you have nightmares. It will take a long time for you to move beyond the trauma you experienced during the war."

"I don't know if I ever will."

"You have the Lord's help. The Lord will help you heal."

He nodded.

"Do you want to come back to bed?"

"No. I never sleep after I have one of these nightmares."

"All right. I'll fix us some coffee, and maybe you can tell me something about the war."

"Daisy." Rafe had let her go, but he grabbed her hand and whirled her back toward him. "The next time I have a nightmare, don't touch me. I just might mistake you for a Hun."

* * *

"I don't think I'll ever be able to step into Molly's room without missing her." Daisy paused in the doorway and looked in.

Molly's room beckoned just beyond the threshold. Even after living with Rafe in their home for two weeks and walking past Molly's door several times a day, her daughter's room still held the power to cause pain.

Rafe stood at Daisy's back, and he laid a comforting hand on her shoulder. "You have a mother's heart."

Daisy placed a palm on her chest. "Molly still lives here, in my heart. Being in Summit again has brought everything back. I see Molly everywhere I look. Especially here, in her room." She sighed. "I suppose in time, seeing her room will get easier."

They both stood for a moment, looking into their daughter's bedroom, before Rafe nudged her inside. "It will be easier once we put her things away."

Daisy halted. "Oh, Rafe. I don't think I can do this!"

Rafe turned her toward him and pulled her into an embrace. His palm cupped the back of her head. He bent his head and murmured in her ear, "Yes, you can. We can do this together."

Her nose burrowed in his faded green flannel shirt. The feel of his warm, muscled strength beneath her face and his arms around her gave her courage. She closed her eyes and leaned against him. "All right. But it won't be easy."

Rafe held her until she pushed out of his arms and stepped toward Molly's crib.

"The first thing I should do is wash her sheets and blankets."

"That would be a good place to begin. I'll put her blocks back in their box."

Tears sheened Daisy's eyes as she lifted Molly's battered brown bear from the crib and stroked its worn fur. Her heart ached with the knowledge that she'd never lay another infant in this crib. This bedroom would remain forever empty, with no baby's cries or toddler's laughter to give it life. She gulped back the lump that formed in her throat.

Rafe had never referred to her confession that they probably could have no more children. Guilt that she'd deprive her husband of sons and daughters weighed on her. Rafe deserved to be a father. He'd been a loving parent to Molly, and he deserved sons, sons she could never give him. Despite his declaration that the two of them would be happy without a family, Daisy couldn't help but feel her husband must wish for children.

She buried her guilt beneath a determination to be the best wife she could be and laid the bear on top of the chest of drawers beside the bed. Turning back to the crib, she loosened the sheets and blanket from the mattress and tossed them on the floor by the door. She crossed the room to the rocker in the corner. Pulling the pink blanket from the chair's back, she added it to the pile of laundry by the door.

Rafe had finished stowing the blocks in their box and had set the container in the toy bin. He'd straightened the books on their shelf and now stood by the window near the crib. "Do you want to leave the curtains?"

Indecision gripped Daisy, and she nibbled at her lower lip. If the curtains remained, she'd always be reminded of Molly. Stripping the room of any vestige of her daughter would be best. "Take them down." She turned her back to the sight of Rafe sliding the curtains from their rod and instead occupied herself with sweeping the floor. She didn't look around when her husband added the pink fabric to the pile by the door.

When the last reminder of their daughter had been removed and the room cleaned, Daisy bundled the dirty linens in her arms. She took a final glance at the forlorn bedroom and walked into the hall. Rafe stepped out behind her and closed the door.

The *snick* of the door closing terminated a period of her life that she could never bring back. Motherhood would forever be denied her.

CHAPTER 28

Denver, Colorado
Autumn, 1922

One morning in early September, someone rapped on the front door, quick staccato beats that signaled distress. Daisy hurried from the kitchen to answer the summons. She swung the door wide to see one of the miner's sons standing on her veranda and struggled to remember the urchin's name. "Can I help you . . . Davey?"

The boy nodded. His hair stuck out over his ears like straw, and his freckled face looked anxious. His boney ankles showed beneath his too-short overalls. "Doc Daisy, my ma wants you to come look at Susie. She's not feelin' so good."

Daisy's professional self leaped to the forefront, and she forgot to ask why Davey wasn't in school. "What's wrong with Susie, Davey?"

The boy shrugged. "I don't know, Doc Daisy. She's layin' around and complainin' about her side hurtin'."

That snippet of information gave Daisy some notion of what Susie's medical issue could be. Several things could cause Susie's symptoms, but appendicitis was the one possibility that Daisy feared most. She touched Davey's shoulder. "Wait here for me. I'll get my doctor's bag and will be right out."

Upstairs in one of the spare bedrooms she'd converted into her medical office, Daisy checked her doctor's bag and added a few items. With the bag gripped in one hand, she darted into the bedroom to change into her serviceable dark skirt and plain white blouse. Dressed for any medical situation, she ran down the stairs and outside.

Davey waited in the porch swing, toeing the chair into motion. He leaped up when Daisy erupted onto the veranda.

"I'm ready, Davey. Take me to your house."

Daisy followed the boy's slight form into the mining community to the home where his family lived. She'd visited Davy's mother during her previous excursions through the mining town, so she'd had dealings with the family. Following close on Davey's heels when he clattered into the small home, she let the screen door slam behind her.

A young woman with a worn face and brown hair bundled into an untidy bun greeted her. "Thank you for coming, Doc Daisy. I hated to bother you when Susie may only have a belly ache, but I'm worried about her."

Hoping to reassure her, Daisy smiled at the woman in her most professional manner. She recalled that this woman was Ada Johnson's friend, Jenna. She'd drunk coffee with the two women in Ada's kitchen one summer morning. "Jenna, I'll look at Susie. I'm sure we can figure out if she just has a stomachache."

Jenna managed a slight smile in return. "Thank you, Doc Daisy. Susie's back here. She's just been layin' around for a couple of days and hasn't felt like going to school." She led Daisy to a back bedroom. Three narrow beds crowded the small space. A shabby rag rug covered the floor. On a cot jammed against one wall huddled a small form. They halted beside the bunk.

Daisy leaned over the child. "Susie, I'm Doc Daisy, and I'm here to help you. Your mother says you're not feeling well. Can you tell me how you're feeling?"

The little girl, who had been curled into a ball facing the wall, straightened her legs and rolled onto her back. She turned a wan face to Daisy. Her chestnut hair clung in damp wisps to her temples. "My tummy hurts. And I'm cold." Susie shivered and pulled the blanket up beneath her chin.

"Do you feel like eating?" Daisy employed a gentle tone, hoping to encourage the child to talk.

Susie shook her head. "My tummy doesn't feel so good."

Daisy straightened and glanced at Jenna. "When was the last time she ate?"

"She didn't want any supper last night, but her pa made her eat a few bites. She didn't eat much breakfast or lunch yesterday, either." Jenna wrung her hands. "Doc Daisy, I've got to tell you that my husband has gone to fetch Doc Irby."

Daisy's glance sharpened. She tried not to reveal her irritation or her fear for the child's welfare. "Thank you for telling me, Jenna. I'm going to send Davey for my husband." She wheeled and hastened into the kitchen. When she reached Davey, who squatted on the floor with his marbles scattered over the planking, she knelt beside him.

"Davey, would you please go to the mine and get Mr. Wild Wind? He should be at the office."

Davey looked up at her. "Sure, Doc Daisy."

Daisy shook his shoulder. "You must hurry, Davey. It's

important that you bring Mr. Wild Wind here as fast as you can."

Davey scrambled to his feet. His eyes rounded with the gravity of his mission. "I'll hurry, Doc Daisy."

"Thank you, Davey. That's a good boy."

Davey spun and dashed across the kitchen. The screen door banged shut behind him. He thudded down the porch steps and sprinted up the road.

For Susie's sake, Rafe must arrive before Jenna's husband and Doc Irby. In situations such as this, the father's wishes would overrule the mother's. If Doc Irby had the final say, Susie's life could be in jeopardy, since Daisy doubted the doctor could diagnose appendicitis. If he misdiagnosed Susie's ailment and her appendix burst, nothing would save her. Rafe's presence might influence Susie's father to allow for a more professional analysis.

Please hurry, Rafe.

Daisy shook herself from her preoccupation and returned to the bedroom. Coming to a standstill, she leaned over Susie's cot. "Susie, I'm going to take your temperature, and then I'll feel your tummy. Will that be all right with you?"

Susie gave a slight nod and reached out a thin hand to her mother. Jenna clutched her daughter's hand and perched on the edge of the mattress.

While Susie lay lax with the thermometer beneath her tongue, Daisy pulled the covers down around the girl's waist. A faded flannel nightgown clad her thin form. "I'll press your tummy in different places, and you tell me when it hurts."

Susie nodded again.

Taking care to be gentle, Daisy pressed the child's stomach, running her fingers over the left side, then her belly button, and finally on the right side. Susie winced after Daisy had lifted her hand.

"That hurts." The thermometer wobbled when Susie spoke.

"Right there? Just nod your head."

Susie nodded.

Daisy pressed again, and her patient cringed, but only after the pressure had been released. Rebound pain, Daisy thought, a sure sign of appendicitis. And the area felt tight, like a drum.

Daisy tucked the covers back around the girl's chin and pulled the thermometer from her mouth, then tilted it so she could read the result. The instrument measured a low-grade fever, another indication of appendicitis. She laid the thermometer on a small table beside the bed and drew Jenna aside, turning her back to the bed and spoke in a low tone so Susie couldn't hear their conversation.

"Jenna, Susie has appendicitis." Daisy tried to make her tone sympathetic as well professional as she gave her dreaded diagnosis. Until recently, appendicitis meant a death sentence.

Jenna's face blanched. "No, Doc Daisy. Don't you think she just has a tummy ache? Maybe if you gave her a laxative, she'd feel better."

"A laxative won't help her. In fact, it could make her condition worse." Daisy gripped Jenna's hands and looked her in the eyes. She must convince Jenna that Susie would need to be transported to Denver for a life-saving operation. If she could convince Jenna that her daughter needed the procedure, perhaps Jenna could persuade her husband to let their daughter go to Denver.

Hurry, Rafe. Hurry.

"Jenna, Susie needs an operation. She should go to Denver, to a hospital where a doctor can do the surgery."

Jenna closed her eyes and pulled her hands free from

Daisy's grasp. She pressed her fists against her mouth. "We can't afford a hospital."

Daisy touched the other woman's shoulder. "Without the surgery, Susie will die. She must have the operation." She drew a breath. "Never mind the money. Mr. Wild Wind and I will cover the cost of Susie's surgery and hospital stay."

"Whatever will Hank say? He won't stand for it," Jenna wailed and wrung her hands. "I don't mean to complain about what your husband pays his men. I heard Hank talking the other day about the hard times uranium mines are having, so I can't complain about the wages. Your husband is generous to his men. It's just that we can't pay for a hospital, and Hank is proud. He won't want charity."

"I hope Hank will see reason and do what's best for his child."

Footsteps tromping across the porch and male voices in the kitchen announced the arrival of Jenna's husband and Doc Irby. Daisy faced the bedroom door, prepared to do battle.

The men halted just inside the bedroom. Hank, a stocky man of medium height, threw his wife an accusing glare. He jerked his sandy-haired head in Daisy's direction. "What's she doin' here?"

"Your wife sent for me, Mr. Irving. She wanted a second opinion on Susie's condition."

Hank snorted. "We don't need a second opinion. Doc Irby's good enough for us."

"Your daughter is very sick. She has appendicitis."

At that pronouncement, Hank's expression paled. He cast another look at his wife, all belligerence wiped from his face.

Doc Irby stepped forward and tucked his thumbs in his suit jacket pockets. He rocked back on his heels. "Appendicitis, you say? We'll see about that."

Before anyone could stop him, he strode to the bed and

jerked the blanket down about Susie's waist. His plump fingers strayed over her stomach, pressing as they moved. When he reached her right side, Susie cried out. The doctor felt the spot once more, then twitched the covers back over her form. He turned on his heel and addressed Hank Irving, ignoring Daisy as though she were a first-year medical student along for observation.

"There's nothing wrong with your daughter that a purge and a dose of my Patent Medicine won't cure. There's no need to get all worked up over a bout of constipation." He reached into an inner pocket of his suit jacket and withdrew a flat green bottle. "Here you go. Give her a teaspoon of that tonight and bran for breakfast, and Susie will be right as rain in a day or two."

Fury exploded in Daisy's chest. Dr. Irby's treatment would most certainly result in Susie's death. She flung herself between the doctor and Hank Irving and faced the doctor. "Susie has an infected appendix and needs surgery. Your treatment will kill her."

Behind his spectacles, Doc Irby's eyes glittered, and his veined cheeks reddened. His walrus moustache quivered. "My dear young lady, I don't understand why you think you're qualified to diagnose anyone. Women are meant to be nurses, nothing more. Leave the doctoring to us men."

Daisy gripped her hands together to keep from hitting the good doctor right in his sneering mouth. She reminded herself that as a God-fearing woman, she couldn't say the words piling up behind her clenched teeth and clamped her lips shut to prevent herself from saying something she'd regret later. Still, Susie's life hung in the balance, and she'd fight for the child as best she could.

She drew herself up to her full height, feeling more than ever disadvantaged by her short stature. "Dr. Irby, I'm a fully qualified physician. I hold a medical degree from one of the best universities in the country. I'm more than qualified to diagnose a case of appendicitis. Susie has appendicitis, and if she doesn't have surgery, her appendix will rupture."

Susie moaned and closed her eyes. Hank crossed to his wife's side and curled an arm about her shoulders. "Doc Irby is a good doctor, Jenna. I'm sure he knows what's best."

Daisy whirled away from the doctor toward the Irvings. "He doesn't know what's best! If you listen to him, your daughter will die."

"Tut, tut, my dear. Much ado about nothing." Doc Irby pursed his lips.

"Don't you 'my dear' me!" Daisy spun toward the doctor and curled her hands into fists. Her eyes flashed.

The doctor turned his attention to Hank and Jenna, who huddled together near the bed. "Your daughter is experiencing a simple case of constipation, nothing more. It's a very common complaint of young children. There's no need to work yourselves into a tizzy."

Daisy was about to launch into a hot reply when a familiar male voice spoke from the bedroom doorway.

"Daisy, what's going on here?" Rafe towered in the aperture, a figure of calm command that cooled frayed tempers by his very presence.

She wilted with relief. Rafe would use his position as the city's foremost citizen and Hank's employer to talk sense into the man. "Rafe, Susie has appendicitis. She must go to Denver, where she can have surgery, or she'll die. Doc Irby insists that she's only constipated."

Rafe raked the bedroom's occupants with a piercing stare. Hank and Jenna remained mute when his perusal fell on them. Though he puffed out his chest in a show of bravado, Doc Irby shriveled to silence beneath Rafe's silent challenge.

Rafe dismissed the doctor with a shake of his head and turned his attention to Daisy. "What makes you think she has appendicitis?"

She rattled off Susie's symptoms.

Rafe listened with an intent expression. When Daisy had finished, he asked, "You're sure she has an inflamed appendix?"

"As positive as I can be without opening her up."

Rafe took a step toward the Irvings and addressed his employee. "Hank, you're Susie's father, so you're the person who has the final say in her treatment, but if Susie were my daughter, I wouldn't want to take a chance that Doc Irby might be wrong."

Every adult in the room thought of Molly. Rafe understood the loss of a child.

Hank flushed. "Jenna and me, we can't afford a hospital or surgery."

"Can you put a price tag on a child's life?" Rafe let his words settle between them before he continued. "I'll pay the hospital and surgical fees. I'll even fly your daughter to Denver." He propped his fists on his hipbones. "You and Jenna go down the mountain on the train and stay with Susie until she can go home. Don't worry about losing your job. I'll see that you still have work when you get back."

"What about Davey and the other children?"

Jenna gripped her husband's shirt front. "They can go to my sister's house. Let's do as Mr. Wild Wind says."

After a moment's indecision, Hank nodded. "All right. Fly Susie to Denver, Mr. Wild Wind. Jenna and me, we'll follow by train."

Doc Irby stalked from the house in high dudgeon, muttering beneath his breath. He glared at Daisy when he brushed past.

A mad scramble to prepare Susie for the trip followed.

Before Rafe left to ready his plane for the trip, he pulled Daisy aside. "Go to the house and get together some things for us. Just pack a few essentials. We'll have an extra passenger for this trip. Susie doesn't weigh much, but every extra pound counts."

Rafe pushed open the screen door and jogged down the porch steps. Daisy returned to the bedroom and drew Susie's father away from the bedside.

"Mr. Wild Wind has gone to get his plane ready for the trip. I'll go to our house and pack a few things. You and Jenna let Susie know what we're doing and dress her warmly. She'll need a blanket, as well. It will be cold in the plane. When she's ready, carry her down to the hanger."

Hank Irving gripped Daisy's hand. "Thank you and your husband, Mrs. Wild Wind, for helping Jenna and me. We're grateful." He paused and gave her a weak grin. "And if you're wrong about the appendicitis, then Susie will have enjoyed a plane ride, and Jenna and I'll have a trip to Denver."

Daisy returned the pressure of his hand, covering their joined hands with her other one. "Thank you for entrusting Susie to us. We'll take good care of her. I know the surgeons at the Denver hospital, and Susie will get the best care possible. You'll find I'm not wrong about the appendicitis." She extracted her hand from his grip. "You and Jenna enjoy yourselves while you're in Denver. Take some time off to see some things. I recommend strolling around the lake at Denver Park. That's where Mr. Wild Wind took me when we first went out together."

"Denver Park. I'll remember that." Hank's mouth curled in a genuine grin. "I think Jenna would enjoy a walk around the lake."

"She would. You can rent bicycles, too, or a boat. And there are booths that sell hot chocolate on cold days. You can buy popcorn, or funnel cake."

"We'll make it a real vacation, when we aren't with Susie."

"You do that. Now, I must go and pack. Don't you worry about Susie."

CHAPTER 29

Rafe shut the door of their luxurious Grande Palace suite and dropped the brown leather valise at his feet. Before Daisy could blink, he whirled her close. She curled her arms about his waist and buried her face in his flyboy's jacket, enjoying the intimacy of being in his embrace. His husky voice spoke into her ear.

"What would you say to a few days in Denver, Mrs. Wild Wind? I thought we should take some time for ourselves, maybe enjoy a second honeymoon." He spent several moments nibbling a leisurely foray across her neck before he continued. "What do you say to that?"

Daisy pushed against his arms enough so she could peer into his face. Her heart beat hard at the warmth evident on his features. "I'd love to, but can you spare the time?"

"I told the mine manager to take over while we're gone. He's not expecting me back for several days."

"You planned this?"

Rafe grinned like a naughty schoolboy caught in a prank. "I figured since we had to go to Denver anyway, we might as well make the most of the opportunity. I think we deserve some time alone together."

Recalling the years they'd spent apart and the few weeks they'd shared since they'd reconciled, Daisy thought some time alone together would be a fine idea, though she couldn't resist the urge to tease. She adopted a mischievous air. "Since we're in Denver, I think I should visit the shops. A new wardrobe would be just the thing to celebrate our marriage. Of course, I'll need jewelry to go with my new outfits. And another purse, as well. I think a purse made of ostrich leather would be the cat's meow."

Rafe growled in her ear, and he tickled her ribs. "You minx. All you're interested in is my money."

Daisy squealed and giggled. "Nope. I didn't marry you for your money."

"If not my money, then you must have married me for my handsome face."

She shook her head. Her blue eyes danced.

"You married me for my muscles?"

She shook her head once more and waltzed out of his arms. "Guess again."

"You married me for my towering intellect."

"Wrong."

Rafe stroked his chin and pretended to ponder. "If you didn't marry me for my money, or my handsome face, or my muscles or brains, why did you marry me?"

"I married you because of your mother."

His mouth dropped open, and his eyes widened. "My mother?"

"Yes, your mother."

"What does my mother have to do with your marrying me?"

Daisy abandoned her teasing and replied in a serious tone.

Her expression turned earnest. "Your mother accepted me into the family the very first time you took me to the Slash L. You didn't warn her that you were bringing me home that first Christmas. You just showed up with me on your arm, yet she never blinked an eye when you presented me to her. She made me feel welcome."

"My mother is good at that."

"She has a warm heart."

"And I'm sure she saw that you were the girl who could tame her fun-loving son."

"I tamed you?"

Rafe snatched her around the waist and pulled her against him. With his hands locked around the small of her back, he gazed down at her with love heating his expression. "Yes, you tamed this bachelor who had vowed no woman would throw a loop over him. I fell for you fast and hard." Not giving her an opportunity to reply, he took her mouth in a long kiss. When he broke away, he pressed her head against his chest and laid his cheek on her hair. "One of the things I liked about you was the fact that you didn't try to rope me in. You never assumed anything."

"I never expected anything." Daisy closed her eyes and enjoyed the feel of his worn flyboy jacket beneath her ear. She breathed in the scent of leather.

"I liked that. I didn't feel hunted. And what I feel for you now is so much deeper than when we first married." Curling a forefinger beneath her chin and tipping her head back, Rafe kissed her again. "Now, Mrs. Wild Wind, let's get down to some serious honeymooning."

Much later, over their linen-draped dinner table in the opulent Grande Palace dining room, Daisy leaned back in her chair. "How did you convince the maître-d to let us dine at this time of the evening?" She gestured toward the other tables. Only a few patrons still lingered over their meals. "Everyone else is finishing up. I'm sure the kitchen is about to close."

Rafe laid down his fork and grinned at her across the table. "I do believe I've mentioned that money talks."

Daisy smiled back. "You act like money grows on trees."

"Money grows in a uranium mine."

She propped her elbow on the table and rested her chin in her palm. She stared at her husband. "I suppose it does."

Rafe reached for her hand. His long fingers curled about her smaller ones. "Daisy."

"Yes, Rafe?"

"What would you think about us flying to the Slash L after we leave Denver instead of going directly back to Summit?"

She perused his intent face. His eyes met hers, unwavering. "Are you ready to face your family now?"

He gave a decisive nod. "It's time for me to go home. It's been too many years since I've been back."

She squeezed his hand. "Going back to the Slash L will make your mother very happy."

"We'll surprise them."

"Your showing up at the Slash L will certainly be a surprise."

"I'll call Cole and let him know when we're arriving. I'll land near the oil wells. That would be the best place for me to bring the aeroplane down. He can meet us there with the motor car and drive us to the ranch house."

"I can't wait to see your mother's face. She'll be especially pleased since your parents weren't able to make the trip to Summit last summer."

"She'll be more pleased to know that I've gotten my heart right with my Heavenly Father."

Daisy ran her thumb over his knuckles and smiled. "That definitely will please her more than anything."

"Both of my parents have been praying for me all these years."

"And I have, as well."

"You've been a steadfast and loyal wife, despite my behavior. I don't deserve you." Rafe's eyes crinkled in a smile. "Have I told you today that I love you, Mrs. Wild Wind?"

Daisy flushed as she thought back to what they'd done together in their hotel room. "I recall you mentioned it a time or two."

"I have years to make up for, so I'll tell you again. I love you, Daisy." He brought her hand to his mouth and kissed her knuckles. "What shall we do tomorrow?"

Daisy thought about all the possibilities that Denver offered. What she'd like more than anything would be to recapture her first boat ride in Denver Park. "Could we rent a boat in Denver Park? I'd like for you to take me rowing."

"Taking you rowing will be my pleasure."

"I should stop by the hospital first and check on Susie before we do anything else."

"We can do that."

"She'll be lonely and afraid until her parents get here."

Rafe's expression turned serious. "Hank will be glad he listened to you. If he'd followed Doc Irby's advice, Susie would have died."

"You convinced him to listen to me."

"I convinced him when I told him we'd cover all his expenses."

"The surgery and hospital bill will probably total more than he makes in six months."

Rafe frowned. "When we get back to Summit, I'll have a

talk with my bookkeeper. I think it's time to give the married men a raise."

Daisy thought of the financial hardships she'd noticed when she'd visited the miners' homes. "I know you're already a generous employer, but so often there's hardly enough money to go around. The men would be grateful for a raise."

"I'll have to consult with Cole before I institute a raise, since he's my partner."

"Cole will agree with you."

"He will. I'll discuss a raise for the miners with him when we visit the Slash L." Rafe pushed his chair back and rose. With his hand still curled about Daisy's, he pulled her to her feet. "Are you ready to retire, sweetheart?"

His endearment warmed her heart. "Of course. It's been an eventful day." She stifled a yawn. "I just realized how tired I am."

Rafe tugged her against him and tucked her beneath his arm. They strolled toward the dining room exit, hips bumping. Daisy leaned into his warmth, secure in his love.

* * *

Daisy paused on the broad, shallow steps of the Grande Palace's arched red sandstone entrance. Waiting at the curb stood Rafe's dark blue touring car, gleaming in the autumn sunlight. She darted a questioning look at her husband's face. "I didn't mention this yesterday because we were busy getting Susie checked into the hospital, but I'm glad you kept your motor car. Now we don't have to depend on taxis to drive us around Denver."

With playfulness dancing in his eyes, her husband stared down at her. "I couldn't get rid of this old lady after I got back from the war. Though I wouldn't admit it, she held too many memories of our courting days. I couldn't sell her."

"I'd rather trust your driving skills than any taxi driver."

Rafe linked his fingers with hers and hauled her toward the automobile. "It may cost me a pretty penny to store my motor car at the airport, but it's worth the expenditure to me. I despise taking a taxi."

When they reached the vehicle, Rafe tipped the waiting chauffer and dismissed him. He ushered Daisy around to the passenger side and opened the door. "Your carriage awaits, madame."

She paused with one foot on the running board and smiled up into his face. "This reminds me of our courting days when you squired me about Denver. Do you remember the times we left Cole and Garnet to themselves while we went places? The two of us riding in your car almost makes me feel like that girl again. You've thought of everything."

He leaned down and dropped a kiss on her lips. "I try."

She slid into the black leather seat, and he closed the door. Watching while he stepped around to the vehicle's front and spun the crank to start the motor, she basked in the miracle of having the old Rafe back. In the past weeks he'd reverted to the man she'd married, and she loved the way he teased her, just as he had before the war.

With the engine chugging, Rafe jogged to the driver's side door and climbed in. He curled one hand about the steering wheel and gripped the gear shift with the other, then slid a look at her. "I considered buying a motor car with one of those new electric starter buttons, but since I'm not in Denver much, I didn't think a new car worth the money. I can still crank this lady."

Daisy patted the dashboard. "I have a sentimental attachment to this car. I'm glad you didn't turn her in for a new model."

They spent some time with Susie at the hospital before Rafe took Daisy to a boutique. He parked the motor car beside the sidewalk that fronted the shop. "We left Summit with just one satchel of clothes between us, so you'll get your new wardrobe." Leaning toward her, he adopted a mock threatening air as he wrapped one hand around the back of her neck and tugged her toward him until their noses almost touched. "Just don't expect me to drop big bucks for you to buy an ostrich leather purse. I'll carry you out of the shop over my shoulder if you even look twice at one."

Unfazed by his threat, Daisy patted his cheek. "I know better than to believe that. You're just a softie on the inside. I could buy two ostrich leather purses, and you'd only grumble while you paid for them."

Rafe turned his head into her hand and pressed a kiss on her palm, then leaned his forehead against hers. "And I know you well enough to know that you won't beggar me by buying two ostrich leather purses."

Two hours later, they left the shop, each wearing one of their new outfits. Rafe had exchanged his jeans and flannel shirt for a muted plaid wool suit and white shirt. Daisy wore a cinnamon-colored suit of wool knit jersey with a skirt that flared about the hem. Brown Mary Jane shoes clad her feet. A cinnamon knitted cloche hat with two blossoms adorning one side cupped her head.

Rafe stowed their packages in the motor car's boot and ushered his wife into the front seat. When he joined her on the driver's side, he affected a starving air. "All that shopping has given me a powerful appetite. I'm about to expire from hunger. What do you say we have lunch before we go to Denver Park?"

They ate lunch at one of the restaurants they'd frequented during their courtship days. When they'd eaten and sauntered back to the motor car arm in arm and laughing together, Rafe drove them to the park. He pulled the roadster into a shady spot amongst other vehicles and cut the engine.

"Let's rent ourselves a boat."

They strolled toward the lake's shoreline, which curved in a gentle semicircle along the edge of the grass. The encircling trees flamed with autumn foliage. Black metal benches sprouted from the sandy beach. The mingled scents of popcorn, funnel cakes, and coffee teased Daisy's nose. The booths that sold these treats rubbed shoulders with each other along the shore's edge. Cyclists tootled down the trails that followed the shoreline.

Since the day was a Saturday, families enjoyed the mild fall weather. Children scampered about their parents' legs. Their voices and laughter filled the air.

Daisy noticed a young couple with a little boy dressed in wool knickers and knee socks strolling toward the water ahead of them. The mother held a curly-haired infant in her arms. The father gripped his son's hand and matched his strides to the boy's shorter ones. The little boy chattered in a non-ending monologue, while his father answered his questions with good-humored patience.

Seeing the family with their offspring reminded Daisy of her own loss. She cut a glance at Rafe. Her husband's attention riveted on the children. His dark eyes burned, and his mouth curled up in a wistful smile. Rafe's reaction to the children brought remorse for her barren condition crashing over her. She could never give Rafe the children he craved. Regret tarnished the outing's pleasure.

The family stopped at a booth where the father purchased a bag of popcorn. She and Rafe continued to the small white building where rowboats could be rented. At the window, Rafe paid for a boat and collected the oars. They stepped onto the wharf. Their footsteps sounded with a hollow thud on the boards as they walked the length of the dock to where their boat was moored.

Rafe halted beside a white rowboat with red trim about the gunwales. He laid the oars atop the seats and vaulted into the craft's belly. The boat rocked. Reaching up for Daisy, he flashed her a grin, his yearning for children apparently forgotten. "The first time you got into a boat with me, I had to pick you up and put you in."

Daisy shook off her melancholia and attempted to match his humorous mood. "I'd never been in a boat before. I just couldn't make myself step off the dock."

"You didn't trust Cole and me to keep you and Garnet safe."

"The water seemed so deep, and the boat so small. I was convinced it would tip over and spill us into the water."

"You trust me now not to tip us into the water?"

"If I can fly with you, I can trust you not to dump me into the water."

Rafe gripped her about the waist and swung her into the rowboat. She settled on the rear seat, while he sat facing her on the center seat. He clamped the oars in the oarlocks and dipped the paddles in the water. The craft eased away from the dock and nosed out into the lake.

The boat cut through the water as Rafe's strong strokes launched them into the deep. Crystal autumn sunlight danced over the wavelets and spangled the surface with gold.

Daisy watched her husband's shoulders bunch with each stroke and remembered how his muscles felt beneath her hands. Their love in its many forms gave her much pleasure. His gaze caught hers, and he smiled at her, the slow, easy smile he reserved for her alone. His eyes spoke of love and intimacy. She let his gaze snare her for several moments before she wrenched her own away. She couldn't allow him to guess her thoughts, so she broke the thread that bound them and trailed her fingers in the water.

Rafe deserved to have children. Clutching his love to herself must make her the most selfish woman in the world. If she truly loved him, how could she stand in the way of his having a family?

CHAPTER 30

Slash L Ranch
Autumn, 1922

Rafe brought the red biplane down onto the flattened prairie dirt with the precision of a surgeon and the skill learned from thousands of such landings. Each time she flew with him, Daisy marveled at her husband's mastery of the craft.

He appeared beside her cockpit and helped her out. She pulled her leather helmet from her head and tossed the headgear onto the cockpit's canvas seat. Rafe leaped to the ground and lifted her off the wing.

A tall man wearing a sheepskin jacket and a brown felt cowboy hat who had been leaning against a parked motor car approached with long, easy strides. She and Rafe ducked around the wing and met Rafe's older brother. Daisy watched while the brothers greeted each other with grins and backslapping. At first glance, the two brothers might have been mistaken for twins. In appearance they resembled each other like two figures cut from the same pattern.

After he'd greeted his brother, Cole turned to her and swung her off her feet in a bear hug. "I'm glad to see you brought this brother of mine around, little sister. The old Rafe is back."

Daisy gripped Cole's shoulders and laughed up at him. "The old Rafe is definitely back, but I can't take any of the credit. The Lord did it all."

Cole set her down and cocked an eye at his sibling. "Now that's a true statement. My little brother always was a stubborn critter, once he took a notion. Only the Lord could knock some sense into his hard head."

Rafe shrugged at their banter and didn't reply, but a shadow darkened his face. Daisy thought it time to turn the conversation into other channels.

"Where's Garnet? I thought she might come with you."

"She wanted to, but to keep your visit a secret, she got Mother involved in developing a new recipe for barbeque sauce. We all know cooking isn't one of my mother's housekeeping skills, so Garnet thought a new recipe would be enough of a diversion to prevent Mother from wondering what we were up to."

"Your mother is a difficult woman to surprise."

The brothers exchanged a sheepish look.

Cole spread his hands in an acknowledging gesture. "Somehow she always seems to figure out our secrets."

"And I'm sure your father knows we're coming."

"I don't even try to keep a secret from him. He knows what we're all doing before we do."

Daisy had learned early on that the sibling's half-Cheyenne father possessed the uncanny ability to anticipate the actions of anyone on the ranch. The capacity to foresee peoples' behavior must have had its roots in his warrior training. No one ever tried to hide anything from the former Dog Soldier.

Cole spoke up. "Well, let's get your luggage loaded and head back to the house. If we hurry, we can make it in time for lunch."

While the men transferred their bags from the aeroplane to the motor car, Daisy looked out over the prairie's swells.

A line of oil derricks marched like triangular wooden skeletons across the prairie, their gaunt silhouettes poking upward into the blue Colorado sky. Daisy remembered the first time Rafe had brought her here to see the oil wells which provided much of the Slash L wealth. She'd been a timid girl then, not daring to hope that her handsome escort might harbor a romantic interest in her. So much of life had passed since those innocent days. She felt like a different person from the unassuming girl she'd been when she'd been Garnet's maid.

They piled into the automobile, with Daisy in the back seat. The motor car chugged along the track that would take them to the ranch headquarters, passing white-faced Herefords grazing on the withered prairie grass.

As the vehicle navigated the dirt road that wound over the vast rangeland, she listened with half an ear to the men's conversation.

"The price of beef is down, so we've taken a hit with the cattle. We've let some of the single men go." Cole cocked his head toward a group of white-faced cows bunched on a hillock not far from the lane. "The slump in beef prices has affected our Quarter horse sales. Ranchers just don't need as many cow ponies these days."

"So, what are you doing about it?"

"Jake has started breeding horses for speed. One day, not

too far in the future, we hope, there will be formal Quarter horse racing. We intend for Slash L Quarter horses to be first in the racing market. Once we get a good crop of racing-quality Quarter horses, we intend to begin promoting the idea of professional Quarter horse races."

"That's not an impossibility. Ranchers and cowboys have been racing their horses ever since ranching got established. Organized racing is just a matter of time."

"And we intend to make a name for the Slash L in the racing world."

"Jake keeps up with what's happening in the Quarter horse circles. He'll make sure the venture succeeds."

Jake was Cole's and Rafe's older half-brother from their mother's first marriage to their father's own half-brother. Jake had taken over the horse side of the vast Slash L enterprise when his stepfather assumed the role of the ranch's head after Clint Logan's death. Daisy reflected on the tangled skein that bound her husband's family together. To outsiders, the family appeared to be a complicated web of relationships. Family members accepted their unusual situation as something natural and shrugged away any resulting snarls.

Daisy's wandering attention returned to the men when their conversation pivoted to another topic.

Rafe addressed his brother. "How is Aunt Coral managing without Uncle Clint?"

"Aunt Coral is a tough lady, but she and Uncle Clint had been married a long time, and they were devoted to each other. She misses him very much."

"And Mother?" Clint Logan had been their mother's uncle and like a father to his orphaned niece.

"She took his death hard."

Rafe nodded and lapsed into silence.

Daisy leaned into the back seat's corner behind Cole and

dozed. The long ride to the ranch headquarters gave her time for a nap.

Rafe's hand on her knee roused her. Her husband had twisted toward her over the front seat's back and squeezed her knee. "Wake up, sleepyhead. We're here."

Daisy gave him a drowsy smile and sat up, then leaned forward and peered out the window. They'd reached the cattle headquarters located outside of the main ranch compound. The motor car eased down the road between the ranch buildings. A complex of barns, blacksmith shops, and corrals greeted them at the prairie's edge, followed by the bunkhouse and cookhouse for the single ranch hands. On the opposite side of the road stood the commissary, schoolhouse that served as a church on Sundays, and married men's houses.

Children played in the schoolyard. Rafe gave a long look at the youngsters when the motor car rolled past. Another stab of remorse at her barrenness filled Daisy.

They reached the adobe wall that encircled the original ranch headquarters. In the Slash L's early days, the wall had served as protection from marauding tribesmen. Now the stockade served a more ornamental function. The automobile chugged between the compound gate's tall pillars and rolled to a stop before the wide veranda steps.

Cole pushed his cowboy hat further back on his head and glanced at his brother. "The family should be at lunch now, so you'll surprise everyone at once."

Cole led the way into the house, a sprawling white clapboard structure with black shutters at the windows. As the family grew, wings had been added on either side, so the house had expanded with the family. Just beyond the foyer, they filed past what had originally been the ranch office on one side and the parlor on the other. Cole stepped into the dining room and paused just beyond the threshold, his hat held against his chest.

Children's chatter and the rumble of adult voices sounded from the room. Daisy gripped Rafe's hand to lend him her support. Returning home for the first time since he'd left to fight in the Great War would be an emotional occasion for him.

"Cole, where have you been? We started the meal without you." Rafe's mother spoke from her position at the end of the table.

Rafe's hand tightened on Daisy's at the sound of his mother's voice.

"I apologize, Mother. I had an errand to run, and I didn't get back in time. I'm glad you didn't hold up the meal for me." Cole's offhand tone didn't hint at the dramatic nature of his errand.

"Ranch meals aren't held up for anyone." His mother's voice chided him.

"I know that, Mother, but I think you'll forgive me when you learn the nature of my errand."

At that cue, Rafe stepped into the dining room and brushed past his brother. He kept Daisy close to his side. His grip on her hand tightened until his fingers bit into hers.

Silence descended on the room. Every face turned toward them. At the far end of the long table, Della Wild Wind gaped at her son. Her face blanched, and for a long moment she sat as if turned to stone.

Mother and son stared at each other until Della shook her head as if to clear it and tossed down her napkin. "Rafe!" She pushed back her chair and launched herself around the table toward him.

Rafe let go of Daisy's hand and met his mother halfway.

His arms closed around her, and he gathered her close. Della buried her face in his jacket and sobbed.

From the other end of the table, a tall, impressive figure rose. Wild Wind made his way to his son and his wife.

Daisy watched the former Cheyenne chieftain approach his son and admitted to herself that, even after all the years since she and Rafe had married, her father-in-law intimidated her. He appeared no less imposing in his flannel shirt and jeans than she imagined he had when he'd worn fringed buckskin leggings and a deerskin tunic. An air of leadership and strength cloaked him, setting him apart from other men, regardless of his dress.

Daisy couldn't imagine what her mother-in-law had felt when this fierce warrior, wearing war paint and clad only in a breech clout, stole her and took her to his village. The years and circumstances had tempered the warrior, but beneath his civilized veneer, Daisy glimpsed the combatant he'd once been.

Wild Wind halted beside his son and laid a hand on his shoulder. Rafe disentangled one arm from his mother and wrapped it about his father's back. The trio stood as an island until other family members crowded around to greet the prodigal.

A tall woman with bobbed golden-red hair left her chair on the other side of the table and circled around the table. Garnet, Daisy's former employer and friend, greeted Daisy with a hug. "It's so good to see you again! When you left here last spring to find Rafe, I wasn't sure how things would turn out between the two of you."

Daisy returned the hug and then stepped back to look her friend up and down. "I had moments when I wasn't sure Rafe would take me back, but we're together again now."

"When we have a few minutes alone, you'll have to tell me all about it."

Daisy nodded and gave her friend another once-over. "I see you're in an interesting condition again."

Garnet looked down at her belly and ran a hand over her bump. A contented smile played about her lips. "Number four is on the way. I told Cole this one must be another boy. I've been feeling movement for weeks now."

"You're getting the family you always wanted."

Garnet glanced at the clan that crowded the dining room and then turned a warm look on her husband. Her hand stroked circles over her stomach. "You of all people know I didn't want any child of mine to grow up alone and without family." She brought her attention back to her friend.

"There's no chance of that here." Daisy couldn't help but laugh even as she and Garnet shared a silent memory of Garnet's own lonely childhood in New York City.

Garnet joined the laughter. "Before we married, Cole warned me about his family. He thought I might be put off by his having so many relatives, but I love it."

Della interrupted them by reaching for Daisy and drawing her into the circle made by her husband and son. Although Rafe's mother was a tall, stylish woman with curly graying hair and beautiful bone structure, Daisy had never felt intimidated by her mother-in-law. Della Wild Wind had always shown her genuine warmth and love.

"Daisy, come here. I want to thank you for not giving up on my son."

Daisy returned her mother-in-law's embrace. "I couldn't give up on him. I love him too much, and our vows included for better or for worse."

Wild Wind, an older version of his sons, sent her a grave

smile. "This cub of mine has found his way home. You have kept the hearth fire warm waiting for him to return."

Daisy returned his smile. "Yes, I couldn't give up on Rafe. I kept the hearth fire burning while I waited for him." She turned her attention to her husband. The look he sent her spoke volumes and made her toes curl inside her Mary Jane shoes. Later, when they were alone, they'd show each other how they'd keep the hearth fires burning now that they were together again.

A petite white-haired woman clad in a black, drop-waisted frock joined their group. Though still beautiful in old age, she appeared fragile despite her erect posture. She took Rafe's hand. "Welcome home, nephew. I never doubted that you'd return one day."

Rafe disentangled himself from his parents' embrace and stooped to enfold the diminutive woman. "Thank you for never giving up on me, Great-aunt Coral. I know I've been a trial to my family."

"My husband taught me the power of forgiveness. There's plenty of that here today."

Rafe set her away from him with his hands on her shoulders and peered into her face. "And how are you doing these days?"

A cloud crossed Coral's face, and her faded eyes betrayed her grief. "Getting through each day without Clint is a struggle, but he's in Heaven now, and to wish him back here with me would be selfish. I have plenty of family to support me."

Rafe glanced at the family who gathered around them. "You do have family."

That comment brought a hoot of laughter from the clan, and from that point on, assorted cousins, siblings, and in-laws besieged Rafe for the rest of the day.

Later, in privacy of their room, Rafe pulled Daisy against

him and held her close. He looked down at her with tenderness. "Thank you for never giving up on me. It was your love and persistence that made today possible. Without you, I would have lived the rest of my life as a frozen husk of a man."

Her gaze traveled over his face. The warm lamplight from a lantern on a table beside the bed cast half his face in shadow. She traced his bold features with gentle fingers. "The Lord would have brought you around another way without me."

"I don't know about that. There's something irresistible about a wife who adores her husband even when he knows he's been wrong." His hand stroked through her hair, then cupped her face. "I should know." His expression heated, and he dipped his head to take her mouth. "What was it you told my father about keeping the hearth fires burning?"

Daisy giggled before his mouth covered hers. "I don't think this is what your father meant when he said that."

With a thumb beneath her chin, Rafe tipped her head up for his kiss. "My father is a wise man. He has many layers, and his words often have several meanings. He knows exactly how important a warm hearth is to a marriage. Now, my dearest wife, let's make our hearth fire hot."

CHAPTER 31

Like a shroud, darkness pressed upon the room. Unable to sleep, Daisy stared at the ceiling. The quilts that draped the bed pressed like a weight upon her. Rafe lay on his side facing her, one hand splayed over her stomach. His steady breathing sounded in her ear.

Around them, the bedroom furniture hulked as blacker shapes in the gloom. Tonight was their last night at the Slash L. These few days at the ranch had helped her husband continue the healing process. He'd reveled in the family's presence, which he'd shunned since the war. She'd watched from the fringe, content to let him garnish the lion's share of attention.

Despite the love the family had showered on them both, a seed of despondency grew. Her defect loomed like a cloud that would mar their future. Would God have restored Rafe to her only to deny him the children her husband desired? Images of Rafe with his family tortured her. He'd spent time playing with his cousins' and siblings' numerous offspring. The children had flocked to him, and each time she watched him give a toddler a ride on his shoulders or stand at the corral fence with Cole's oldest boy discussing horses, her barrenness acted as a goad that pricked her heart.

She turned her head to look at his face, so close to hers. His features appeared as a pale oval in the dimness. Though she couldn't see the details of his countenance, her memory painted each one as though it were visible. She imagined the way his lashes formed dark crescents on his cheeks as he slept, and how the lines in his face smoothed out, making him appear younger than his forty-one years. Tousled hair fell over his forehead. Daisy almost gave in to the impulse to smooth the wayward curls off his face, but she resisted the urge to touch him.

If she cherished him with the love that put the loved one's welfare above one's own, could she chain him to her side when she knew he desired children? Could she continue to revel in his love, which he lavished upon her, when she couldn't give him what he craved most?

Another part of her argued that their marriage vows made a sacred covenant before God that shouldn't be broken. They'd agreed to stay married until death parted them. Even during their four-year long separation, neither of them had taken steps to dissolve their union. Daisy clung to that truth. Though she felt selfish for staying with Rafe when another woman could give him a family, the Biblical principal of marriage overrode all else.

Her indecision put aside, she surrendered to the urge to touch him. Her fingers strayed over his rumpled hair. She loved its soft, springy texture. Her hand then trailed over the curve of his shoulder, feeling sinew beneath her palm. She cupped his smooth muscles, tracing the form that was uniquely *Rafe*. Her husband, her man.

At her touch, he stirred and muttered, though he didn't waken. The hand that splayed over her abdomen roamed to her back and pulled her closer. She rolled onto her side so they lay face to face. Snuggling the blankets around her ears, Daisy sighed and laid her hand on his chest, thrilling at the simple intimacies marriage afforded.

* * *

Cole's motor car chugged to a stop near Rafe's biplane. On the return trip, Daisy sat up front with Cole, while Rafe shared the back seat with his mother. Della Wild Wind hadn't wanted to say her goodbyes at the ranch house and had accompanied her sons to the plane. She'd clutched Rafe's hand during the whole ride.

Cole swiveled to address his brother and laid his arm along the seat's back. "Well, little brother. You survived your first visit to the Slash L. Don't stay away so long next time."

"Daisy and I will be here for Christmas."

"Thank you, Rafe! That will be the best Christmas present you could give me." His mother gave him a tremulous smile. "Having you back at the Slash L will be like old times."

Rafe leaned close and pecked her on the cheek. "You can count on us being here." He freed his hand from her grip and swung out of the vehicle.

Cole transferred the luggage to the plane while Rafe performed his pre-flight check. When everything had been inspected to his satisfaction, Rafe wiped his hands on a rag and strolled to the group watching from beside the motor car.

"We're all set, Daisy. Let's load up."

With Rafe and Daisy settled in the aircraft and the engine throbbing, Rafe taxied the plane into the wind. The biplane trembled and then surged forward when Rafe released the brake. Oil rigs flashed past beside them. Cole's motor car receded into the distance. The craft lifted into the air, and the earth dropped away beneath them.

Rafe circled once over the oil fields and buzzed low over Cole's motor car, waggling the plane's wings. Cole and their mother waved at the biplane cruising overhead.

Rafe turned his crate toward the mountains. The billowing prairie, a patchwork of sere flatland broken by hillocks and ridges, fell away beneath them.

Daisy had worn a wool suit for the trip, but the chill air aloft made her shiver. She tucked a quilt about her legs and thrust her gloved hands between her knees, grateful for her leather flying jacket's warmth.

The engine's monotonous throbbing lulled her into a sleepy half-doze.

Sometime later, a change in the motor's rhythm jerked her into awareness. She peered over the plane's side. They'd left the prairie behind them, and now the Rocky Mountains surrounded them. The aircraft droned between high mountain ridges. A rocky river twisted and foamed in the narrow valley below them. Snow layered the granite peaks that loomed above them. Spruce and fir trees growing on the undulating mountain shoulders thrust their dark green branches toward the sky. On the lower slopes, aspen leaves shimmered like gold coins.

Lulled by the engine's regular cadence, she leaned back in the canvas seat. She'd just closed her eyes when the engine sputtered again, then settled back into its normal tempo. Moments later, the motor coughed several times.

Daisy's heart lurched. Her breathing snagged, and she curled her hands into fists. Her ears must be deceiving her. She must be imaging the engine's faltering stutters. Rafe was a careful mechanic and maintained his aeroplane with meticulous diligence. A mechanical problem couldn't be possible.

Yet, when the motor faltered once more, she had to admit that a mechanical failure might be a possibility. Her imagination wasn't conjuring the spluttering rhythm.

Another cough. The engine hesitated, then caught. The aircraft's throbbing drone sounded like sweet music in Daisy's ears. She breathed again and unclenched her fists. Perhaps they'd arrive in Summit without incident, after all.

Minutes later, the engine coughed, fired, and died. Before her eyes, the propeller slowed and stopped spinning. Silence filled the air. Through her leather helmet's earflaps, only the rush of wind streaming past the aeroplane could be heard.

For the first stunned moment, her brain refused to process the fact that a crash seemed inevitable. Her mind froze. Then, as the biplane began to lose altitude, reality blasted away denial's blessed numbness. They were going down. For whatever reason, they'd crash.

With gruesome clarity, details of every crash landing that Daisy had ever heard about screamed in her head. *Blood. Fire. Broken and smashed bones.* She reined in her galloping imagination and reminded herself that Rafe piloted the aircraft. Rafe, a skilled veteran flyboy who had successfully brought in wounded planes during the war, would navigate the crash in as safe a manner as possible. She prayed as she'd never prayed before, imploring Almighty Providence for safety.

The craft sank earthward, though it still glided onward. The mountains on either side loomed higher as the aircraft lost altitude. The narrow valley that slashed through the ridges rushed up at them. On their left, the tumbling river foamed over rocks and boulders. A narrow ribbon of craggy shoreline rolled past below them. Trees and bushes on the mountains' shoulders to their right nearly brushed the biplane's twin wings.

Somehow, Rafe kept the plane aloft far longer than Daisy imagined possible. The earth skimmed past beneath its wheels, and still, Rafe fought to keep them airborne. When at last the craft sank in its final descent, Daisy gripped the cockpit's rim and braced herself for the impact. Rafe kept the nose up, though the wheels jarred on the flinty shore before they collapsed.

When the aircraft skidded into the earth, the jolt shook Daisy to her bones. Rocks tore at the undercarriage. The craft raked a furrow along the river's edge. A river boulder ripped the left wings from the plane. The fuselage slewed, then righted and plowed on.

Daisy's neck whipped at the ricochet, and her knee smashed against the cockpit's side. The back of her head thudded against the interior partition. The machine shuddered as it continued its mad rush along the shore. The ship hammered against rocks and river debris, which tossed the aeroplane upward before it slammed back against the ground. Fir trees growing from an outthrust knoll grabbed at the aeroplane's right wings and tore them from the frame. A boulder in their path halted the aircraft's advance when the craft smashed into the crag. The crash flung Daisy against the cockpit's front rim, and her forehead collided with the edge. She bounced back against the seat with the crate's abrupt halt.

For a heartbeat she sat motionless, unable to believe that they'd survived, when a finger of flame dancing around the cowling alerted her to imminent danger.

CHAPTER 32

Fire. The very thing Rafe feared most. Her mind raced. If she stayed in the plane just a few moments longer, she very likely wouldn't survive. Her death would free Rafe to marry again. He could still have a family.

Daisy closed her eyes against the flames' mesmerizing vision. Her death would be swift. An explosion would end her life without the prolonged suffering of being scorched. If she loved Rafe enough, she should be willing to make the sacrifice. He deserved to have children.

Rafe's frantic voice sounded in her ears, shaking her from her stupor. He reached over the cockpit's side and jerked at her lap belt's buckle. With the strap freed, he grabbed her arm and hauled her over the cockpit's side. Gripping her hand, he dragged her away from the wreckage in a mad sprint.

Behind them, with a whoosh and a roar, the aircraft exploded. Rafe flung Daisy onto the stony ground and covered her with his body. The impact drove the breath from her lungs and ground her head into the shoreline's pebbled surface. She lay immobile, both winded and scraped.

At last, Rafe rolled off her onto his side, and she lifted her head. Peering over her shoulder, the conflagration that engulfed his red biplane met her gaze. Fire consumed the fuselage. Flames licked at nearby trees. Heat from the blaze rolled toward them and seared their faces. She glanced at her husband, who propped himself on one elbow and stared at the wreckage. His face betrayed no emotion, though she knew he must regret the loss of his aeroplane.

She curled her fingers about his forearm. "Rafe."

He turned his head in a slow arc and met her concerned gaze.

"I'm sorry about your plane."

He shrugged and returned his attention to the inferno. Together, they watched the flames devour the aircraft. When nothing remained except ashes and twisted metal, Rafe shoved to his feet, then reached down and pulled her upright. "Are you hurt?" His fingers feathered over her scratched face and probed the lump on her forehead. "You have a goose egg."

Daisy flinched at his touch. "I hit my head on the cockpit rim."

He ran his hands over her limbs. "I don't think you broke anything."

She shook her head. "I didn't. I'd know it if I did." Reaction set in, and she began to shake. "I think I need to sit down."

Rafe carried her to a nearby knee-high boulder and lowered her onto its smooth surface. When he'd settled beside her and wrapped both arms about her shoulders, he tucked her into his embrace. She nestled her head beneath his chin and closed her eyes. The river's burbling rush sounded in her ears. Songbirds called from the trees. She let nature's peace lap over her in a calming wave. When she felt able to talk, she lifted her head and peered into his face. "Do you have any idea of what happened?"

His chest expanded beneath her when he took a deep breath. "I can only guess the fuel I bought in Denver had some dirt or trash in it. That could have clogged the lines."

Daisy shuddered. "The Lord spared us from death. And I'm very glad I was flying with you and not some other pilot. I can see why Will says you're the best pilot he knows."

Rafe shrugged away her compliment. "The Lord gave me a skill for flying."

They sat in silence for a time before Daisy's curiosity compelled her to ask questions. "Is anyone expecting us in Summit?"

"I called the mine manager from the Slash L office before we left to let him know we were on our way home. When we don't show up, he'll know something's wrong. And I promised my mother I'd telephone the ranch."

"She'll worry when she doesn't hear from you."

"She won't give my father any peace until he sends out a search party. The problem is, they don't know where to look."

"How far are we from Summit?"

"As the crow flies, we're about twenty minutes from there. Since we're on foot and must cross mountainous terrain, we'll have a three to four-day hike."

Daisy contemplated the challenges they'd encounter. "That's another reason I'm glad I'm with you. You know how to trail and live off the land. If anyone can get us safely home, you can."

Rafe ruffled her hair and gave her a one-armed squeeze. "When Cole and I were growing up, learning to track and survive off the land was a lark. Who knew that my father's training would be put to good use one day?" He gave her another once-over. "You scraped your knee. We should clean it."

For once, Daisy ignored her medical skills and let Rafe care for her. Letting him carry her to the river's edge and seat her on a rock, then bathe all her scrapes with his flyboy's white scarf seemed like bliss. The water stung, but Daisy sucked in a breath and told herself not to be a sissy. When he'd cleaned her injuries, Rafe squatted before her and patted her face and knee dry with the other end of his scarf. When he'd finished, he curved his palm about the back of her calf and looked into her face.

His eyes darkened with emotion. "If anything had happened to you in that crash, I don't think I could have lived with myself."

She tangled her fingers in his hair and leaned forward to kiss him. "We both survived, thank God."

Rafe wrapped a hand around her neck and took control of the kiss. Their joy at having survived a crash landing lent the kiss a fervor that shook them both. They gloried in life and loving. Rafe broke off the kiss and buried his face in the curve of her neck. His hand clenched in her hair. "Daisy, Daisy. You're the most precious thing in my life. I was an idiot to waste those four years away from you. This brush with death has given me a whole new perspective."

She wrapped her arms about his shoulders and nodded against his cheek. "We'll make up the time."

"The Lord has given us another chance. I mean to make the most of what He's given us."

After a moment, Rafe pushed back and looked into her face. "We should leave now and try to make as much distance as we can before dark. Can you walk?"

Daisy flexed her knee. "I think so. I'm afraid I'll slow you down, though."

"No matter." Rafe pushed aside his leather jacket and patted the Colt that hung from a gun belt about his waist. "I have matches for a fire and enough ammunition to keep us fed, even if we take a week to walk out of here."

They set out traveling west along the river's course. Unable to put much weight on her injured leg, Daisy hobbled at a snail-like pace. Reluctant to admit how much walking pained her, she gritted her teeth and kept putting one foot in front of the other. With an arm about her and half supporting her, Rafe matched his strides to her limping gait.

They spent the night in a protected hollow, leaning against a tree, and dined on roasted rabbit. The night grew chilly as the moon climbed into an obsidian sky. Their breaths hung like vapor in the chilly air. Daisy huddled within her husband's embrace. Rafe's arms about her and a campfire kept them from freezing.

Four days later, they made their slow way along a ridge on the lower slope of a mountain. Aspen leaves showered them like golden rain and made a carpet for their feet. Daisy wrapped her legs about Rafe's waist and clung to his neck, giving him the appearance of a misshapen gorilla. By the second day, her knee had throbbed with such painful intensity she could scarcely hobble, so Rafe had knelt before her and instructed her to climb onto his back. With him carrying her piggyback, they'd made better progress than when she'd tried to walk.

Now Rafe halted. He lowered her to a sitting position and propped her against an aspen tree's smooth, pale bole, then stretched the kinks out of his back. "Will you be all right if I leave you here for a bit? I'd like to scout around."

Daisy nodded and rested her head against the tree. "I'll be fine." She surveyed her husband between narrowed lids.

A dark growth of beard obscured his jawline. Dirt

smudged his jeans. Snags and stains marred his white flyboy's scarf. He resembled a disreputable smuggler, but despite his deplorable appearance, he oozed strength. She felt safe, no matter that wilderness surrounded them.

Brushing aside his leather jacket, Rafe loosened the thong on his holster and pulled out the Colt. He held the weapon out to her, butt first. "I'll leave my six shooter with you. Do you remember how to use it?"

"I can use it if I have to." She took the revolver from him and laid the weapon in the leaves at her side.

He stood over her, his fists braced on his hips, and stared down at her. "If you need me, fire off two shots in a row."

"All right."

Rafe didn't move. He still stared at her, indecision plain on his face.

Daisy made a shooing motion with her hands. "Go. I'll be fine."

He stooped and kissed her, then straightened. "I won't be long." He wheeled and set off up the ridge at a jog.

When he'd disappeared over the summit, Daisy fingered the lump on her forehead. The injury still pained her, though she hadn't mentioned that fact to Rafe. If she had a mirror and could see her reflection, she guessed that her forehead would sport a colorful purple and yellow bruise. Rafe had jokingly informed her that she looked like a boxer who'd come out on the losing end of a match.

Next, she felt the tender spot at the back of her head. A lump had developed there, as well. Her head had ached ever since the crash, but she didn't think she had a concussion.

She closed her eyes and tipped her head back against the tree again, taking care to avoid the bruise beneath her hair. She wrapped her arms around her and huddled into her jacket. In the mountain elevation, nighttime temperatures dipped into the lower range. During the day, bright sunlight at least lent the illusion of warmth as long as they kept moving.

Rafe had done his best to keep them toasty when they'd stopped for the night. He'd built their campfires in sheltered places. Leaves or evergreen branches had served as a cover for them while they'd slept. Her husband's woodsman's skills had kept them alive. Still, as grateful as she was for Rafe's knowledge, she'd be glad when they reached Summit.

She inspected the wool skirt Rafe had purchased for her in Denver. Dirt smudges and leaf stains soiled the fabric. A three-corner tear where she'd snagged the skirt on a fallen tree branch marred one side. The strap of one of her Mary Jane shoes had broken. She scratched her itching head and grimaced. A long soak in a hot bath, a shampoo, and clean clothes would make her feel human again.

Daisy had lost track of how long she'd been sitting there, half dozing, when her eyes flashed open at the sound of male voices. As far as she knew, she and Rafe were the only people for miles in any direction. Should she call out to get the men's attention, or remain motionless and hope they didn't see her? She sat in tense silence with one hand wrapped about the six-shooter's grip and held her breath as the voices came closer.

Daisy clutched the aspen's trunk and struggled to rise. If the men encountered her, she preferred to meet them on her feet instead of seated on the ground. With one hand braced against the tree for balance, she rested her weight on her good leg and managed to stay upright. With the weapon concealed at her side, she waited.

Bundled in jeans and sheepskin jackets, several male figures appeared between the trees. She recognized Rafe in the lead and wilted against the aspen's trunk.

When the group halted before her, Rafe pulled the Colt

from her limp fingers and jerked a thumb toward the men. "I ran into a search party who has been looking for us."

Cole stepped forward and swept her up into a hug. "I'm so thankful you're safe."

Daisy hugged him back. "What are you doing here?"

"When Rafe didn't call the ranch the day you left to let us know you'd gotten home, my mother telephoned the mine office. The mine foreman admitted that Rafe's plane hadn't arrived in Summit and was overdue. When you still weren't back the next morning, my mother wouldn't rest until she'd convinced Father that something had happened to the plane. We drove to Denver and took the train to Summit. No plane crashes had been reported over the prairie, so we assumed that you must have gone down in the mountains closer to Summit. We set out looking for you from the town."

"I'm thankful you listened to your mother, and I'm so glad to see you."

Cole squeezed her again and released her. "We're glad to see you, too, little sister." He grinned and pointed to the lump on her forehead. "Even if you look like a purple-faced raccoon with two black eyes."

Daisy turned to the other men clustered about her and Cole. These men worked for Rafe, miners who had volunteered their time to search for them. She gave them a warm smile. "Thank you all for helping Cole search for us."

They returned her smile with shy looks and shuffled their feet.

Cole pulled a six shooter from its holster and fired three shots into the air. "Father is heading up another search party. We thought if we divided into two groups, we had a better chance of finding you. These shots are a signal to Father that you've been found. He should join us as soon as he locates us."

Early in the evening, the weary search parties straggled down Summit's main street. Shadows pooled between buildings. Lights shone from café windows and cast golden oblongs across the boardwalk. A chilly evening breeze wafted from the mountain peaks as they trailed along the walkway. The men looked unkempt, disheveled, and dirty. A makeshift stretcher, constructed of sapling poles thrust through the sleeves of two jackets, carried Daisy. Her husband and Cole held the poles' ends.

Their progress along the boardwalk gathered attention. Diners leaving Katie's Café watched the group trudge past. Word of their safe return must have spread, for they hadn't yet reached Montgomery's Emporium when Katie sprinted toward them from her café. As she reached the stretcher and came to a halt, she grabbed her friend's hand. Her eyes widened when she spied Daisy's colorful lump.

"Daisy, I was so worried. Thank God you're safe. Are you hurt very badly?"

Daisy looked up into Katie's worried face and squeezed her hand. "No. My knee is bruised, so I can't walk. The rest are just scrapes and bumps."

"I'm so glad to hear it. Now, if I can do anything for you, anything at all, you let me know."

Daisy squeezed Katie's hand once more. "I promise."

They continued past the hotel and the church. Miners turned off toward their own homes, leaving the three Wild Wind men and Daisy.

As they neared the end of the road, Edith rose from a porch rocker at her rented house and hurried down the steps. She stopped beside Rafe, stylish as always in a dusty blue wool jersey suit and matching jacket. "I was so worried when I heard that your aeroplane had crashed. I'm glad you're safe."

Rafe tipped his head in her direction and acknowledged her greeting with a weary nod. "Thank you. And Daisy is safe, too."

Edith spared a glance for Daisy. "And you, too, Daisy."

Daisy tried to be gracious. "Thank you, Edith. I'm alive only because of Rafe."

Edith couldn't seem to help herself. She clutched Rafe's arm. "You could have died."

Rafe shrugged her hand away. "I could have, but I didn't. Thank you for your concern, but we need to get Daisy inside. She's been injured."

Edith stepped back a pace. "Of course. I just wanted to welcome you home."

The door to Rafe's house opened, and Della Wild Wind erupted onto the veranda. When she saw the group in the street, she skimmed down the steps and flew to her son's side. "Rafe!"

Since both hands clutched the ends of the sling's poles, Rafe couldn't return his mother's frantic embrace, so he bent his head and bussed her on the cheek. "Mother. I hear you set the cavalry on us."

"I knew something was wrong when you didn't call the ranch. Mothers have a way of knowing these things."

Rafe managed an exhausted chuckle. "I won't argue with that."

Della Wild Wind loosened her hold on her son. Turning to Daisy, she bent over the stretcher and patted her daughter-in-law's cheek. "I see you took a nasty bump when you crashed, but we'll fix you right up. My husband's people have an herbal salve that will heal you in no time."

Her mother-in-law's solicitude proved to be the final straw that swept away Daisy's desperate grip on her composure. She couldn't stop the tears that sprang to her eyes and dripped down her temples into her hair. Words refused to form.

Rafe's mother patted her cheek again. "Don't try to talk. You've had a terrifying experience and are worn to the bone. You'll feel better after a hot bath and some food." Della Wild Wind straightened and turned a stern eye on her son. "Rafe, get your wife inside so we can take care of her."

Rafe grinned down at his mother. "Of course, Mother." He tightened his grip on the poles' ends, ready to carry Daisy into the house.

The group trudged up the veranda steps, taking care not to tip Daisy off the stretcher, and left Edith alone in the street.

CHAPTER 33

Summit, Colorado
Late Autumn, 1922

Daisy leaned over the sink and peered out the kitchen window. She watched as Rafe strolled up the street toward the mine with his loose, easy stride. Her hungry gaze burned over his tall form, from his black cowboy hat, short jacket, and jeans to his low-heeled boots. She loved him so much that just the sight of him made her heart thump with exquisite pain and closed her throat. Her love made her doubt her ability to carry out her plan.

When Rafe made an abrupt turn toward the house instead of continuing to the mine's office, Daisy drew back from the window. A moment later, she heard his boot heels pound up the steps and thud across the veranda. The door opened.

"Daisy!" Her husband's voice bellowed through the house.

She hurried into the great room. "I'm here. What's wrong?"

Rafe lunged at her. He scooped her up and twirled her about, then grinned down at her. "Nothing. I got the notion to pay my wife a visit before I returned to the office."

Daisy took pleasure in the feel of his arms around the small of her back and his chest against hers. She wrapped her arms about his neck and peered into his face. His eyes crinkled in a smile. She laughed up at him. "Silly man. What kind of a notion is that?"

"A very good notion. I had a yearning to kiss my wife."

She gripped his hat brim and swept off the headgear, then flipped it toward a nearby chair. She thrust her fingers into his hair. "Well, what are you waiting for?"

"I'm not sure. What am I waiting for?"

"While you're figuring it out, I'll kiss you." Daisy leaned closer and went up on tiptoe.

"No, you don't. I came here to kiss you."

"Well, then. You'd better get on with it."

His eyes heated, and he bent his head. His mouth covered hers, and for the moment, Daisy forgot her plan. Rafe's kiss made her forget everything except the two of them, ensnared by passion. When Rafe finally lifted his head, he left her breathless. She dropped her forehead against his chest and waited for her pulse to quiet.

"I ought to have a notion like this more often." His husky voice sounded above her head.

"Mmm . . ." She couldn't speak.

Rafe let her slide down his front until her feet touched the floor. "As much as I'd like to continue this, I have a meeting with my accountant. I'd better go." He gave her a peck and snatched his hat from the chair. After jamming it on his head, he paused by the door. With exquisite tenderness, he traced her lips with his thumb. "I'll try to get home early tonight, and we can pick up where we left off."

Daisy nodded and savored his gentle caress. She watched as he turned to leave, then flung a question at his back. "Is Will still here?"

Her husband paused with one hand on the doorknob and glanced at her over his shoulder. "He's getting ready to leave now."

"I think I'll run down to the hanger and say goodbye."

"He'd like that."

When Rafe had gone, Daisy leaned against the door and closed her eyes. Her legs threatened to collapse beneath her. The thought of the scheme she was about to set in motion terrified and grieved her. In the few weeks since the plane crash, she and Rafe had grown closer together. She gloried in his love, yet guilt at her barrenness gnawed at her. If she truly loved Rafe, she should set him free to make a life with someone else who could give him the family he deserved.

She pushed away from the door and flew up the stairs to their bedroom. At the dresser mirror, she borrowed Rafe's comb to tidy her hair. When she'd styled her hair so that her sunny tresses framed her elfin face and tucked under her chin, she laid down the comb and inspected her reflection. Her drop-waisted emerald-green wool frock hung straight from her shoulders to her knees. Leaning closer to the mirror, she scrutinized her face. The pale image that stared back at her betrayed the gravity of her plan. She pinched her cheeks to give them color and whirled away from the looking glass.

Daisy paused long enough to pull her hip-length coat from the wardrobe and shrug into the garment before she skimmed down the stairs. She hurried outside before she could turn craven and change her mind. Her reluctant feet took her down the street and to the airfield where she'd find Will.

Since last August's festival, Will had developed the habit of flying into Summit every couple of weeks during his mail run. True to his word, when the Postal Service issued Will his new Standard JR-1B biplane, he'd flown the crate to Summit.

Rafe had been like a boy with a new toy.

Daisy's thoughts took her back to how Rafe had circled the craft and run his hands along its lacquered sides. He'd caressed the arched wings and commented on the reinforced tail skid. He and Will had removed the cowling and discussed the engine, one of the best available. The Standard's engine could haul the plane at faster speeds than other kinds of airships could achieve.

Will had let Rafe test fly the aircraft, and her husband had fallen in love with the aeroplane.

Her memories lent a bittersweet tang to her mission.

The autumn sun gleamed in the mountain air. The aspen and maple trees on the lower slopes had shed their leaves and now lifted skeletal branches to the sky, while the encircling peaks wore snow's sugary mantle. The view caught at Daisy's heart. After she left Summit, she'd miss the beauty of the season's changes.

When Daisy reached the airfield, Will was finishing his pre-flight inspection. As she approached, he wiped his hands on a rag and stuffed the cloth into a back pocket of his tan flying jodhpurs. He strolled toward her and grinned down at her, his hazel eyes glinting.

"To what do I owe this honor? I thought we said goodbye at lunch."

Daisy tried to return his smile and failed. She attempted to adopt a breezy attitude and failed at that, as well.

Will took a closer look at her face. "Daisy, what's wrong? Has something happened to Rafe?"

She shook her head and gulped. "No, Rafe is fine." She sucked in a breath. "Will, do you remember last summer when you told me that if I needed help, to ask you?"

Though he nodded, a wary expression crossed his face. A lock of curly auburn hair fell over his brow. He shoved the strands off his forehead with one hand.

Daisy took a breath and plowed on. "I need your help."

"All right. What kind of help do you need?" With his features set in a guarded cast, Will planted his booted feet wide and scrutinized her.

Daisy raised her gaze to his face. She gulped again and forced out the words in a rush. "I need you to help me leave Rafe."

Shock replaced the wariness on Will's handsome countenance. Grabbing Daisy's arm, he whirled her around his aeroplane's wings toward the back of his plane. He jerked her against the white canvas fuselage and pinned her there. With an outstretched arm on either side of her head, he glared down at her. "What did you just say?"

Daisy jutted her chin at him. "I said, I need you to help me leave Rafe."

"That's what I thought you said. Lady, have you lost your mind? Rafe is crazy about you."

"I know. And I'm crazy about him."

"Then what's the problem?"

Daisy met his fierce stare. "I can't give him more children."

Will let out an explosive breath and spun away. He took one step and pivoted, arms crossed, and scowled at her from beneath lowered brows. "Has Rafe complained about that?"

She shook her head. "He hasn't blamed me, but I know

he's disappointed. He loves children, and he deserves to have a family."

Will stared at her for a moment. Tension twanged in the air between them. "I won't ask why you can't give Rafe more children. It's none of my business, but I can't imagine it would be enough for Rafe to want to dissolve your marriage."

"It's not him. It's me. I must give him a chance to have a family with someone else."

Will stepped closer and loomed over her. Once again, he caged her between his outstretched arms and spoke through clenched teeth. "No. I won't do it."

Daisy quailed, though she refused to let Will see how he intimidated her. She gave him back his stormy glare with one of her own. "You promised to help me."

"Not with something like this." Will looked her up and down. His expression softened a bit. "Daisy, I'll admit I envy Rafe for the fact that you love him. If anything happened to him and you were left alone, I'd be the first man in line to offer you marriage."

Will's admission ratcheted up the tension between them. Daisy gaped at him. She closed her mouth. "Thank you, Will. That's very kind."

He snorted. "Kindness has nothing to do with it." With a shake of his head, he shoved off the plane's fuselage and stepped back. "But Rafe is very much alive, and I won't do anything to come between you. I won't help you leave him."

She gripped her hands together. "Please listen to me. I have it all worked out. I'll take the train to Denver one morning when Rafe is busy with the mine. All I need you to do is to fly me from Denver to another city where Rafe won't find me. I can't stay in Denver. He'll look for me there. I can get a job in a hospital in New York. I have family in the city."

"This is the most hair-brained scheme I've ever heard."

Will brooded and leveled a dark stare at her. "Have you discussed this with Rafe?"

"No." Her voice sounded small to her ears.

"I suggest you discuss the situation with him to find out how he really feels before you go haring off alone."

"You know how Rafe is. He'll do the honorable thing and tell me that us not having children doesn't matter."

"Lady, what you're doing isn't honorable." Will let the brutal truth hang in the air between them. "Have you considered the fact that Rafe might not remarry?"

Rattled by Will's blunt words, Daisy tried to speak with more confidence than she felt. "He will. He wants children."

"So you think, but you haven't brought up the matter with him to find out for sure."

Put like that, the weakness in her argument glared at her. Still, she'd made up her mind, and she wouldn't shy away from this opportunity for Rafe to have a family. She pressed both palms against the plane's skin and pleaded. "Won't you help me?"

Will pivoted and presented his back to her. With his hands on his hips, he stood as resistant as an inflexible statue and stared past the hanger to the mountain peaks. He didn't reply.

Daisy eyed his back and gave him time to consider before she spoke again. "If you won't help me, I'll find someone who will."

Will spun and stalked toward her, then halted. He cocked an eyebrow at her. "You're just stubborn enough to do it, too." Crossing his arms, he eyed her with a meditative stare. His mouth formed a hard line.

Daisy returned his gaze and waited for him to speak. Although shudders rippled through her, she refused to abandon her scheme. Rafe deserved a family.

Will took two steps toward her and propped his fists on

his hips. He impaled her with a glare. "You don't seem the type to run. I had you pegged as a gal who could face anything."

Daisy goggled at him. "Run? What do you mean, run?"

"Well, what do you think you're doing? You think you can't give Will children, so you're going to bail on your marriage. You'd *leave* him? That's running, in my book."

Chills shivered down her spine. "I'm not running, I tell you." His logic speared her heart, a dart whose aim struck true. Gulping in a breath, she squeezed her eyes closed against the tears that threatened. When she could speak without breaking down, she opened her eyes again.

Will hadn't moved, though his face wore a rueful look. When he caught her watching him, he wiped his features clean of all expression.

"I'm not running." Daisy's shoulders slumped. She might never recover from the sacrifice she was about to make. Tipping up her head, she met Will's gaze and stretched her hands toward him. "I love Rafe so much, I won't stand in his way. I'm getting out of his way so he can have a family. Don't you see? It's because I love him that I'm leaving him." She swallowed.

Will rumpled his hair with both hands. "Daisy. . . I see your point, but you can't do it." He lowered his hands and sighed.

"Why can't I? It's the right thing to do." Pain stabbed her heart even as she spoke. "I must stop thinking about me, and consider what's best for Rafe."

"Leaving him can't be the best thing for Rafe."

Daisy didn't comment. She brought her gaze once again to Will's face. "Will you help me?"

He took the final step to close the distance between them. Leaning down, he thrust his face near hers. "If for no other reason than to protect you from yourself, I'll do it." He straightened. "But you'll do as I say. I won't leave you in a situation that I think is risky for you."

Daisy fought to force the words past the lump in her throat. "As long as you get me out of Denver, I don't care what happens after that." Despite her plan, her heart plummeted now that Will had agreed to help her. What had seemed vague and distant before had become an uncomfortable reality.

Will lifted a hand toward her as though he would caress her face, but he let his hand drop without touching her. Instead, he skewered her against the aircraft with a piercing stare. "I hope one day, I'll be fortunate enough to have a woman who loves me with the same sacrificial love you feel for Rafe."

"I hope you will, too. You deserve a special lady."

When Daisy walked away from the airfield, she felt Will's gaze pinned against her back. Blinking back tears, she lifted her face to the sky. How the sun could shine when her heart was breaking?

CHAPTER 34

Two weeks later, Daisy laid her shopping basket on the counter of Montgomery's Emporium and waited for Edith to ring up her purchases. She normally avoided the shop, but the gift she wanted to buy for Rafe could be found only here in the Emporium.

Edith pulled each item from the basket and punched the price into the cash register. Though her face registered curiosity, she held her tongue.

Daisy's purchases piled up on the counter. Items of clothing, sleepwear, and a pair of woman's leather gloves mounded beside the register. The last article, a long, fringed gray cashmere scarf that she'd chosen for Rafe to replace the one that had been ruined during their trek through the mountains, topped the stack.

"Do you want to pay cash, or shall I put this on Rafe's account?" Edith gave her a close look that made Daisy uncomfortable.

Daisy pulled her wallet from her purse. "I'll pay cash for this."

When she'd paid and Edith had folded her purchases into a fancy paper bag, Daisy turned to leave. Edith's voice behind her made her pivot.

"I don't know what Rafe sees in you, but he's happier now than I've evah seen him. I hate to admit that you're the woman for him, but I'm glad to know he's happy."

Daisy acknowledged Edith's grudging admission with a nod. "Thank you."

Back at their house, Daisy added her purchases to the satchel she'd already begun to pack and fastened the snap. She folded the cashmere scarf with loving hands and placed it on Rafe's pillow. Rounding the bed, she drew open the drawer of the lamp table on her side and withdrew an envelope with Rafe's name scrawled across the front. For long moments, she stared down at his name. Inside the envelope rested the letter she'd written explaining why she'd left and urging him to remarry.

This letter represented her final personal contact with her husband. She didn't expect to see him again. From this point on, their dealings would be handled through a solicitor.

Daisy laid the envelope beside the scarf on Rafe's pillow and gave it a final glance, then lifted her coat off the bed and shrugged it on over her green wool frock. With the satchel clutched in a tight grip, she left the house.

Only when she'd boarded the train for Denver and the locomotive had left the station did the finality of her scheme hit her. She'd done it. She'd left Rafe and Summit. While the coach swayed and clacked its way through the mountains, Daisy stared with unseeing eyes out the window. Her thoughts beat inside her skull and gave her a headache.

Since she'd ridden the train to Summit last spring, so full of hope, she'd reunited with Rafe and found happiness she hadn't thought possible. Today, she rode back down the mountains to an empty future without her husband. She refused to listen to the voice whispering in her ear that perhaps she was making a mistake.

Just before he'd left Summit a few days ago, Will had given her the details of her escape. Rafe had left them in Katie's Café and returned to the mine, and Will had glanced over his shoulder to make sure none of the other diners was listening. "Get a ticket on Friday's train to Denver. I'll meet you at the depot, and we'll take a taxi to the airport."

Daisy had nodded, her heart at her feet. "I won't take much luggage. Just a satchel."

Will's eyes had crinkled in a reluctant smile. "I'm glad you're a sensible girl, and I won't have to convince you not to bring a mountain of trunks that my aeroplane can't carry."

"I've flown with Rafe enough to be aware of the weight limit." And she'd never again fly with her husband in his new biplane.

"I'll fly you all the way to New York City myself."

"Will, you can't. That's too much. All I'm asking is for you to fly me out of Denver."

His mouth firmed, and his hazel eyes hardened as he sent her a look across the table that withered her objections. His satin over steel tone brooked no argument. "Do you think I'd actually drop you off somewhere and let you find your own way to New York? Think again, lady. I'm not leaving you until I've delivered you to your family, and I know you're safe."

Daisy fiddled with her spoon and then lifted her gaze to Will. "Thank you, Will, for helping me. You've been a good friend."

"I don't know what kind of friend would help his buddy's wife leave him." Will grimaced and shook his head.

Now that her escape plan had a definite date, Daisy's heart lodged like an icy lump somewhere near her stomach. She hesitated, then burst out with something she'd wondered about. "Have you ever been in love, Will?"

His glance flicked to her face before it skittered away and focused on something over her left shoulder. Before his expression shuttered, she read the truth on his features.

"I think you know the answer to that question."

She hung her head. "I'm sorry. I shouldn't have asked, but I wondered if you'd ever experienced the pain of love. Love hurts, Will. It hurts so much." She crumpled the napkin that lay beside her plate, then tossed it onto the table. "I'd be the most selfish woman in the world to stand in the way of Rafe having a family. I know I'm doing the right thing to set him free, but it hurts so much."

Now, with the first step toward her goal accomplished, Daisy leaned her head against the train seat's back. Her despair gnawed at her, but she stiffened her resolve. Nothing —not heartache, not the pain of separation nor the images of Rafe married to another woman with a houseful of children— would make her change her mind.

Instead of dwelling on her doomed love, she buried her emotions beneath her goal and focused on her future. She should have no trouble finding a job in New York City. Female doctors there were few, but at least she wouldn't be the only woman doctor in the city. And seeing her family again would be a treat. She hadn't visited them since she'd returned to the States from France after the war.

Perhaps she should find a job where she could help children. Helping heal other children might help relieve the pain of her own empty arms. After several years, her time with Rafe and her life in the Rockies would seem like a fading dream.

Like a reel of one of the new moving pictures running in an unending loop, Daisy's thoughts pivoted back to their final day together.

Yesterday, her husband had left Summit for an unexpected meeting. He'd told her that he and Cole were traveling to Chicago on business. She'd been distracted by her own plans and hadn't questioned the sudden nature of his trip. He hadn't mentioned the meeting earlier, so something must have come up regarding the mine. With Rafe in Chicago, she didn't have to worry about him discovering her absence for several days.

She blocked her mind to the memory of their poignant love making on their last night together. Such thoughts only brought her heartache and weakened her resolve.

At the Denver station, the locomotive shuddered and groaned its way to a halt. The whistle screamed, and cinders rained down upon the sidewalk. Passengers spilled onto the platform.

Daisy scanned the crowd that pushed and shoved in the depot. She didn't see Will. Anxiety clutched her. She hoped he hadn't been detained. Now that she'd left Summit, she wanted to get on with her life and depart Denver as soon as possible. She hardened her resolve. Nothing, absolutely nothing, would stop her from doing the best thing for Rafe. In time, he'd understand that she'd done the right thing and would thank her for it.

When the last passenger had disembarked and she was alone in the coach, she reached beneath her seat and dragged out her luggage. The walk down the aisle to the exit seemed too short. She paused at the top of the steps and looked down at the platform below. Once she left the train, she'd put one more barrier between herself and Rafe.

While she hesitated on the passenger car's step, stubborn

love thrust through the barren soil of duty, but with ruthless determination, Daisy tamped down the betraying emotion. Love wouldn't deter from doing the right thing. She must be strong.

With one hand gripping the rail, she squared her shoulders and descended the stairs. The crowd on the platform had thinned. Only a few people scurried across the boardwalk, intent on their own business. She took a step and scanned the area. Will still hadn't arrived.

She'd taken one more step when someone behind her grabbed her arm and whirled her about. She squeaked and swallowed a scream. Her bosom thumped into a hard male chest. Daisy looked up into her husband's furious dark eyes.

"Rafe! What are you doing here? I thought you were in Chicago."

Rafe glared down at her through narrowed eyes and replied through clenched teeth. "More to the point, what are you doing here?"

Daisy swallowed and threw out a diversion with a question of her own. "How did you know I'd be here?"

"Will told me."

"Will told you!"

Rafe clamped his fingers around her upper arm. "Yes. Will told me. Did you expect him to help you leave me and not inform me of your scheme?"

"I expected him to honor our agreement."

"Then you have no notion of the male honor code. Will would rather cut off his right hand than betray me with you. He only went along with you to prevent you from haring off on your own."

Daisy narrowed her eyes. "You never had a meeting in Chicago, did you?"

"No." Rafe clipped out the word.

"You lied to me."

He put his nose in her face. "What do you call what you did to me?"

Daisy had never seen him so furious. She'd pushed Rafe's sunny disposition over the edge into a simmering rage. "I'm sorry." She forced the words past her tight throat.

"Sorry! You're sorry? Is that all you can say?"

Refusing to quail beneath his temper, she stiffened her spine. "What do you expect me to say?"

Rafe ground his teeth. He straightened. "I won't discuss this with you here, in public. I'm taking you back to the hotel where we'll have our conversation in private. Apparently, you need reminding about the nature of our wedding vows." He tore the satchel from her hand. With his other hand still clenched around her upper arm, he spun them about and stalked toward the exit.

Daisy trotted beside him as he towed her along. She knew better than to ask him to slow down.

People whom they met on their way to the street took one look at Rafe's savage face and gave them a generous berth. His sheepskin jacket made his shoulders appear wider, and wearing his heeled riding boots, he seemed enormous. No one seemed willing to cross over six feet of irate Western male.

Rafe's motor car waited along the curb. He dragged her around to the passenger side and wrenched open the door. After tossing her bag over the back of the front seat, he stepped aside. "Get in."

Without a word, Daisy slid into the automobile. Rafe slammed the door.

Neither spoke on the drive to the Grande Palace Hotel. Rafe paid grim attention to his driving, and Daisy huddled in her seat. Despite the waves of outrage that rolled toward her from her husband, a luminous glow filled her. Now that she'd been discovered and Rafe wouldn't let her leave, she could remain with him without the guilt that had plagued her. They could stay together after all.

At the hotel, Rafe left his motor car with a parking attendant and dragged her into the resplendent lobby. In forbidding silence, he hauled her up two flights of stairs to their room. Once inside, he slammed the paneled door and dropped her luggage where he stood. When he loosened her hold on her arm, Daisy whirled away from him and backed a pace.

Rafe stood with his back to the door, arms folded. His cowboy hat rode low over his brow. His eyes glittered just beneath the brim. Color smudged his cheekbones. His nostrils flared, and his mouth made a hard slash. For long moments they regarded each other as two antagonists, although Daisy felt no fear of her husband. Rafe might rage, but he'd never lay a hand on her. A curious sensation of peace flowed through her.

At last, he rasped in a voice tight with control. "I feel like turning you over my knee and spanking you, but that's no way to treat a grown woman. I guess I'll have to resort to other means."

Daisy waited, her gaze on his face.

"I want to hear from you why you thought you needed to indulge in these absurd shenanigans."

"If Will told you I was leaving you, I expect he told you why."

"I want to hear it from your own mouth."

They stared at each other across the carpet. Now that the moment of reckoning had come, Daisy's reason for leaving Rafe seemed inconsequential. "I know how much you love children, and I can't give you any. I thought that if I was out of your life, you'd find another wife who could give you a family."

Rafe narrowed his eyes. "You really thought that."

Daisy nodded. "Yes."

"Did you ever consider consulting me about the matter to see what I thought?"

"I knew you'd be honorable and tell me it didn't matter." Her voice sounded small, even to her own ears.

"Of course, I would have told you that. I love you whether or not you can give me more children. It would have been the truth, and not just a matter of honor."

Daisy didn't know how to respond.

"Tell me one thing."

She waited. Their gazes locked.

"Do you love me, Daisy? Really love me?"

Her eyes widened at his question. How could he doubt her love? "Of course, I love you. That was the whole reason I left you. I loved you too much to be so selfish as to stay married to you when I was depriving you of something I couldn't give you."

He blew out an explosive breath. "Leaving me is an odd way of showing your love."

Her reasoning sounded ridiculous coming from him. She defended herself in a terse voice. "It was for your own good."

He chopped the air with the edge of one hand. "From now on, let me decide what's for my own good. Don't do me any favors."

Daisy hugged herself and waited for him to continue.

"Did you consider that I love you more than any children you might give me? That my love for you is unconditional? That without you, my life is empty?"

Daisy shook her head.

"No, you didn't consider that, and you didn't give me the opportunity to tell you. You just decided what was best for me." Rafe took a stride toward her. "You might leave me, Daisy, but as long as you live in this world, I could never marry another woman, even for ten children."

Her tongue couldn't form words. She waited in mute silence for him to finish, unable to look away from his face.

Rafe took another step toward her, and another. He halted before her, so close that she had to tip back her head to keep her gaze on his face, but he didn't touch her. "Did you mean the words 'til death do us part' when you said our marriage vows?"

"Of course, I meant them."

"Then you promise never to leave me again?" His face lost its forbidding expression. A vulnerable light shone in his eyes and plucked at Daisy's heart.

They stared at each other. His body heat radiated toward her, and she yearned for him to enfold her, to draw her into his warmth. She wanted to feel his body against hers. "I'll never leave you again. I'll stay by your side, until death parts us."

Rafe cupped her face. His fingers speared into her hair, and one thumb stroked across her cheek. "Do you believe that when the Lord spared us in the plane crash, it's because He has a plan for us? He has something for us to accomplish together?"

"When you put it like that, I do."

"So do I. And I can't do it without you. Whatever the plan is, we must do it together. Perhaps it's just for me to be the best mine owner in Summit. And to be a godly husband to you." Rafe slipped her coat's buttons from their holes and slid the jacket from her shoulders. He tossed the garment onto the bed behind her and pulled her into his embrace.

She wound her arms about his neck and raised her head for his kiss. His lips covered hers, and he branded her with his passion. When she could breathe again, she nestled her face into his chest. "And I'll be the best wife I can be."

EPILOGUE

Summit, Colorado
Autumn, 1923

Despite the struggle to give birth to Rafe's baby, joy filled Daisy's heart. The impossible had happened. She and Rafe were going to have a baby. Even as the thought cheered her, she clutched the sheet and bit back a moan.

The lowering sun slanted through the bedroom windows and filled the room with luminous gold, though Daisy had no notion the afternoon waned. Time had ceased to exist. She measured time as the interval between one contraction and another.

Della Wild Wind bent over the bed and wiped Daisy's face with a damp cloth. Daisy clutched her mother-in-law's arm and raised her head. "Rafe. I want Rafe."

Rafe's mother smoothed back Daisy's sweaty hair. "He'll be here as soon as he can. You just relax now and try to bring his baby into the world."

Daisy dropped her head onto the pillow. Clasping the sheet as another pain gripped her, she closed her eyes and tried to relax. She clenched her teeth to keep from crying out.

When the pain subsided, she went limp. Her medical knowledge monitored her progress. She seemed to be stuck in this stage of childbirth, and her mind flitted through the possibilities that could prevent her labor from advancing. How different delivering a baby was when one was the mother and not the doctor. The doctor could sympathize with a laboring mother, but the mother was trapped in her body and had to deal with the pain. In these moments, Daisy would have preferred to be the doctor.

Della Wild Wind perched on the edge of the bed. Daisy forced open her heavy lids. "How long has Rafe been gone?"

"Since early this morning."

"Shouldn't he be back soon?"

"He'll be back as soon as it's humanly possible. We just don't know what he had to deal with when he arrived at the hospital." Rafe's mother smiled down at her. Her French braid swung forward, and with an automatic gesture developed from long practice, she flipped her rope of hair over her shoulder. "He'll hurry back to you as soon as he can."

Daisy couldn't muster the energy to return a smile. She fretted over her husband's absence. That morning when her labor pains had begun two weeks early, Rafe had flown to Denver to fetch the doctor who had promised to deliver her baby. Aside from the desire to have her husband at her side, she wanted another professional opinion on her labor.

Daisy scowled at her enlarged stomach, which mounded up beneath the sheet. She'd be glad when her waistline returned to its normal slender shape, and she could see her feet again.

Another contraction made her gasp. When the pain released her from its grip, she said, "I want Rafe's baby. I do. But it hurts so much."

"I know. I had five babies myself." Della leaned forward to wipe Daisy's face again.

Through the open windows, the faint drone of an aeroplane engine sounded as dusk crept into the corners of the bedroom. Daisy lifted her head. "That's Rafe! I can hear his plane."

Rafe's mother cocked her head at the windows. "He made it in time. You'll have your husband back in a few minutes. He'll be here when the baby comes."

They both remained silent, listening. The sound of the aeroplane's throbbing motor grew louder as the aircraft approached the runway and began its descent. A distinctive change in tone resonated when the biplane's speed slowed as the craft leveled out just above the grass. In her mind's eye, Daisy followed the process Rafe's plane made during its landing. From her experience of flying with him, she knew he always cut the engine when the wheels were six inches above the ground. Now the engine spluttered and died. Silence followed.

Daisy suffered through two more contractions before footsteps thudded across the veranda. The front door opened and slammed shut, and then footfalls pounded up the stairs. Rafe burst into the room still wearing the cashmere scarf Daisy had given him, his flyboy's leather jacket, and jeans. When he reached the bed, he knelt and braced both elbows on the mattress, then took Daisy's hand.

"How are you doing, sweetheart?" Concern tightened his features. With his free hand, he stroked her hair away from her face.

Rafe's presence soothed her jangled fears. Renewed strength flowed into her body. Della rolled her head toward her husband and managed to smile. "Better now that you're here."

"I'm here, and I won't leave you. I'll stay right here with you until our baby is born."

Another spasm wrenched her.

"Squeeze my hand, as hard as you can."

She focused her attention on his face and clutched his hand. He held her gaze as if by that very contact, he could transfer his strength to her. As the pain increased, she tightened her grip on his hand with every bit of energy she still possessed. She gritted her teeth and tried not to moan. When the contraction had ebbed, she wilted into the bedclothes and closed her eyes.

"Daisy, Dr. Wilson is here."

Daisy pried her eyes open once more to see Dr. Wilson standing behind Rafe. The doctor resembled a stork with glasses. He gave her a reassuring smile.

His reputation and bedside manner had been one of the reasons she'd chosen him to attend the birth.

Dr. Wilson leaned over the bed. "Your husband was anxious to get me here, Mrs. Wild Wind. He whisked me right away from my hospital rounds. Now, he and I will wash up, and then we'll see what we can do about getting this baby born."

Daisy labored into the night. She had a hazy consciousness of Rafe and Dr. Wilson discussing the slim chance she'd had of conceiving after her ectopic pregnancy and the possibility of more children.

She gritted her teeth. Leave it to men to talk about having more babies before she'd even birthed this one. Why had she wanted a baby, anyway? Before she could answer her own question, the contractions spun her away from their conversation into the serious business of bringing her child into the world.

Rafe provided her with a lifeline. He stayed at her side, soothing, cajoling, and at times bullying her to keep her with him when she wanted to give up. When her body seemed too exhausted to fight any longer, Rafe hovered over her.

"You're almost there, sweetheart. We'll have our baby soon. Stay with me. Don't give up." He stroked her cheek.

Daisy hung on, encouraged by her husband's presence. She clung to his hand.

At one point he leaned over the bed and kissed her forehead. He brushed her damp hair away from her face and cupped her cheek with his palm. "You're so beautiful, Daisy. You take my breath away."

Daisy had never felt less beautiful in her life. Her stomach looked as though she'd swallowed a watermelon. Her sweat-streaked hair clung to her scalp. Perspiration dewed her upper lip. Without doubt, dark circles must smudge the skin beneath her eyes. Fatigue made her limp, but she tried to smile and squeezed his hand. "I don't need a mirror to know you're stretching the truth. Quite a bit, in fact."

His dark eyes glinted down at her. His voice sounded husky in the night's quiet. "No, it's true. You've never been more beautiful to me than you are right now."

In the dark hours after midnight, she delivered her baby. The infant squalled with lusty cries as if protesting his entrance into the world.

With her child's wails sounding in her ears, Daisy subsided into the mattress, exhausted but no longer tormented by pain. Only half aware that Rafe had moved to the end of the bed where Dr. Wilson dealt with their offspring, she closed her eyes and dozed.

A hand on her shoulder roused her. Rafe lowered himself to the bed beside her, a blanket-wrapped object in his arms. He bent toward her and tipped the bundle so she could see their child's face.

"We have a son, Daisy."

She rolled onto one elbow and peered at the swaddled infant. A shock of black hair covered his skull. The baby stared back at her out of hazy eyes from a red, wrinkled face, though even at this early stage, Daisy detected Rafe's features in their son. "He has your nose."

Della Wild Wind leaned over them from the other side of the bed. "That's the Wild Wind nose. All the men have it."

When Daisy had been cleaned and the sheets changed, Dr. Wilson and Rafe's mother left them alone with their son. Rafe settled himself on the bed beside his wife and offered the infant to her. She leaned back against a mound of pillows and cuddled the warm little scrap against her bosom. Fierce maternal love swamped her. All the hours filled with pain might never have been. Each contraction had been worth the effort to bring her child into the world.

Rafe kissed the top of her head. "Thank you, Daisy, for this wonderful gift."

She looked into her husband's face, so close to her own. She smiled at him. "Thank you, Rafe. It wasn't just me. This baby is a gift we gave each other."

He leaned closer and pressed his shoulder against hers. Together, they stared down at their son, who chewed a fist and squirmed. "If I could have spared you the pain, I would have. The hardest thing I've ever done is to watch you hurting and not be able to do anything about it."

Daisy turned her attention from the infant to her husband.

"But you did do something. Just by being here with me and holding my hand, you gave me the strength to keep on. I couldn't have gotten through the birth without you."

Rafe kissed her mouth with gentle passion and then touched the baby's nose. "We haven't decided on a name for him yet. Have you had any more thoughts about a name?"

She laid a hand on her son's warm tummy. "I thought it would be nice if we named him after your great uncle, Clint Logan. Your Uncle Clint was a godly man, and he founded the Slash L dynasty, so I thought honoring him would be appropriate. And the name would please your mother and your Great Aunt Coral."

Rafe stroked his son's cheek. "Clint Logan Wild Wind. I like it. Mother will love it."

Clint Logan Wild Wind's face puckered. He opened his mouth in a piercing wail. One fist emerged from his blankets and waved in fierce demand.

Rafe chuckled. "He's hungry."

Daisy laughed. "I'd better feed him. If he's anything like his father, he won't want to wait for his breakfast."

She loosened the ties of her nightgown and put the baby to her breast. With their heads tipped together, she and Rafe watched their little miracle suckle his first meal.

Daisy's heart filled. She'd come to Summit a year and a half ago, not knowing what the future held. Now, she had everything she could ever desire. She had a husband who adored her, a healthy child, and a home of her own. The Lord had filled her cup full and running over.

If you enjoyed Valiant Heart, please take a moment to leave a review on your favorite retailer, Goodreads, and/or Bookbub.

. . .

Want to stay up-to-date on all of Anaiah's new releases and sales? Sign up for our readers' newsletter!

ABOUT THE AUTHOR

Colleen Hall wrote her first story in third grade and continued writing as a hobby all during her growing-up years. Writing her Frontier Hearts Saga has allowed her to combine her love of writing with her love of history and the West. In her spare time, she enjoys spending time with her husband and family, working Monty, her Morgan/Paint gelding, reading, and browsing antique stores. She lives in South Carolina with her husband and family, one horse, and two very indulged cats.

You can learn more about Colleen on her website: https://www.colleenhallromance.com/

ALSO BY COLLEEN HALL

The Frontier Hearts Saga

Her Traitor's Heart

Wounded Heart

Warrior's Heart

Wild Heart

Made in the USA
Columbia, SC
24 April 2024